THE NIGHT COUNSELLOR

L K PANG

For Isabel, Florence and Leo

"Who looks outside, dreams; who looks inside, awakes."

Carl Jung

CHAPTER
ONE

1953
Jane

"D o you remember your name?"

We sit across the table. My last appointment of the day. The room is bare, concrete cast. Dim light cuts through from the narrow opening near to the ceiling, too high for anyone to reach. The smell of bleach lingers over the newly mopped lino that stretches across the surface in one homogenous sheet, blending seamlessly into the walls.

My pen hovers over a folder of notes labelled on the front with *Patient A*. I take my gaze away from her, careful not to come across as overwhelming but it does little to encourage her to speak. After more silence, I flit my eyes towards her again and see that she focuses on something invisible on the table. Her hair, long and greying, is braided loosely down her back. Her hands are under the table where I cannot see. I assume that she rests them on her lap. I wonder who braided her hair and study her face where her skin smooths over her delicate, pale cheekbones.

"My name is Jane. I'm your counsellor."

I speak in short sentences, making a point to pause in between to let the information sink in.

"I am here to help you."

"Dr Blythe has invited me to assess you over the following months. I will be spending time alone with you each day for an hour. Since this is only an introduction, I won't be here for that long. But I would like to ask you a few questions if I may?"

I wait to see if there is any reaction. There is none.

"You are in the Beaumont. Do you know why you're here?"

They like to call the Beaumont a retreat and rehabilitation centre. We all know that it is a mental asylum, renamed just a year ago as a weak effort to extinguish its harrowing reputation. An attendant in a spotless white lab coat at the door tells me that the patient has been here for two months and has never spoken once. When they brought her in, she was draped in a large woollen coat belonging to one of the guards. They found her walking along the roadside by a farm near the Beaumont at dawn, wearing nothing, covered in blood. Her hands clutching a name on a piece of ripped cotton.

I open the folder and skim through the brief diagnosis from the psychiatrist, Dr Blythe.

Patient Details:

Name: Unknown

Date of Birth: Unknown. Suspected to be mid-late twenties.

Gender: Female

Address: Unknown

Date of Entry: 1ˢᵗ January 1953

Symptoms: Mutism. Waxy flexibility.

Diagnosis: Stuporous Schizophrenia
Treatment: 100ml Largactil every 6 hours

There is a photograph of the creased material they found her with. My eyes take it in. A name, surrounded by splatters of liquid. More blood.

Gina.

The name is inscribed, but not with pen – something rudimentary. A stick? No. Possibly with a nail or the tip of a finger. I place the photograph of the note in front of her.

"Do you recognise this note? Did you write it or was this given to you?"

Again, nothing.

"It says *Gina*? Is that your name?" I ask. "You were holding it in your hand when you were found. Where were you going?"

I pause and study the photos they took of her when she arrived. Distressed, shocked, lips gaping, dark hair in a tangled mess.

"Do you remember what happened to you?"

I turn around to see the guard still standing at the door, staring at the wall opposite him. "I know it's frightening in here. You may have suffered. You are safe now. You can trust me. Can you look at me to show you understand?"

Not even a flicker in her eyelids suggests that the patient can hear me, or if she can, that she recognises Gina as her name or a name she knows. She continues to stare at the table. I watch the slow rise and fall of her chest. Her lips remain still, relaxed into a permanent thin line just above the round of her chin.

I swallow. I agreed to taking this job as a counsellor, as someone who could help a patient's healing through conversation, a new form of treatment. I was unaware that this was what I would be faced with. I see if she can follow some basic instructions. Sliding a piece of blank paper towards her, with a pencil on top of it. I ask,

"Please could you pick up the pencil?"

Her eyes stay transfixed on the table as if there were no pencil, no paper.

A slow steady breath flows out of me. Can she not hear me or is she unable to move? I scan her notes again… *Waxy flexibility,* the inability to move without guidance or aided posturing. I have an urge to approach her and move her arms to see how she will respond. Could I? Would Dr Blythe truly mind if I physically examined her myself? I'm curious and don't allow myself time to talk myself out of it.

"I'm going to move a bit closer to you now and I'm going to try and lift your right hand up. And then your left." I walk around the cream melamine table and perch on its edge. Gently, I place my hand under her right wrist and lift it up to the height of her shoulder. She follows the movement easily. I move my hand away, so it no longer supports her wrist, and her hand stays in the air in front of me. I do the same with the other hand and once again, I let go. Now two hands hover over her thighs, as if they were suspended by thin puppet strings. Her expression remains still. I lightly guide her hands back down to her lap and return to my seat. I clear my throat.

"Thank you for letting me approach you. From now on, I will be spending time with you. Speaking to you, showing you things. Maybe we could even go out for short walks. There are beautiful gardens here that we could potter around. Or we could arrange to take a trip somewhere further afield. Otley is not far from here. We could see some of the countryside or visit some shops. Would you like that?"

The door opens, breaking the silence with the creak of its metal hinges and my heart sinks at how fast time has passed. A guard steps in.

"Time's up, Mrs Galloway," he says.

I nod at him in acknowledgement and look back over to her with a meek smile.

"It's time for me to go now. But I will return tomorrow."

I rise and make my way to where the guard waits with the door ajar.

"How do you know that she has been able to speak before this?" I ask him before I leave the room. He merely shrugs in response. Turning to glance back at her, I see that she is still in the same position she has been all along. Over the last few years since the end of the War, I have worked alongside different psychiatrists who have treated women, victims too traumatised to speak on the aftermath of their abuse or tragic accident, but it perplexes me to see one as still as this.

The guard leads me down the corridor to reception, past the cells, each one padded with rubber, stained brown at the edges. Here, it is not quiet. Here is where the women wail, scream, laugh and curse. I peer into each individual unit I pass and clock each lost soul in my mind until one stares directly at me through the small opening. She grasps at the bars with her fingers, and I look straight into her eyes, wild and dark like a starless night sky.

The clank of the door from the room where I had just walked from catches my attention. A guard leads Patient A out the door.

Her arms are thread into long sleeves which wrap around the back of her waist. She shuffles across the floor in bare feet, and her gown reaches just below her knees. Her eyelids are still lowered, and I wonder if I will ever get to see her eyes properly and what colour they could be.

"This way, Mrs Galloway," the guard says, retracting my thoughts.

"Why is she in a jacket?" I ask, watching as they lead her into her cell.

"Just for precaution," the guard responds.

"But has she shown any violent behaviour?"

"Not yet."

I watch her enter her cell and look back at the other woman who seems to have disappeared, but the mirror in the corner of the ceiling shows me her body curled up on her mattress. I hear her scratchy voice singing.

"*Rock-a-bye baby, on the treetop. When the wind blows, the cradle will rock.*"

I look above the woman's door and take a mental note that she is in Unit 5. As we reach the final door, she appears back at the window.

"Sweet dreams!" she screams suddenly, making me jump. The words echo off the walls, setting off more cries and cackles from other cells.

I approach the reception to retrieve my belongings. As I exchange my visitor badge for my coat, woollen cloche hat, leather gloves and bag, a woman in a white dress with a wide nurse's cap makes a beeline towards me along the length of the corridor, her heavy keys jangling against her hip as she struts.

"Did she speak?" she commands.

I blink at her, baffled by her directness. Her eyes set in her hard, bony face, flicker towards my file.

"Patient A. Did she speak?" she confirms.

"No, she didn't," I say.

"Do you think she ever will?"

The heat rises in my cheeks.

"It's going to take some time. But I hope I'll be able to help her."

She nods. "We don't have much time. The police ring daily to ask questions. If she doesn't speak soon, we'll have to resort to harder measures."

"The police?" I ask. "We are talking about the same patient?"

"Didn't you know? They suspect that she has something to do with a murder. A farmer discovered a woman's body near to where they found Patient A."

So that's why they put her in a strait jacket.

"That's it? They were just in a similar location. It's not sufficient proof."

"She was covered in blood, Mrs Galloway. That is sufficient enough. We're in the Beaumont now. Here, it's guilty until proven guilty. If you think this new talking therapy technique is going to get her to confess to anything, she'd have to be stupid as well as mute." Her face is stern and I struggle to formulate a response quickly enough. I pan over to her name tag resting on her chest. Minerva Tolsy.

"Nurse Tolsy, I don't feel comfortable speaking about my client so contentiously at reception, especially without any facts. I don't work with the police. I am not here to interrogate her."

She stiffens her back and a frown stretches across her face.

"Of course, Mrs Galloway." She gathers some files and turns to the receptionist.

"I'll be clocking off soon, Susie."

She turns her eyes back towards me and Patient A's documents.

"Shall I file that away for you?"

I hesitate for a moment and then hand the papers over to her. With that, she walks back into the main wards, leaving me blindsided. Why did Dr Blythe fail to mention to me the patient's link to a death? I look back at the receptionist who gazes at me blankly.

"Is Dr Blythe in today?"

"Sorry, no. He's in Wakefield hospital until Thursday."

"Who is in house today?"

"Just Nurse Tolsy."

I want to ask more questions, but our conversation is cut short by the ring of the telephone. The hands on the clock behind the desk have just reached three o'clock and I realise that I'll miss the next tram home if I don't leave now.

From the tram stop, I look back at the hospital building that symmetrically spreads across the foot of the hill, like a blanket of grey, dirty grit. Standing at the centre is the imposing clock tower, a relic from past asylums with only one onerous meaning.

The tram home to Bramley, north of Leeds, drops me off a short walk from my home, a small apartment on the first floor above a chemist. I wave a brief greeting to Mr Nichols, the pharmacist, as I pass and enter a lobby through the side door.

Only now do I feel my exhaustion. My ankles feel like they're weighed down by iron shackles as I heave each foot up every step and dig around my bag for my keys. I unlock the door and swing it open.

Kirsty, the neighbour, turns to give me a wide welcoming smile.

"Oh, you're back!" she says and my world, in an instant, feels lighter. The way she moves makes her appear like there is a wire crinoline under her yellow, buttoned dress, her wide hips sway from side to side as she wipes down the counter one final time and brushes her hands over her the apron she borrowed from me.

"Thank you for staying. I didn't realise I'd be so late. How is he?" I sigh, dropping my bag on the table.

"He's fine. Fast asleep now. I gave him some toast and a glass of milk before bed. He didn't have a temperature or anything."

My five-year-old son, Jasper, needed to be picked up from school early today because he was feeling unwell. I hate to inconvenience anyone, but there are few in Bramley that don't judge me for raising a child on my own, and there are even fewer that I trust. She smiles warmly at me and takes the apron off. It brushes against her bobbed hair, and she smooths it back down with her hands.

"I thought I'd do a bit of cleaning whilst I was here. I hope you don't mind. Just wanted to help a bit."

"Thank you, you really didn't have to."

The kitchen is sparkling with everything put away, adding to my guilt some more. I look through my purse which only has a ten shilling note left in it. I take it out and hand it over to her, but she waves it away.

"Goodness girl, no. Help doesn't cost money! I'm happy to do it, any time. I don't have anyone I need to look after."

"Kirsty, I really don't know what I'd do without you."

She declines the cup of tea I offer and says she should get back to prepare her supper, so I see that she steps back into her own apartment and I gently close my front door before checking on my little boy's room. Jasper snores softly in his bed, holding onto his soft toy rabbit with his covers tucked up to his chin. His face relaxed, mouth slightly open, long lashes resting softly below the lids of his eyes, and I watch the rhythmic rise and fall of his breath. I brush his fringe away from his forehead and plant a gentle kiss upon it, inhaling the sweet scent he still retains from infancy.

"Night Jay, I love you," I whisper into him.

He stirs and reaches his arm out from beneath the covers, stretching it over my neck and pulling me in towards him. I take these few seconds to nuzzle my nose into the warmth of his skin and wish my whole day could be filled with this tenderness.

I have a wash in the bathroom – the water is barely warm, so I make it quick and slip into my nightgown. I scrub and hang last week's dirty laundry up and finally sit myself at the small dressing table by my bedside. I curl my fair hair into each hair roller and gently massage cream into my tired skin, the stillness of my new nameless patient sitting firmly in my mind.

CHAPTER

TWO

"Your tea, Ma'am."

Mabel carried a tray of tea and cream scones over to the table by the window where I was sitting with a book. The empty crockery rattled against each other despite her quiet, fluid steps. Her old hands steadily decanted every item from the tray onto the lace tablecloth. She rested the tea strainer over the cup, delicately lifted the teapot and poured the hot liquid into it.

"Thank you, Mabel. Have you received any news from Charles this morning?" My husband worked in the tobacco industry, importing the finest cigars from exotic places. Always away on business, hardly to be seen at home. I lifted the strainer off the cup and stirred a little milk into the tea.

"Not since yesterday, Ma'am. I suspect he's rather tied up at work because of everything that's been happening at the Palace."

"The Palace?" I asked. Is that what he called his office these days?

Mabel stepped back. "Have you not heard?"

I blankly stared at her.

"Why. King George?" She paused. "He died – this morning."

"Died?" I repeated, unable to comprehend the word.

"Yes, Ma'am, in his sleep. The whole country is mourning. It's ever so sad. Died so young. And so unexpected."

I turned my gaze to the view outside the window where the rest of the city lay, suddenly feeling hot and stifled by the stagnant air indoors. I rose to open the window a little, welcoming a gust of winter inside although it sent a shiver through me.

"I suppose Sir will be trying to cover all of his staff," Mabel continued.

"Yes… I suppose he will be," I reflected, unsure exactly of how many days it had been since I left the house or last saw Charles. There was an unusual hive of activity on the streets below. The world outside seemed like it had tipped sideways overnight.

"Would you like anything else bringing?" Mabel asked as she cleared away the last teacup and saucer.

"No, that'll be all, thank you Mabel."

Mabel was about to leave.

"Actually, please could you turn the wireless on for me? The Home Service." It was just to her left. She twisted the dial until it had reception and closed the door behind her before there was a subtle click in the latch.

I put my book down and stood by the window. Holding on to my middle, protecting a baby that was no longer there. For nearly two weeks, I had felt a deep, sad emptiness that I was sure could never be filled again. My loss drained every ounce of colour

I ever had in my already pale skin, turned my hair into a thinning, grey and brittle wig.

I watched as the crowds below gathered around a makeshift newspaper stand. The radio crackled and a man's voice stiffly made his announcement through the speaker.

"His Majesty, King George VI, has died peacefully in his sleep at Sandringham House. The official announcement from Sandringham, given at a quarter to eleven, said the King retired in his usual health, but passed away in his sleep and was found dead in bed at half past seven by a servant…"

I looked around the room in our London town house, surrounded by cardboard boxes and felt a shift in my mood. The resignation I wore over our relocation, now wavering and fragile.

In three days' time, we were meant to leave everything I've ever known behind and move to West Yorkshire, where I knew no-one, apart from my husband's mother, Lillian. Charles said the fresh northern air would do me good. That it would help my health and my chances to grow a baby, for us to finally have a family. Lord knows how much I had tried. Was a change in scenery and farm air really going to change anything? Dread washed over me afresh and without saying a word to Mabel, I grabbed my coat, leaving the tea to go cold and the scones to go stale.

Outside, the cold, damp air hit my chest with a sting. People queued up before the newspaper stand with a large headline, "The King is Dead. Long live the Queen!" A suited man handed out papers and one by one, men and women eagerly grabbed their own copy to capture and preserve a slice of history in the making. I joined the back of the line.

"Georgina?" I turned to a familiar woman's voice calling me.

My eyes widened with a mixture of surprise and regret over coming outside. I should have known that someone would have recognised me.

"Agnes."

"What are you doing here? You should be resting in bed. Could Mabel not have come down?" Her eyes travelled down to my stomach.

"Oh, I'm fine." I lifted my hand instinctively to rest over it.

"We're all ever so worried about you. I'm always at home with the children if you never need a friend to talk to."

"Thank you, Agnes." I politely declined, not wanting to spend my last days at home in the presence of children, as awful as it sounded. "That would be lovely, I'm just not quite ready yet."

"Well, you take care of yourself," she said as she noticed that I was already at the front of the queue and the stall holder was waiting, expecting me to buy a paper. "Isn't it awful. The county is in turmoil and the Princess is in Africa!"

"Yes. Very sad," I replied feebly.

I watched her gaze cast my emancipated frame with the pity I had begun seeing all too often.

"I do mean it when I say you can turn up whenever you need to, Georgina."

I thanked her courteously, handed over three ha'pennies to the seller's grimy hand and Agnes finally left me in peace. I stood away from the crowd and unfolded the paper before me to read the words under the headline, next to King George VI's portrait.

King George VI was 56, and was known to have been suffering from a worsening lung condition. Princess Elizabeth, who is at the Royal hunting lodge in Kenya, immediately becomes Queen at the age of 25. She has been informed of her father's death, and is preparing to return to London, but a thunderstorm has delayed the departure of her plane.

She is expected back tomorrow afternoon, when she will take the Royal Oath which will seal her accession to the throne.

I buried my head deep into the words as I made my way back towards the front door to my house and a new sadness crept in. A grieving for someone I never knew. I thought about poor Elizabeth and how she might have felt. How awful it must have been to lose her father whilst simultaneously being forced into a life of duty so suddenly. Life was too short to do something forced upon you.

As soon as I stepped inside, a wild panic choked me. I needed to stay here, in my home! I started to tear the tape off the boxes and with one box, I unwrapped everything from inside at a frantic speed. Soon, seven boxes were emptied with half the items back in their shelves and the other half of them scattered on the floorboards and rugs. I didn't really know what I was going to do with it all once I had unpacked them but freeing everything from its bound state gave me a surge of relief each time.

Mabel knocked on the door and stepped in. She gasped at the mess I had surrounded myself in. "Ma'am!"

"I… was just trying to find something. I couldn't remember where I had packed it."

"Would you like me to help?"

15

"No, no. Don't you worry yourself over this. I caused this problem, I will solve it!" I got onto my feet, felt the blood drain from my head and stumbled back. I grasped onto the nearest piece of furniture my hand found to steady myself.

"Ma'am, you should really rest as much as you can. That's why I'm here."

"I know, I just – I thought I could manage it. I'll be fine Mabel, really." I dusted my dress down.

"I was about to ask what you would like for dinner tonight? The fishmonger delivered some fresh haddock this morning. Perhaps I could poach it in milk for you?"

"That sounds delicious, thank you, but I'm not that hungry." Mabel looked at me. I knew what she was thinking. If she wasn't my housekeeper, she would have told me that I needed to eat and keep my strength up, but I knew that she dared not to, and I was grateful for that. Just the mention of food turned my stomach and I could feel the taste of bile work its way up to my throat. I managed a false smile for Mabel. "You go ahead and have some yourself, it's only good whilst it's fresh and I wouldn't want it to go to waste."

The evening drew in quickly and the glow of dimmed lamp lighting from the street filtered in. I stared outside the bedroom window until I saw the glare of a car's headlights turn down the road. Its engine chuntered as it slowed to a halt outside.

A gentleman with a hat shielding his face climbed out the back of the car holding his suitcase in one hand and a cane in the other and disappeared near the entrance of our home. The front door opened and shut firmly. I heard the rustling of his footsteps and his pace quickened as he headed upstairs, leading with one step louder than the other.

The bedroom door slowly opened, and Charles poked his head through the door.

"Darling?" The warmth of his voice immediately made me well up with tears.

He approached me in slow limping steps and took a seat next to me on the windowsill.

"How are you feeling?"

"Much like how I look. Rotten. Exhausted."

"You always look beautiful to me, my dear wife."

I wasn't sure that a flippant compliment was enough to make up for his latest disappearance, but it did do something to light a flame inside that I thought had long been extinguished. I focused on his mesmerising blue eyes, and I tilted my face towards him, taking in the scent of his cologne and cigar smoke.

"I don't want to move, Charles. Please, can we not just stay here?"

He sighed, so low it was almost a grumble.

"You know it's for your own good, Georgie."

"I don't see how. All my friends are here."

"But you don't even want to see your friends anymore. You've been isolating yourself and I worry about you all on your own."

"I have Mabel."

"Mabel is only here whilst you're not feeling well, and she will be retiring soon."

"And what about the King?" I ask. "I want to visit him."

"But… He's dead."

"I'd like to see him lying in state."

He took hold of my hands and brought them to his chest where his tweed waistcoat met his shirt.

"I'm not sure you're able to stand in a queue for hours?"

"It won't be until next week. I'll feel a lot better by then."

He was quiet in thought for a long moment as I watched him pull his thoughts together, praying that he would agree.

"How about this. You go and see the King – lying in state. We move up to our beautiful new cottage. And then we just give it two months. And if you really hate it, we can move back. This house will still be here."

I eyed him closely.

"One month," I said.

"Seven weeks."

I was tired but I still let out a chuckle and he stroked my cheek with the back of his finger. I leaned into his touch.

"I promise you; you won't need it. You'll love it."

"How can you be so sure?"

"Because I chose it for you. And, I didn't want to say too much as I wanted it to be a surprise. But since you look like you need cheering up right now… Mr Hosta intends on opening a cigar shop in Leeds where I will be stationed mostly, which means I'll be home with you a lot more."

"Really?"

"Yes. Every night! You'll be sick of me!" he laughed.

The resentment I harboured for Charles coming and going as he pleased started to fade away. Seeing him again, my loneliness disintegrated into ash and my heart reopened with hope. His familiarity, everything I had ever felt for him, the gratitude, love and respect, rushed through me. He shifted uncomfortably beside me. The windowsill was not wide enough for the both of us.

"How is your leg?" I asked, observing the one he cannot straighten fully.

"It's been niggling a fair bit today. Just need a bit of rest, I think. Now – are there any leftovers? I'm absolutely famished! The food just isn't the same abroad!"

We headed down to the kitchen for a little supper together. My appetite had returned slightly at his return although I was mindful not to eat too much. I still wanted to hang onto that feeling of hunger a while longer and found satisfaction in watching Charles eat and drink eagerly. I realised that no matter where I lived in England or anywhere else in the world, I was not at home unless he was there. So, if moving to the north was what he wished for us, then I would be happy to do it.

CHAPTER

THREE

Tram 329 leaves from Jasper's school and descends into the valley towards Crowbeck and the clouds sink as though they are burdened by lead. Once through, the tram takes the long lane up towards the hospital where the clock tower stands guard. Like a watchful eye, there is no escape from its tall gaze.

Tulips and daffodils have bloomed along the driveway up to the entrance, but they do little to ease the unsettling feeling I carry once I'm inside the grounds. Even the birds in the trees do not sing. Beyond the hospital campus, there is woodland and a trainline which serves only the hospital, and in the far distance further up the hill, a house, white in colour, stands alone, near to where Patient A was found.

I notice a broken pane of glass in one of the sash windows on the first floor. Its clear edges, jagged and sharp, dangerous enough for someone to cut their flesh on it. Through another window,

21

someone's face catches my attention; a patient with an unnerving gaze, stares down at me, challenging me to look away. I enter through the large doors. The receptionist is different from yesterday.

"Jane Galloway. Here to see Patient A, please."

"Morning Mrs Galloway. Here's your visitor badge. You're a little early. They're just about to have some dinner. Would you like to go through to the dining room? You might be able to grab a cup of tea whilst you wait."

"Yes, thank you. Where is it, please?"

"Down the right corridor, through three sets of gates. The dining room is on the left."

The passage of corridors feel like a rabbit warren. Gate after gate, a monotonous thrumming emanates from dulled fluorescent lights that intermittently flicker and cast an eerie glow against the tiled walls. I finally reach the first set of double doors. On my left, a door opens to the Orange ward, clearly denoted by its paint on the walls. An attendant wheels a woman out who fixes her eyes on me so hard that she turns her head at an awkward angle whilst the wheelchair still moves ahead. I catch a glimpse of the room inside. Rows and rows of metal beds are knitted closely together, barely with space to stand in between.

The dining room in contrast looks nearly empty. There are some armchairs to the side, upholstered in faded green vinyl, similar to those you would see in the reception of a local school. And along the length of the back wall, there are canteen tables with small vases of flowers upon each one as an attempt to provide warmth to the room. It is a vast space, with grand arched windows near the top of high ceilings that crescendo into a central glass dome. Yet, with no views to the outside and attendants standing by each solid wall, watching and listening, the room hangs with an oppressive, claustrophobic air. I wander past several groups of patients and attendants who follow me with their gaze as I reach the counter where there is tea and coffee. An unpleasant concoction of smells linger in from the kitchen, a jarring blend of fish and cleaning products.

The room feels too cold and I long for my coat which I had to leave with the rest of my possessions at reception in exchange for Patient A's file. I wrap my hands around the delicate cup of hot tea and wait. There are only two patients that have visitors. One elderly man with a younger woman, perhaps his daughter. They both sit in silence in armchairs at the end of the room. He appears to be heavily sedated as his head lolls to the side and his back is so relaxed, he almost slips off the chair. The other patient is a young woman, not far from being just a girl. An older woman with similar older features sits with her. The girl's cries and pleads to go home echo off the walls whilst the older woman hushes her and tries to hold onto her hands.

A bell rings down the corridors, I detect the look of relief on the woman as an attendant comes to collect the girl, and all the patients from the wards start to line up along the edge of the dining room.

"Retrieve trolleys!" A male attendant shouts across the room like a military command.

Four patients immediately walk towards the kitchen and wheel out trays with each patient's meal.

"Take your seats!" he sounds again.

The patients migrate to their seats in a trance-like state and wait for the trays to be served to them. I watch them, stirring their spoons around dented metal bowls filled with congealed, lumpy soup, and I question where I'm getting the smell of fish from.

In the far corner, I see her. Patient A, being fed by a female attendant. The attendant carefully spoons the soup into her mouth. She only opens it slightly so most of it doesn't make it in. It reminds me of when I was weaning Jasper onto solids. The attendant wipes runny cream goop off her chin.

As though she senses my stare, she pauses, turns her head, and we lock eyes. Embarrassed, I shift my gaze away from her. When I look back, she continues to feed the patient. I decide to address the distance between us and head over to them. I sit myself on the nearest plastic chair. It feels like they both do not see me.

"Hello, I'm Jane. I am this patient's counsellor."

The attendant pauses with her spoon in the air between the bowl and Patient A's mouth. She smiles at me politely with cold brown eyes.

"I'm Mary," she says.

"Mary, lovely to meet you."

"And you," she says without meeting me in the eye and she spoons another bit of soup into the patient's mouth.

"You are in charge of feeding all of her meals?"

Mary nods.

"Do you care for her in any other ways?"

"Most of her needs. Toileting. Bathing. Dressing."

"Which other patients do you care for?"

Mary shakes her head.

"Just her," she says.

"Ever since she was admitted?"

She nods again gently. It was unusual for an attendant to be dedicated to just one patient.

"Have you seen any changes throughout the weeks?"

"No, none."

I watch the slow rise and fall of her hand whilst she feeds her patient, the soup bowl not getting much emptier. Mary stops and rests the spoon against the bowl, and she looks at me with an intent but steady expression.

"Are you here to help her talk again?" she asks me.

"Yes, Mary."

Mary looks back over to Patient A.

"She will never speak. It's a pointless effort." My smile fades as her words prickle uncomfortably against me.

"No efforts are pointless, Mary. We do what we can to care for these individuals." Mary ignores me and continues with the feeding. "I'm due to have my appointment with this lady in ten minutes," I say, then I speak directly to the patient in a softer voice. "I look forward to seeing you then." I gently place my hand on top of her forearm resting on her lap and notice that Mary's eyes fall to it.

I find a place away from the pungent aromas to write my reports. Dr Blythe and I are to meet for the first time to debrief this afternoon and he will want to know my progress. As I carefully scribe notes down onto thin, lined paper, I sense a movement behind me and a light fanning of air at the back of my neck.

"You again," a woman says, almost in a whisper. Her voice comes strangely like an apparition, with her body following closely behind it. I jump and turn to face her inky eyes, recognising her instantly as the one in Unit 5 on my first visit.

"Hello," I say. "Finished your meal?"

She shakes her head and stands in front of me. Her posture stooped.

"Disgusting. Not proper food. Got any fags?" Her request somehow validates her existence, as though the mention of fags would make her seem more real and I relax a little.

"Cigarettes? No." My eyes flow over her body, her frame so slim I can almost make out where the ends of her bones meet at the joints. It does not look like she eats or enjoys many meals here.

"What's your name?" I ask her.

"Cleo," she grins by lifting one corner of her mouth in a shape that looks more like a grimace, baring me her blackened and broken teeth.

"And how are you, Cleo?"

"Ha! No one has asked me that in a long time."

"I'm sorry to hear that." I look around the room and take in the rows of resigned beings.

"And how long have you been here Cleo?"

She shrugs. "I can't remember not being here."

My eyes scan back over to Mary and the patient, and Cleo follows my gaze and starts to hum her lullaby again.

"Why do you sing that? Does it remind you of your childhood?" I ask her.

She shakes her head and continues to hum, closing her eyes and then starts to giggle.

"What's so funny Cleo? Why don't you share the joke with me?" I smile.

She opens her eyes and stares at me. Her mouth opens as if she is about to speak but seconds pass and I find her unnerving.

"She talks in her sleep," she finally says.

The mumbling statement catches me off guard.

"I'm sorry?"

Cleo's eyes dart to the side. "I know, I know! I'll tell her later. One thing at a time!"

I watch the empty space to the side of her head where she looks towards.

"Cleo?" I say, and she returns her focus to me. "Could you repeat to me what you said please? Who talks in her sleep?"

She nods but her attention drifts again.

"Is there someone else talking to you?" I ask.

"Michael. Pa hates Michael. He never visits me, but Michael does." Her voice trails off into something incoherent. I feel as though we are having two separate conversations and I want to steer it to just the one.

"Is Michael always with you or can you tell him to leave for a bit?"

"Sometimes. He always disappears after they've zapped me." Nervous laughter follows. She gives me that grin again, but it doesn't extend beyond her lips. Her eyes remain unlit.

"He likes you," she says.

The attendant standing guard interrupts us with another command.

"Clear trays, chairs on tables!"

Within a second, the room is filled with the clammer of metal and plastic crashing into each other. I take a deep breath.

"Cleo. You said someone talks in their sleep?"

She swallows. "That woman. She can't speak until night."

"What woman?"

"That one." She nods over to Mary who now wipes her patient's mouth and starts to clear the tray away.

"The patient Mary is with?"

Cleo nods, then lifts her hand to push something invisible away.

"Are you sure it's her you can hear?"

"Yup, clear as day."

"What does she say?"

"She calls out names, the same ones over and over again."

My attention sharpens.

"Which names?"

She shrugs.

"She must be cursed? Ghosts haunt her at night."

Cleo stops talking as soon as Nurse Tolsy wheels in a trolley lined with plastic cups. She reaches a female patient sitting alone by the wall, momentarily turns her head towards us, and Cleo's eyes shift down to her feet.

"Mildred! Time for your medication!" Tolsy commands. I watch Tolsy's manner as she stands over the patient, checking that she swallows the pills down. Mildred gives her mouth a clumsy wipe with the back of her sleeve and Tolsy travels to the next patient further away from us. Cleo is still hesitant to speak, her dark eyes sinking further in. I suspect that Nurse Tolsy's presence intimidates all the patients.

"Cleo. Who is the charge nurse in the evenings?" I lower my voice.

"Nurse Weaver. She's the nice one. There aren't many of them."

"Is Nurse Weaver here every night?"

She shrugs again.

Nurse Tolsy closes the gap in between us. Her expression remains stiff when she reaches our table.

"Mrs Galloway, I see that you're getting acquainted with our Cleo. She's quite a character." I nod at her in acknowledgement. "It's time for your medication, Cleo." She hands over a small cup with two pills and a larger cup filled with water.

Cleo stares at the pills, unwilling to move.

"Come on Cleo, we haven't got all day. You want to feel better, don't you?"

"Michael's gone, nurse. I don't think I need them."

"You need to take them, so he doesn't come back. Be a good girl now, you don't want to end up in an isolation cell again because you can't control yourself, do you?"

I watch Cleo awkwardly place the pills in her mouth and drink the water, wondering what Cleo had done to deserve the punishment before. Tolsy turns to me.

"Raymond, our attendant, will be collecting you in five minutes." She takes the cup off Cleo and walks over to the next patient.

"You have to be careful of what you say around her." Cleo whispers so quietly that I have to strain my eyes to listen.

"Why is that? Is she unkind to you? You don't like the medication you have to take?"

"A dead man follows her. No one can see him, not even her. But I can."

I study Cleo, wondering if anything she says is really the truth, or merely her own reality.

When it's time to see Patient A, Raymond leads me into the room where I first met her.

"You'll start to know your own way around soon," he says, jangling his own set of keys that are all shapes and sizes in his hand. He swiftly swipes up the key to the room as if he has done it a million times that day, and swings the door open for me. "In you go, the patient will be in with you in a jiffy."

Mary brings her in and ushers her on to her seat. I jot carefully into my notebook. *Able to walk, slightly assisted.* Without even a glance in my direction, Mary leaves the room.

"Hello, how are you?" I ask her, smiling. "Do you remember me from yesterday? I'm your counsellor, Jane Galloway."

I lift out a photograph album from my bag.

"I thought I would bring you this. Some pictures of my family and share with you a part of my life so you can get to know me more and about where I am from. And it may also help you reflect on your own life too. Your life before you came here. You may find some similarities."

I turn to the first page.

"This is Jasper, my son playing in the gardens at Harewood House, and this is my mother, next to him. She's passed away now but she loved spending time with my son. I look at her picture now and really notice her resemblance in me."

Whilst I speak, I watch her closely, only glancing at the photographs every so often, curious to know if she has a family of her own.

"This is my son on his first birthday with his father." I'd forgotten to remove that photograph from the album and do not linger upon it for long, turning the page again so that it is out of our sight. A laugh escapes from me when I see the next image.

"This is me with my cousin at the seaside when we were young. It was freezing that day, but we still wore our swimming costumes and ran into the water for a dip. The sea was ice cold! Do you like the beach? I find that it is a very peaceful place to be in. My favourite beach is at Sandsend, quieter than Scarborough, and they sell Jasper's favourite ice cream."

One by one, I describe pieces of my life captured in one small piece of card, hoping that she will relate to some of it, that the places and the shapes will trigger some response. But another hour passes without her speaking and the guard comes in and takes her away again.

When I walk past the cells this time, I make a point of looking into Cleo's, and I see her sitting on her bed to the side of the room. She catches my eye and gives me her special grin, putting a finger to her lips.

Shhhhh… she mimes.

CHAPTER

FOUR

1952
Georgina

Charles drove us down the long, winding lane towards the house with a car full of our belongings past Leeds, through towns and villages before we reached Crowbeck and even then, we hadn't quite arrived. Lush, green fields with grazing sheep and frolicking lambs lined each side of the lane, as we approached a cottage with a gable ended porch and cream walls. Lavender and rosemary bushes hugged its footings and wisteria climbed the end of the house, not yet in season to flower, and I thought that we had finally reached our new home. But to my surprise, Charles did not stop the car.

"Where are we going?" I asked.

"That's my mother's house," he said as he took the car a distance further up the lane and a much grander building came into view. He slowed the car and pulled up just in front of it. I stared up at the red bricked mansion with ivy elegantly positioned up its frontage.

Charles grinned. "This – is ours."

My bottom lip dropped, and I stared at it, dumbfounded, unable to believe that this mammoth building in comparison to our London townhouse was ours.

"How?" I breathed as we climbed out the car.

He laughed. "Remember when I said we could afford more space up here? Come on, I can't wait for you to see the inside!"

A stone portico framed huge freshly painted double doors with 'Crowbeck House' engraved on a stone plaque to its side. Charles swung the doors open dramatically, bowed and bent his arm, allowing me to thread my hand through to link it. I couldn't blame his enthusiasm; the hallway alone was wider than the entire width of our previous home.

"It was built in the 1700s, home to England's most treasured writers for some time. It needs a little updating but there's plenty of time to do that. Mother knows some local decorators that could help, in fact. Here – do you like the sitting room? Look at that fireplace!"

"It's glorious," I said, still suffering from shock.

"There's plenty of room, you'll never get bored. There's a library, a study, games room… Come, upstairs!"

We momentarily passed the kitchen and the smell of warm pastry wafted towards us. The staircase elegantly swept up to a landing that overlooked the hallway and onto the front doors, downstairs. Charles led me into each bedroom, each one as large as the next, nine of them in total. He swung me around and caught me by my waist, lowering his eyes to level with mine and laughed.

"Aren't you going to say anything?"

"I – Charles this really is beyond anything I ever imagined but, it's so big! What would we need all this room for?"

"Our family!" He opened out his arms, extending his cane to emphasise his statement.

"But–"

He lowered his tone, and his eyes softened.

"Darling, there's no pressure. The house is for you and me. If our dreams to fill it with one to twenty children come true, then even better. I just want you to be happy." He lowered his hand down to the base of my belly. "But I do have a good feeling about this." I mustered a smile, saddened by the prospect that it all may just lead to disappointment for him. Not only could I not promise him children, but I could not promise him my own happiness either. As if sensing my doubt, he pulled me towards him and held me for a long while.

"You were kidding about twenty children, weren't you?" I mumbled into his chest.

"Yes," he chuckled, lifted my chin and placed his lips over mine. I felt their warmth emulating through and the urge to grip on to the collar of his jacket possessed me, pulling him tighter towards me. Then a woman's call echoed through the hallway.

"Hellooo?"

I pulled my lips away from Charles. He smiled and pushed my hand off his chest. Leaning over the balustrade, he called,

"Mother!" I let out a discreet sigh and we headed down the stairs.

"Hello, Lillian," I greeted her, trying to appear effortlessly cheerful. I opened my arms and felt her robust frame embrace me.

"Charles! Georgina! Oh, how wonderful! Let me take a look at you!" She held me at arm's length and inspected me up and down. "Goodness girl, did your maid not feed you? I'll make sure that's taken care of here. You won't ever have to miss a meal again! There is already a pie and roasties in the oven!"

My smile started to wither. Already I felt as though she wanted to control everything and change me – change my relationship with Charles.

"Mother, that sounds like just what we need!" Charles said as he left to move the suitcases out of the car.

"Let me help you," I shouted after him.

"No, it's alright. I think it might start to rain soon. You can help Mother set the table!"

I managed to stomach a little of Lillian's hearty dinner although it had been a while since I'd had anything so stodgy and rich, and my stomach cramped in protest. Later, I found Charles in the master bedroom, gazing out of the sash window into the gardens with his hands on his hips, looking proud of his achievement in claiming these new grounds as his own. I saw a patchwork of fields as far as the eye reached, with rooftops of Crowbeck lining the horizon, and threatening over it was a brewing storm cloud, drifting closer towards us.

He turned to me and stretched out his arm and I wrapped my own around his waist, drawing in the scent of his cologne lingering on his loosened shirt.

"What do you think?" he asked softly.

I searched for any doubt in his eyes and find nothing but contentment. A slice of hope that I rarely saw and dared not disturb. Sorrow filled my heart in a way I could not shift nor explain, no matter how hard I tried or how lucky I knew I really was.

"I think… you're right. We'll be very happy here," I said.

He planted a tender kiss over my lips once, twice, then at the side of my jaw just below my ear, and again down my neck, the base of my throat where the skin dipped into the valley of my collar bone. I took in a gasp of air, feeling the heat rise in my blood and my pulse quicken.

Taking my hand, he led me to the bed and gently guided me onto it, slowly making his way on top of me. I leant up towards him, eager to get another kiss but out of nowhere, a loud crunch came out from underneath the mattress. Charles lost his balance and fell on top of me. I screamed out in shock, thinking the floor was going to swallow us up, and the sides of the mattress folded over on either side of us as the slats on the timber frame snapped.

We burst into laughter, and I covered my eyes with my hand.

"Perhaps we need to go shopping for a new bed in the morning," he suggested.

For the first time in months, we made love and the contentment he felt began to flow its way into my own heart.

The next couple of days flew by with our time taken up by unpacking boxes and finding new homes for every item. I found him one afternoon in the garden with a spade, boots and a shirt rolled up to his elbows, planting fruit trees into the earth. My attention turned to a gap in the hedge, an arched opening, delicately swathed in red. A little wooden gate with an iron ring separated me from what was on the other side. It drew me towards it, and when I crossed over the threshold, I felt as though I had wandered into somewhere so magical, that only pixies could exist here.

The archway continued into a pergola of climbing roses which led me further into a garden abundant with more red blooms, filling the air with their alluring scent. A sweet little gravel path led me to a fountain – a cupid, balancing on the tips of its foot, spurting water out of its arrow into its pond. I sat on an old bench and allowed my mind to rest, bathing in the small patch of treasure I had found.

That night, Charles and I lay in bed, and he turned to me.

"I have to leave for Luxemburg in the morning."

"Luxemburg? Already?"

"I know, I'm sorry darling. It wasn't the plan. I wanted to stay here with you for at least a couple of weeks, but this is a new client, he wants me there, and I have to show willing." I lay still, silently staring up at the gloomy ceiling where a woodlouse crawled its way towards the lampshade.

"I thought you were starting a new shop in Leeds?"

"Yes. Very soon, I will be. I just need to tie up some loose ends. You understand, don't you darling?"

My mood sank, knowing that I had heard *soon* too many times before, and silence fell between us.

"Darling?" Charles shuffled closer to me and stroked a strand of hair away from my forehead. "I'll be back in no time. I promise."

I woke the next morning, reaching out to my side for a final hug only to find that he had already left. His side of the bed was perfectly made with a neatly wrapped gift and a small card on his pillow. I sat up, my satin gown draping coolly around me, and I unravelled the twine around the present. I lifted the gift out of its wrapping. It was a book of some sort, leatherbound with an imprint of a rose on the front. I looked at the back and flicked through the pages, all of which were blank.

I opened the card.

My dearest Georgina,

I'm sorry that I cannot be by your side as you settle into our new home. Here is a little journal for you to voice your thoughts and dreams. I hope that it provides you with the comfort you need whilst I am away. I will miss you every second of each passing hour.

All my love,

Charles.

I sighed and headed downstairs when I heard the click of the front door. My heart leapt with anticipation.

"Charles?" I called out.

Perhaps he had changed his mind and cancelled his trip because he wanted to spend more time with me. Or maybe he had just forgotten something. It didn't matter if he had, I only wanted to see him, even just for a minute. Disappointment immediately sank in when I saw Lillian standing in my hallway with a wicker basket full of enough food for a week.

"Georgina! Good morning!"

"Good morning, Lillian. I didn't realise you had a key."

"Oh, didn't you? Charles gave me one before he left yesterday. Said it would be good to keep an eye on you and make sure you're settling in."

"Did he?"

"Yes, well he could hardly expect you to manage this place all on your own, could he? It's so handy being so close by, isn't it? Now, let's see. Have you had breakfast yet? I have half a dozen of freshly laid eggs from my hens today." She bustled straight into the kitchen and pulled her apron on.

"I'm not hungry."

"Nonsense, child. That's why you're so slim. You'll be fit for nothing soon other than a gardening rake."

I momentarily looked up to the heavens for some peace.

"I feel as though I have a bit of headache coming on. I think I'll just head back to bed for a bit if that's alright."

"The headache is because you don't hydrate yourself enough. I'll make us a good vat of mutton stew. Perfect food for fuelling. You go and rest and I'll call you when it's ready."

The thought of hot mutton simmering in its gravy juices first thing in the morning was not appetising in the slightest. I closed the bedroom door tight and opened the window to let the wafts of cooking out into the cold air, wishing for Charles' return. Is this what life was going to be like now? Just his mother and I?

From the top window, I studied the scene again and noticed a cluster of buildings set a distance away from the centre of Crowbeck, monumental in appearance and symmetrically planned out with a clock tower at its centre. I wondered what the building could be and that perhaps I should go and explore the town more fully tomorrow.

CHAPTER

FIVE

1953
Jane

r Blythe's office is simplistic and clean, almost empty yet somehow distinctly smells of old books. He is a man of small stature, slightly balding at the centre of his head. He taught me psychology at the University of Leeds. After I had finished my studies, he left at a similar time to me to work in psychiatric wards and we kept in contact in a professional manner although as the years went by, I saw him more like a distant uncle than a mentor. He knew I had more aspirations and that ultimately, I wanted to work in clinical psychology, but just before I qualified in my doctorate, Jasper was conceived. When my husband had left me, and I was alone to look after Jasper, I desperately needed a job but no one who knew me wanted to hire me as a counsellor. Like being abandoned by the man I loved wasn't hurtful enough, I was being rejected from society too. But Dr Blythe wasn't like anyone else – he always went out of his way to check up on me and offered me a role whenever there was one.

When he started at the Beaumont, he called me and asked if I was interested in a new role, one that the hospital hadn't seen before. Already I knew that the offer would be controversial.

"Jane, please. Come in – take a seat. How are you?" he asks as he gestures towards the chair opposite him. His accent is an unusual blend of somewhere in the South with a hint of an Irish inflection at the ends of his sentences.

"I'm fine, thank you," I say as I sit down.

"It's good to see you again." He peers over his spectacles. "How are you finding the Beaumont?"

"I've not quite made up my mind yet."

"I see. That good?" His eyes light up as he smiles. "Tell me, how have you been getting along with our patient?"

"She remains… unresponsive."

He studies me and nods his head slowly.

"You do look a little uncertain, I must say. What's wrong, Jane?"

"I – I just don't know if I'm suitable for this role."

"Why not?"

"Dr Blythe," I sigh. "I'm a counsellor, not a psychiatrist like yourself. I don't know if I'm able to help her – I haven't been trained."

"Tell me if I'm wrong, Jane, but I was under the impression that you wanted to qualify as a clinical psychologist?"

"I do."

"Do you doubt my own judgement of character?"

"Well… no, and I'm truly grateful for this opportunity."

"Then take my advice, and don't turn it away." His kind eyes grow stern. "Grab chances like this with both hands."

"It would be more helpful if there was a way to find out what used to interest or stimulate her… You found her walking along a farm track near here? She can't have been planted there in the middle of the road out of nowhere. She must have lived locally, there would be people who recognise her, who know her?"

Dr Blythe shook his head. "No one has come to claim her."

"What about all that blood on her when you found her? Do you know how that happened?"

His eyebrows furrow into a perplexed expression.

"You don't know? Did you not go through her file?"

"Yes, I did but there is no mention of it, just the photograph of her note."

I hand it over to him to check. He puts his reading glasses on and flicks through it.

"Very strange. It should be in here."

He closes it and I stare directly at him.

"What about the body the farmer found in the field nearby?"

"How do you know about the body?"

"Nurse Tolsy said the police have been calling. They're accusing the patient of committing the murder. Why didn't you tell me about this earlier?"

He takes his glasses off.

"I didn't want to share that information with you so soon. I was afraid it would hinder your relationship with the patient. We are trying to build trust."

"It's hardly possible to build trust if you hide important information from me that could stall the progress of my client. What happened Dr Blythe?"

"On the same night they found Patient A, a body of a woman was also found further up the track. She was inside a car… Both the car, and herself, were burnt to something unrecognisable." I swallow back the alarm I feel upon hearing this. Dr Blythe clearly sees my reaction and continues. "No one knows what happened but, what if the two incidents were connected? Do you think you could continue, knowing that she was responsible for someone's death?"

I take a moment to consider this and choose my words carefully.

"Until there is sound evidence of this, and until she shows any visible signs of violence, then yes – I will continue."

He leans back and pats the table.

"Well then. Good."

"I want to also discuss about Cleo."

"Cleo?"

"In Unit 5."

"Cleo… Cleo…" He recites, whilst rubbing his chin to try and jog his memory. "Ah! You mean Charlotte?"

I reply with a blank expression.

"Charlotte! She thinks she was Cleopatra in a past life. What about her?"

"She's drawn my attention, twice now, about Patient A. She says that Patient A talks at night."

"Cleo said that? She's schizophrenic. How can you be sure what she's saying is reliable?"

"Yes, I know, it might not be. But she has told me about this on more than one occasion, and it is about the same patient, not any other patient in the hospital. It makes it something worth considering. *And*, it also may well be possible! I would like to investigate it."

Dr Blythe peers at me.

"Talking at night? Is she awake at night and talking, or is she sleep talking?"

"I can't be sure."

"Well, I suppose there would only be one way to find out."

"Could I visit? One night to assess her in her cell?"

He lowers his head and scratches it. I can see that he is thinking about it at least, so that's not a straight no.

"There are fewer guards at night, and you can never trust the night attendants, they are either asleep whilst standing or playing billiards in the games room." He taps his fingers on her file in deep thought and then comes to a decision. "She may not be convicted, but we can't take any chances. It's too risky."

"If I could think of a way to make it work, would you permit it?"

I think I'm about to get somewhere with him because he pauses and I can almost see the cogs of his mind turn. Just as he is about to open his lips to speak, there is a knock at the door, pulling us out of our conversation.

"Not now!" he calls out to the person on the other side.

"Dr Blythe. It's Minerva."

He glares at the door and sighs.

"Come in."

The door opens and Nurse Tolsy sees me straight away. Her lips form a straight line of disapproval.

"Yes?" he asks.

"News from the castle, Doctor. Sir Feyman's back from his travels."

Dr Blythe nods. There's a change in his expression that I can't quite describe, but I am unable to see if this news is welcome or not.

"Thank you, Minerva."

Dr Blythe turns his attention onto me again.

"Right, where was I?"

"Ah, yes. Hmm."

He rubs his chin. "I'll think on it. Carry on with what you are doing for now. Maybe take her for a walk next time. The fresh air will do her good. Have one of the attendants help you."

"Thank you, Doctor. Just out of interest, do they know who the deceased is?"

"I thought you might ask that," he says. "As a matter of fact, no, they don't. Oddly, no one has come to claim her either."

I rise from the chair and head to the door.

"Jane?" I turn back and his eyes seem to soften, and I wait for him to say something else.

"I hired you, not because I know that you needed a job – I could have given you any job – but I wanted to give you *this* job. I believe that this patient needs someone like you to help her. You see things that others can't."

I stare back at him, letting the words he says in his graceful, measured manner sink in. He observes me with a quietness that lets me know he trusts me.

"Thank you, Dr Blythe."

I leave in good time to pick Jasper up from school. I wait at the gates. One of the teachers opens the front door and the pupils come flooding out. My little Jasper rushes past them all and runs towards me with a large smile, his school bag bobbing away on his back. I hoist him up into my arms and kiss him on the cheek when I see his teacher, Mrs Mensa, wave me over. I look into Jasper's eyes.

"Is everything alright, Jay?"

"Yes," he says nonchalantly.

"Mrs Galloway, could I have a word please?" Mrs Mensa calls over to me. I sense the seriousness in her tone and I know that it won't be good news.

"Go play," I tell Jasper, pointing him in the direction of the playground and face Mrs Mensa.

"Jasper has been having some run ins with his fellow pupils."

"What do you mean?"

"He threw a punch at another boy in the playground during the lunch hour. We don't tolerate bad behaviour in our school Mrs Galloway, as you know, and Mr Gibson disciplined him fairly." I stare at her, horrified, knowing my son will have been subject to the headteacher's cane that otherwise permanently leans against his desk, ready to strike against the next insubordinate act.

"Why did he punch the boy?" I ask.

"He was teasing Jasper for not being good enough to have a father."

"Well, then I'm not surprised! How would you feel if a group of people picked on you about your circumstances that are beyond your control?"

"Mrs Galloway, it doesn't matter what caused his anger. He must learn to control it and it would be appreciated if you could see to it that he does."

"Yes, Mrs Mensa," I say, swallowing down all the tempestuous words in my mind. It would not do for me to start an argument against school authority. I shift my hot glare over to Jasper in the playground. "Jasper! Time to go!"

I last saw Jasper's father on Jasper's second birthday. I fell pregnant out of wedlock, a scandal to all those surrounding us, but Jasper sprung himself upon us with his arrival so we did what anyone would do and called for a shotgun wedding. We were in love – it was all we needed, and I was too young and foolish, thinking our love would last forever.

First it was another woman's lace glove I found in the back of his car, but he denied it and said he was simply giving a co-worker a lift home when the rain was particularly bad one evening. Then it was one of her stockings scrunched up in his inside jacket pocket. But being the fool that I was, I still gave him another chance. I had no choice, I wanted to keep our family together, and I worried about what others would think.

It was on the day of Jasper's party in the Village Hall that I caught his father with her in the store closet as I looked for a pan and sweeping brush. It turned out to be one of the other mothers from school all along. I told them both to leave in an instant. She dragged her son away from the party as I brought out the cake and we all sang *Happy Birthday*, and everyone wondered why they had to go so suddenly. My husband continued to pretend that everything was normal, to save face and for Jasper's sake, but

I couldn't stop the tears from welling up in my eyes and I acted like they were stinging from the smoke coming from the candles.

Part of me felt like she wanted me to catch them so she could finally have him all to herself. Back at home, I screamed at him, hit him with my fists until they turned raw, but he never once retaliated or shielded himself against my onslaught of rage, fuelled more by his silence. He wasn't going to repent or beg for my forgiveness. He just wanted to pack his things up and go, so I yelled at him to leave. I could not quite believe it when he really did leave for good. Was it me? Was I really that bad as a wife? A lover? So bad he had to have another? I often think that my career aspirations were too high for him. I wasn't like the other women in Bramley and maybe I was studying and working so hard that he felt left behind… So he left me to punish me for it.

Jasper's halfway up the steps of the slide. He looks at me and shakes his head. Mrs Mensa doesn't know what else to say to me and watches me with a boggled stare as I struggle to retrieve him.

"Come on, Jay! You can play at home!" I start to leave towards the gate and turn my back against her. Seeing me go, he runs to grab hold of my hand, half tugging me back, whining and I feel the gaze of everyone burning into us as we go and the journey along that path cannot be short enough. Finally, we turn a corner. Out of sight and earshot, I say,

"Who did you hit today, Jasper?"

He stops tugging at me and starts to shrink by my side and as a wave of realisation strikes him, his face fills with guilt.

"Duncan was nasty to me. He said I wasn't normal." His voice wobbles as he speaks and water wells up in his eyes. I stop and kneel down to meet him.

"I know he hurt your feelings darling, but you mustn't lower yourself to their level. If you hurt them, you'll get yourself into trouble too, and you're better than that. You're Jasper Galloway!" I smile and kiss him on the tip of his nose.

Back at home, I help Jasper prepare for his bath and inspect the flesh on his bottom, rosy and pained from Mr Gibson's cane. I rub some salve over its tenderness.

"Mama?"

"Yes?"

"Do you think my daddy will ever come back? Because if he did, then maybe the children wouldn't be horrible to me?" A lump rises to my throat. I cannot answer Jasper's questions, but whilst I dress him, I find myself fantasising about his father's return. He would suddenly appear at the door, crying with regret, begging for us to take him back, and I could love him again – just for Jasper's sake.

At night, disorientated and unsure at what hour it is, I am woken by Jasper's murmurs.

"Please, Daddy!" he screams with whimpering sobs following on. I gently stroke away the tension in his arms, fists and kicking legs and shush him back to a deep sleep but it is enough to wake me fully and I lie next to him, thinking that the thought of his father leaving him must have cycled around in his mind all evening. He was so small; I didn't realise that he would have a memory of this but I suppose a parent leaving your life on your birthday would leave a mental scar. Does he bury his pain, only able to release it in his dreams?

Patient A appears in my thoughts. Her head hanging low, her body sitting stiffly on a hospital stool. If she talks in her sleep, she too may be able to expose memories she cannot voice in her waking hours.

CHAPTER

SIX

1952
Georgina

orning barely broke the dull skies. I woke in my bed alone again and stroked the sheets where Charles would have been lying and sauntered from room to room, staring at each empty space.

I paused at one of the central bedrooms where sunlight generously poured in, and pictured how sweet a crib would look in the corner. A neatly weaved basket with a delicate laced veil hung from the ceiling, draping around its sides. A little girl, making gurgling noises as she woke. I looked out into the gardens and imagined her in a year's time, taking her first steps, tentatively holding on to the trunks of the trees Charles planted that would be flourishing with blossom and ripening fruit. In three years' time, she would run out from behind the door in surprise, squealing with the delicious sound of laughter after winning a game of hide and seek with me. A faint, hopeful smile rose to my lips.

I took a seat back at my dressing table. My reflection in the mirror too honestly showing my sad, tired eyes and a frown that seemed to carve permanent lines above my brow. The colour of my skin, pale and sallow, lacking any make up as I didn't see anyone apart from Lillian anymore.

I looked upon the book Charles gifted to me, its cover – warm and soft to the touch. I lifted a fountain pen and put it to the paper.

My name is Georgina. My heart pumps nothing but lead. It sits in my chest and every breath is a struggle. I am not ill. I am just so… sad. Disappointed, angry, resentful, lonely… and sad.

I hovered the pen over the next blank space and took a second to acknowledge the slightest relief of pressure I felt from writing those words.

Before I was married, I used to live in London. We lived on the second floor of a town house in Parsons Green with my parents. It was just big enough for the three of us in a busy neighbourhood. It was 1945. At the age of 17, I was too young to be conscripted for war work so I used to walk across the Thames to Putney each day to help the greengrocers there for 12 shillings a week, enough to buy myself a new dress or shoes every so often. I remember that walk so well, the river glistened under the mid-morning's rays and there was something strangely joyful in being able to breathe in the pungent fumes the engines of cars choked out. I was young with my whole life before me. I felt alive.

Once the war had ended, I didn't think I could feel any luckier. And then I met Charles one night at a dance with some friends. He was the only one sitting down at a table watching everyone else wearing out the soles of their shoes to the music. Even from across the room he had a charm. I had to walk over.

"Why aren't you dancing?" was the first thing I ever said to him. He smiled and waved over to his leg.

"Injury from shrapnel!" he shouted over the music.

I pulled out a chair next to him to sit on and we talked until the music ended and the lights flicked on, like we had known each other all our lives. I didn't care that I only danced to one song that night. I don't remember a single day after that when I didn't smile.

He asked me to marry him on our one-year anniversary since that very night and of course I said yes. He landed a really good job with a tobacco company and my parents were so proud to have him as their son-in-law. Not long after our wedding, I fell pregnant. We were so close to having everything we needed. Until I lost our first child. And then our second…

Couple after couple, our friends started to have children of their own and for some unbearable reason, God did not want to grant us a baby of our own. I started to shy away from our friends' invitations to parties, especially when their children were about. And after one too many declines, the number of invites lessoned until they petered out altogether.

We stopped trying just to save the disappointment. Charles started working away more. Taking on roles in Europe and even the Far East. With the extra money it bought him, we were able to buy a whole townhouse for ourselves nearer to Central London and he hired Mabel to help. I had given up all hope for having a family until three *months ago when I conceived again! I thought that this was finally it! Our child had come. One day, I felt butterflies in my tummy and was sure it was kicking. Charles was extremely excited and was convinced we were to have a boy. We started to clear out the spare room and bought a small crib… The next day, I started to bleed… and our hearts broke all over again. I was inconsolable and poor Charles did not know what to do with me. I suppose that's why he travelled away so much, to avoid my miserable company.*

Then he landed the job in Leeds. I really wasn't sure. But Charles said it would be a welcome change for us. Nothing we had done so far had worked in our favour. Perhaps a new location, more open space and new friends would help. He was very convincing and waved away my reservations.

"An adventure!" he said with his large, handsome smile – I was never able to resist that! "If we really hate it, we'll move back in a heartbeat."

Well, I'm here now. I hate it and we have not moved back.

I underlined the last sentence with a heavy stroke of ink and petulantly flicked the pen across the book. I heaved out a sigh and stared out the window where the grey building spread its fingers across the landscape. The peculiar clock tower was beckoning.

CHAPTER

SEVEN

1953
Jane

asper sits in his school uniform eating warm porridge and scrambled eggs whilst I sip on a strong cup of tea. He looks like a miniature grown man in his tie and braces, with his hair neatly combed to the side, and I watch him tenderly whilst he jiggles his feet and hums on his stool as he eats.

"Did you have a bad dream last night, Jay?" I ask him.

He spoons a mouthful of porridge into his mouth whilst he thinks.

"I don't think so, Mama. But anyway, I never remember my dreams. So even if I did have a bad dream, I don't think I would know."

"I suppose that could be a good thing. To not remember the bad dreams."

He nods his head and chews.

"Mummy heard you sleep talking."

He looks at me with amused, wide eyes and chuckles.

"Was I? What did I say?"

I decide not to tell him. "Nothing much." I glance at the clock. "Eat up, time for school."

He slides his arms into the sleeves of his blazer and we step outside. Some mothers walk their children out at the same time, but no one greets us as we head towards the gates of his school, and I shy away from any eye contact. He runs ahead when he sees his friend and the top of his satchel flaps up and down.

"Wait! Jay! You forgot your cap!"

He comes back to me, and I slide his woollen cap on snugly over his head. He tilts his head up, plants a wet kiss on my lips. "Don't forget what we talked about last night," I whisper. He nods and heads in and I turn back towards the tram stop, ignoring the other mothers in my path.

At the stop, a man with a face I recognise instantly beams his smile across at me. It's Richard, the local police constable who lives on the same street as us. He looks impeccable in his navy-blue uniform with round silver buttons neatly centred down his tunic and his hat tucked under one arm. I quickly check that my hair is in place before he gets too close.

"Fancy seeing you here," he says. "Don't you normally take the route down to South Leeds?"

"I did, but I've been relocated for a new client at the Beaumont."

"Good! That's exactly where I'm heading to now. Car's in the garage. May as well ensure everyone behaves on the tram whilst I'm on duty."

"I'm sure they will once they see you on it," I smile. "Why you heading to the hospital?" Our tram approaches and we step on to it. All the benches are full except for one space left in the middle. He extends out his hand, offering the seat to me. I shake my head, choosing to stand with him and the tram sways as it sets off down its tracks again. A couple of young women in the corner throw doe-eyed gazes towards him and giggle to themselves. He must be quite the heartthrob of Bramley although he seems unaware of it and his expressions remain focused on our conversation.

"There's a mute patient in there that I need to check in on."

"Patient A?"

He turns to me, surprised. "Yes, you know her?"

"She's my patient."

"Ah. That should be interesting."

"Is it to do with the murder? You're not charging her for it, are you?" My voice lowers.

"Not today, Jane. Not today. Why? Has she spoken yet?"

"No." I hesitate for a moment. "But it is my job to try and get her to."

The conductor heads towards us and we show him our passes.

"Well, the way it's looking, she might be better off staying mute," he says solemnly. I don't answer that in case I end up saying something that will end up as condemning evidence. He notices my change in mood and changes the subject to something lighter.

"How's everything else going? Jasper doing well?"

"He punched someone at school yesterday for calling him abnormal."

"That's my boy!" Richard laughs.

"I would have found it amusing too if Jasper hadn't got a good spanking out of it. So yes, it's going well," I say, shaking my head in dismay.

His face falls. "Sounds like you need a drink one night."

I'm not sure if that is an invitation, but it makes me smile. Our conversation distracts us from the tram's route, and we reach the Beaumont before we realise. Richard places his hat on and straightens his back as we enter the hospital.

"Here to see Sir Alexander Feyman," Richard says, and the receptionist picks up the receiver. Once she has announced his arrival, she places the receiver down and turns to me.

"Good morning, Mrs Galloway," her voice carrying a dull, lifeless tone.

"Morning," I say as I follow the daily ritual of clocking in, handing my possessions into reception and receiving Patient A's file.

"I'll see you later," I say to Richard, and he smiles and nods at me. As I walk down the corridor, a man, distinctly tall and smartly dressed in a pinstripe suit walks past me. The presence of him is so prominent that I find myself staring at him and am surprised to see his eyes directly meeting mine and they do not leave. It unnerves me and I shift my gaze away until he passes. I turn around to see him shake Richard's hand and head to the dining room.

As soon as I get there, I am challenged by Nurse Tolsy, who instantly subdues my mood.

"You're early again I see."

"I like to make use of the day fully. It's good to assess the patient in her surroundings before some one-to-one time."

Really, I want to be early so that I can talk to Cleo about my patient's sleep talking some more. Tolsy studies me sceptically as if she can sense my ulterior motive.

"I see. She's being bathed by Mary currently. You'll have to wait here."

The other patients are getting their morning dose of medicine, several different sized tablets in a cup and a separate cup of water for each one. In the vast space, I realise that Cleo's striking presence is missing. Perhaps she is being bathed too, I'm told that they go three at a time throughout the week.

Mary walks in with my patient shuffling next to her, their faces almost mimicking each other in their lack of interest. Mary's eyes lock onto mine, and I head over to them.

"Good morning, Mary," I say and turn to the patient. "Good morning, how are you feeling this morning?" I know not to expect a response and I follow it up with a smile.

"The sun is out. Shall we go for a little stroll? Mary, perhaps we could take a wheelchair just in case it gets a little tiring?"

She nods and heads to the storeroom for one. When she returns, she guides the patient into the chair. I am still unfamiliar with the layout of the building and ask Mary which doors are best to leave from to access the gardens and she simply answers me by wheeling the patient forwards. We pass a couple of attendants who nod their heads at me as I walk alongside Mary.

"Do you know where Cleo is this morning?" I ask her.

"ECT."

Electric shock therapy must be what Cleo meant by being "zapped". The image of her body held down by several attendants makes me wince internally. Unable to protest with a large rubber block placed into her mouth, convulsing from the electrical current so hard her bones may snap.

"How often does she go through that procedure?"

"It used to be once a week but they're not seeing any improvements, so I've heard that they're going to be increasing it."

We walk around the meandering paths within the gardens slowly and I stoop down to describe everything we see to the patient, the shades of colours and the patterning of the landscape. I point out the patients who are tending to the shrubs and the birds that flit down, twitch their heads and fly off again. She stares out into the middle distance, not quite focusing on anything and I am not sure if she is aware of any of her surroundings or of the changes between inside and outside.

I look towards Mary.

"Mary, would you mind if you left us alone for the last twenty minutes of the session?"

Her face changes almost as though I might have offended her.

"It's alright. Dr Blythe has permitted me to. It'll be perfectly safe."

She glances around her. We both know that there are plenty of guards and other attendants around to watch over us and she looks down at the patient. After an awkward amount of hesitation, she leaves obligingly without saying a word and I think to myself, how strange she seems.

When Mary is finally out of earshot, I bend down to meet the patient in the eye.

"I hope that this is pleasant for you, it's nice to get some fresh air, it clears your mind. It would be nice to know your name so I could address you properly. You have a name. Do you remember it? Could you say it?"

Her head dips slowly, but I don't think it's intentional. I place my finger under her chin and ease her head back up. I pause, thinking I should bring my letter cards next time. Perhaps she will be able to indicate what her name begins with, even with a subtle glance or a gentle lift of her finger. I ponder over my next choice of words.

"I met Dr Blythe and he told me about your tragic incident. I don't know what it was you went through, but it must have been painful and terrifying enough to stop you from speaking."

"I've been told that you have nightmares… and that during them, you speak. My son has nightmares too. It breaks my heart to think that anything could hurt him. Fills me with complete fear. If something bad has happened to you, I am here to offer you support."

Her expression does not change, and the strength of my words only tickle the breeze around her.

"If I'm being completely honest with you – and I want to be, because I'd like you to trust me." I look directly into her eyes, willing them to meet mine. "I believe that you can hear me. To tell you the truth, I haven't given you the best sessions I had hoped to deliver over the past few days. I've been very distracted. My son is having trouble at school, the other children are being nasty to him and all of a sudden, I'm thinking about his father who left us. It has really sent me off kilter. I feel off balance and I don't know how to reset myself. There's no one I can really talk to about this. Ironic, isn't it? Since I'm a counsellor."

I'm suddenly aware at how inappropriate I'm being. Sharing my thoughts and emotions so openly with the patient as though the tables were reversed and she was the counsellor, not I. There is no structure to what I'm telling her. It's scrambled bits of information, I'm vocalising whatever feelings come. The space between us somehow feels sacred and no one else's but ours. How I wish she could answer me but somehow knowing that she could not, also brings me some solace. I knew that even if she was able to give me eloquent guidance, I would object to it anyway. Her silence feels selfishly comforting, safe in the knowledge that she will not reveal my secrets to anyone. And deep inside, there is a hope that if I can be so vulnerable with her, she may learn to do the same in return.

A strong gust of wind hits us. The patient's hair whips across her face, and I see Mary marching over in the corner of my eye with a blanket.

"Let's go back inside before you catch a chill."

And another session passes where I feel defeated. It is near to the end of the week, and I have still not managed to make any progress. Not even a slight movement of her eyes, a prickling of her ears, a change in her breath.

We amble back indoors, and I bid them both farewell. Before I leave, I feel a pull to go and check up on Cleo. I am directed by one of the attendants to her bed in the Blue ward – a medium secure zone for potentially dangerous patients undergoing medical care and more guards are in place to keep watch. There, Cleo lies, pale and still as a corpse. Her breathing, hardly detectable and I'm wary that she won't be able to recognise me the next time I visit.

As I rest my eyes over her lifeless body, I anticipate the harder measures Patient A will be forced into if my therapy fails to work and it fills me with apprehension. I do not want her to become another lost soul lying amongst this sea of iron beds, but I feel helpless, unable to figure out how I can stop it from happening.

I approach reception who is manned by a young lady, not much older than twenty. She seems different to the one last time, somehow friendlier and more open to conversation. I hand over my visitor tag and she passes over my belongings with a warm smile, her eyes kind and gleaming through her large glasses.

"Lovely dress," I say, glancing at the bright, floral patterning.

"Oh, thank you! It's from the little boutique in Crowbeck. I kept seeing it on display in the window and went there during my lunch hour last week as soon as I was paid!" Her radiating smile is infectious, proving that you can work in a psychiatric hospital and possess warmth.

"How long have you been working here?" I asked her.

"Me? Oh, only a month. Just to earn a little money because I still live with my parents."

"Do you like it here?"

"Um. Yes and no. I don't think I'll stay for too long. Just to get some experience. My name is Ruth, by the way."

"Nice to meet you, Ruth."

Her friendliness somehow sparks an idea in me. I remember the charge nurse in the evenings that Cleo mentioned was the nice one.

"Please could you tell me what nights Nurse Weaver is in charge?"

"Nurse Weaver? Every night."

"What times?"

"They switch over at seven o'clock," she says with another smile.

"Thank you. Is there any way at all, that I could come and visit the patients during the evening hours?"

"The evening? There's no one here to man the desks after seven. That's when I clock off."

"Perhaps Nurse Weaver could let me in?"

"Maybe. I would have to have a word with the doctor."

I lower my voice. "Oh, I don't want to trouble anyone with more paperwork than they need. A patient of mine needs some urgent care and the doctor is such a busy man. If it helps, you can tell Nurse Weaver that I'd like to speak to her?"

Ruth pauses for a moment.

"Alright. I can leave a message with her. When would you like to come?"

"Tomorrow too soon?" I would need to check if Kirsty would be fine to look after Jasper, but I want to hold a time down now whilst this pleasant receptionist is here.

"Tomorrow is a Saturday?"

I nod.

"It's in the diary and I'll let Nurse Weaver know tonight." She gives me a final, broad smile and I thank her.

* * *

The phone rings later in the evening right after I finish bathing Jasper. I usher him into his room with his towel wrapped around him and rush back out to pick up the receiver.

"Hello?"

"Hi Jane, it's Richard."

"Oh hello, is everything alright?" I am immediately nervous at the sound of his voice, worrying that he's about to bring me bad news about the patient.

"Everything's fine! Don't worry, I'm not ringing to talk to you about business."

"Oh." I wait for his next words with apprehension.

"I uh, hope you don't mind me calling. I just, uh, wondered if you'd like to take up the offer of that drink one night?"

"Oh," I say again. My heart begins to flutter.

"Mama!" Jasper calls from his bedroom.

I ignore his call and pull up a dining chair to sit down, unaware of how long I am silent for.

"Are you – still there?" Richard says.

"I…"

"Sorry, it's too soon. And too late to call. I should have–"

"No – I'd love to. Really."

His breath faintly exhales on the other end of the line.

"Do I sense a 'but'?"

"It's difficult at the moment, with Jasper. I don't feel right leaving him to go on a date, or a drink, I mean."

"I understand."

"I don't know if you'd be happy to. But I was thinking of taking Jasper for an ice cream on Saturday if you'd like to come?"

"Saturday. Yes. That would be nice. Shall I pick you up?"

I laugh. "No, it's alright, we can meet you at the playground first?"

"Great! I'm completely a fan of the monkey bars!"

"Mama!" Jasper's voice now rings out from his room impatiently.

After a hurried and awkward goodbye, I wander into Jasper's room feeling a slight state of shock. During our call, I felt the giddiness rush to my head like a schoolgirl with a crush, but now whilst I crouch down on Jasper's rug, the reality of helping my son with his pyjama selection hits me and the prospect of meeting Richard feels unwise. It's not a date, is it? I decide that I am to treat this occasion as time with a friend. I'm just getting to know him a bit better, that's all. It's never harmed anyone to befriend a policeman.

CHAPTER
EIGHT

1952
Georgina

*L*illian bustled in with a basket of fresh groceries, pouring her restless energy around the kitchen.

"I'm putting on a spread for us this afternoon! I don't know what's come over me, but I'm ever so hungry. Have you heard the news? They're finally ending the rationing on sugar! We should make some cakes later!"

"Oh, Lillian." I stopped at the door of the kitchen, and she paused to scan her eyes from my head to my toes, seeing that I was fully dressed with a coat draped over my arm. "I was about to head out into town actually."

"Now? Why don't you eat first? I can't eat all this bread on my own!"

"I already had quite a large breakfast, thank you. You go ahead, I'll have what's left over when I'm back." Lillian's face fell. "Sorry Lillian, I saw what a lovely day it was and thought I'd make the most of it. Had I known you were coming…"

"Not to worry. You have a good time and get some fresh air. It will do you good. Plenty of jobs for me to get on with here."

She lowered her head and brushed her hands off on her apron, a gesture of disappointment and I felt a twinge of guilt. She was my family, the only family I had up here – she was probably as lonely as I was. My eyes rested on her for a moment and an urge to hug her came over me. But instead, I resisted it, thanked her and left.

It took me nearly an hour to reach the centre of Crowbeck. I regretted wearing my new heels not long after I had left, and I tried to flag down every bus and tram there was but none of them wanted to stop. I was glad that I had not lost my way and felt relief to finally find the main street with all the shops and eateries. I needed somewhere to sit down and hang my coat after warming up from the walk.

A thick quilt of smoky cloud obscured the sun, it was only a matter of minutes before it would start raining. No sooner had the thought entered my mind, a shower of cold rain poured down from the heavens and I cursed as it drenched me without mercy. A quaint little coffee house across the street seemed like the perfect refuge and I ran across the tramlines to get to it.

The door in opened with a loud "ring", signalling my entrance to everyone inside and all heads turned towards me. I brushed the rain off my hat and coat and a waitress came to hang them up for me.

"Eating with anyone today, Miss?" she asked, her accent broad and friendly.

"Just a table for one please," and she led me to a small table by the corner near the window, opposite several rows of booths.

The place was dusted in pastel pink and had stained glass lamps at every table. I ordered a pot of tea and a scone and took my time observing all the customers and passers-by, studying the clock tower in the distance.

"Would you like some more hot water, Miss?" the waitress said, referring to the empty teapot.

The rain had passed, and I politely declined.

"Just the bill, please."

"Certainly, Miss. Not hungry?" She cleared the plate with the scone I had halved and lathered with jam and cream, but hardly touched. I ignored her question.

"Would you mind telling me what that big building is over there please? The one with the clock?"

"What, the Beaumont? It's the mental hospital. You must be new here if you don't know that already?"

"Yes, I am. I'm from London."

"London, you say! Well, hope you like life up here. But stay away from the hospital – once you're in, you're in for good!"

I settled the bill and opened the door with another "ring" – the bell didn't care for my wish to leave quietly. I faced the clock tower, reminding myself of the waitress's advice, and thought it best to heed to it. My feet had had enough anyway, and I felt a chill reaching in from my damp coat.

On the return home, I passed the butchers and some cuts of beef laid out on a metal tray, garnished with parsley, caught my eye. They looked like they were good quality although I didn't know much about meat or cooking, and I definitely didn't eat much either. But I thought I would do something kind for Lillian after everything she had done for me, and the guilt I felt from leaving the house this morning still lingered, so went inside.

Back at Crowbeck House, Lillian was still in the kitchen ironing some bedsheets, her sleeves tightly rolled up passed her elbows. The windows were wide open to let the steam out.

"Ah, you're back! How was it?"

"Lovely, although I did get caught in the rain."

"That's funny, it was dry up here."

"I bought us some pork chops! I'll cook for us tonight?"

"Not from the butchers on the high street surely, they charge a premium in that shop! Don't cook it on my account, put it in the freezer. It'll do for Charles when he's back."

"Lillian, it's my treat, please." I smiled at her, and the corners of her mouth turned awkwardly like she'd never been used to anyone spoiling her with something special.

I seared the meat that evening, though Lillian insisted on helping me with the vegetables. I thought I had overcooked it, judging by the length of time it took her to chew and swallow each mouthful.

"Have you heard from Charles?" she asked, gulping another portion of food down her throat. I take my time cutting my own meal up, my appetite somewhat diminished after inhaling the smell of pig fat and meat over the hob.

"He did call me last night before bed. He said he was stuck on land somewhere near Amsterdam, something about the storm coming and ships not wanting to set off in this weather. But he should be arriving at Hull by the end of tomorrow."

"He does work hard, doesn't he? He's just like his father was." John, her husband, died in the Great War. I could have only imagined how it must have felt for her only son to then be sent out for the Second. Perhaps that is why she is the way she is, always so desperate to mother. She helped me wash the dishes afterwards and wiped the final bits of crumbs off the surfaces. I switched the wireless on, and we listened to some music before the news. The reader announced that an actor had just been convicted guilty for homosexual offences and was sentenced to eighteen months in prison. I listened intently whilst Lillian tutted under her breath.

"Terrible behaviour, I never knew that he was capable of such things!" she said as she put the plates back in the cupboard. I wasn't sure how to respond but a feeling of unease sat in the pit of my stomach, and I let some silence settle between us until the news finished.

"Do you like it here, Georgina?" she asked, studying me.

"Um. I don't really know yet."

"It's early days. I was once like you, moving from a large city to a small town. People are tight and it can be hard to integrate yourself if you're not forward. There are good people here though. You'll soon find out and settle in."

I looked at her and thought that I wasn't thinking of staying beyond the summer.

"Right, I'll leave you in peace, my dear. You go and get yourself some rest. And thank you for dinner," she says.

"You're welcome. I'm sorry it was a bit dry. I'll try better next time." I folded my arms across my chest as I watch her put her coat on and thread her basket through her arm. She paused in front of me, held out her spare arm and wrapped it around me. I wasn't expecting an embrace, and my arms were locked in position against her chest. She pulled away from me, not seeming to notice how cumbersome the hug felt, and I returned her warmth with a smile.

I turned the radio off and had a long soak in the bathtub, contemplating my day. In my robes, still warm and damp, I sat at my dressing table again and wrote another entry in my diary.

CHAPTER

NINE

1953
Jane
Saturday

We sit across from Richard at the ice cream parlour that's been decorated like an American diner and Nat King Cole's *Mona Lisa* plays from the jukebox. The waitress brings us three plates full of waffles with vanilla ice cream, drizzled with chocolate over the top.

"Wow!" Jasper cries in awe and we laugh at his sweet amazement over it.

"This really is enough sugar to last us for the week!" I say.

"Yes, I'm not sure I'll be able to finish all of this. You'll have to help me out Jasper, do you think you can manage it?"

Jasper gives him an eager nod.

Richard adds a spoonful of sugar to his coffee. He looks different in his own clothing and out of his uniform. His stance is more relaxed, and he appears more comfortable in his own skin.

"Is this a regular weekend treat?" he asks.

"Gosh, no. I couldn't afford that!" I laugh. "I wanted to be extra nice today as I'll be working nights for quite a while."

"Nights? Where?"

"At the Beaumont."

"With Patient A?"

I nod.

"Why nights?"

I suddenly realise that he too is involved with my patient's case and have to be careful with what I say.

"I'm just – monitoring her sleep patterns to check for anything unusual."

"Ah."

"How's everything going with the case?" I divert the questioning towards him, and he sighs.

"Nothing's presenting itself as evidence at the moment. We might close the case next week. Could have just been a very unfortunate accident."

"Have you managed to find out who the woman was?"

"Not yet. We have our suspicions. It's a bit of a mystery. Her body was badly burnt – barely recognisable. She was found in the car near the grounds of the house right at the top of the hill, behind the Beaumont. We've been knocking at their door a few times, but the occupants are nowhere to be found." He sighs. "Anyway, it could have been a sad accident – a fault in the car or a lit cigarette on the seat, anything could have caused it." His eyes flick over to Jasper. "It's a good job that this sort of thing doesn't happen often. Let's talk about something a bit lighter?"

I smile. "So, what's a decent, young police constable like you doing stuck here where nothing much exciting happens?"

He laughs. "I like it here. Nothing much exciting suits me just fine. I'd like to think I can settle down one day and have a family. That's the life I hope for and I am very fortunate to have what I have now, I wouldn't want to be in the middle of murder investigations every day of the week."

I smile at this, taken back by how grounded he seems. Maybe I am just too cynical after the experience with the men I have had. He stops chewing his mouthful of waffle, caught in the spotlight under my gaze.

"Sorry," I say. "I'm not used to hearing men sounding so thoughtful about their futures." He looks at me and glances at Jasper. I wonder what he's thinking and whether he has his own suspicions about my history.

"I'm sure your little man here is going to grow up being just as thoughtful." He places another spoon of ice cream in his mouth. "I had an absent father growing up too."

I part my lips in surprise. Perhaps that is why he is so gentle natured.

"Story for another time," he says. "Want a reason for you to come out for ice cream again."

Outside the ice cream parlour, Richard bends down to meet Jasper and extends out his hand for a little handshake and fixes his eyes on me.

"This was really nice. Thank you... Fancy doing it again sometime?"

"Yes, but it has to be my treat next time." I turn to Jasper. "Say thank you to Richard for the ice cream and waffles."

"Thank you, Mr Richard!"

Richard ruffles his hair. "You're welcome, Master Jasper!" Jasper lets out a sweet chuckle. Richard stands up tall, puts his hat on and places a hand on my arm, planting a gentle kiss on my cheek. I catch the scent of his warm scented aftershave; my heart skips a beat and heat rushes to the skin his lips touched.

"Great to see you, have a good evening. Oh, and uh, take care heading over to the hospital tonight." He tips his hat, bowing his head slightly and walks down the path. I inhale and put on my biggest grin for Jasper.

"Do you want to do something a little bit cheeky and go to the cinema before I have to head back into hospital?" He squeals in excitement and tucks his hand firmly into mine.

* * *

The evening arrives quickly, and I leave Jasper and Kirsty at home once I've changed him into his pyjamas and settled him into bed.

"Don't you worry about a thing Jane, we will be fine!" Kirsty says, waving me off down the stairs.

I arrive for 8pm when I know that all the patients have retired in their wards or cells. The night air makes the skin on my cheeks tingle. Light dapples on the damp ground from the reception doors. I ring the doorbell and my pulse quickens with anticipation. A guard accompanied by a female nurse opens the door.

It is Nurse Weaver greeting me, just as Ruth said she would. I sense an instant warmth emanating from her smile. Sandy curls come out of her loosely tied bun that's partially covered by her cap, and she wears a thick cardigan over her uniform. How unlike Nurse Tolsy she is.

"Mrs Galloway. You're here to see Patient A?" she asks softly in a tuneful, southern Irish accent.

"I am."

"Right, but I'm afraid that she's asleep."

"Yes, it's why I'm here actually. I'd like to access her in her cell and monitor her whilst she sleeps."

"Oh? We don't usually allow visitors in the cells."

"I'm her counsellor. Dr Blythe has approved access during all hours as part of the police enquiry," I lie. "I wanted to pay an impromptu visit so that I know I'm here when everything is as normal, and no special preparations have been made that may disturb the patient's routine. I will report my visit to Dr Blythe first thing in the morning."

There is a scepticism in her expression as she listens, and I am sure that I have come to the end of my luck. Any moment now and she is going to turn me away.

"I see…" she says.

A clang in the distance coming from one of the dorms can be heard and an attendant steps out.

"Nurse?" he calls down the corridor and I am grateful for this distraction against Nurse Weaver's studying gaze.

"I'll be over in a tick," she calls to the attendant before turning back to me. "Very well. I'll quickly walk you over now. I won't be able to stay in the secure block as I have to manage the patients who might go on their nightly wanders."

The corridors are quiet at night. The day-time fluorescent lights are switched off and only a dim glow emanating from brass lanterns against the walls guides us. I hear our gentle footsteps on the marble floor. Our shadows cast over the murky green tiled walls and follow us along our path. All the gates and doors are shut. Each time she opens one, she makes sure that it is closed again after letting me through.

We reach Patient A's cell, and she turns to me.

"You'll need this."

She takes a brass flashlight hooked against the wall beside the door and passes it to me.

"I'll be outside when you're ready to come out. Just give the door a tap. The door doesn't open from the inside."

"Thank you. Will you give me an hour before coming through?"

She nods and opens the door. The patient lies still on her bed in her otherwise empty room. Her ankles are chained to the foot of it with thick, metal shackles. She faces the wall with her back turned to me. A grey blanket, ragged and threadbare, cloaks her frame. Nurse Weaver briefly checks that all is in order, nods at me and closes the door with a click. I am immediately plunged into darkness and a chill ripples through my body. It takes my eyes a few seconds to adjust, realising there is a soft orange glow coming through the barred opening in the door from the night light out in the corridor. My breath quickens as I fumble with the flashlight, feeling for the button.

A beam of light fills part of the room and I shine it across the bed, relieved to see that the patient has not moved an inch and that her eyes are still closed. I slide down and sit on the floor, leaning my back against the wall furthest away from her. In the darkness, my heart flutters and my palms are clammy. I rest the flashlight beside me, propping it up at a slight angle so that I have a clear view of her. I take a note of the time. A quarter past eight.

And I wait.

I wait for what seems a long time, until my thoughts ease, my breathing settles and I start to feel accustomed to this unusual setting. My bottom becomes numb and starts to freeze from the cold seeping up from the concrete. Although it is uncomfortable, I find it hard to keep my eyes open in the dull light and stillness. Another ten minutes, I think, and then I'll give up. Maybe Dr Blythe was right, and I let myself buy into Cleo's wild thoughts when I should have stayed at home with my son. I reach for the flashlight to turn it off.

And then.

A murmur comes through. I swiftly turn and watch her. She still faces the wall, but I see that her cover has slipped, and notice the shadow of her spine curve down the line of her back.

It is quiet again for a while.

"No…" she breathes.

My heart stills, waiting for more.

An endless amount of time passes even though it is only seconds.

She bolts up. Her back straight and her legs out in front of her, ankles tugging at the chains.

I gasp at the sight. I have never seen her move unguided until this moment. Fear grips hold of me. Could she be dangerous?

"No – no, we can't go through with this." Her voice comes out as a hoarse whisper but so clear I hear every intonation. My flashlight shines just below her body and I see that her eyes are wide open. Their dark pools reflecting only the dim light. I cannot fathom what I am seeing. The patient who has always been so still and unengaging, moves and talks right before me. She faces the wall opposite her as though whoever she is talking to in her dream, is really there.

"It's wrong," she whispers again.

Her head turns slowly towards the wall where I am sitting. Her eyes lower, aiming directly at me. My heart thumping, I try to shuffle backwards, wanting to sink into the wall behind me. My leg knocks the flashlight over. It falls to the floor, making an unbearable clatter. It rolls towards her bed and then stops just short of going under it. The cell darkens with the only illumination coming from beneath her mattress, highlighting the contours of her cheekbones. My breath quickens. Her eyes, burn into mine, and I am sure that I have woken her. I know that her feet are chained, and she cannot rise, but I still feel vulnerable. I reach my fist out to the side and tap quietly at the door. She turns as if she can hear the knock and I freeze, praying that Nurse Weaver will release me.

"He's here! Leave! Leave now!" I jump, my chest, heaving in short, sharp breaths. There is a change in her expression – the indifference I have been accustomed to falls away and is replaced with something raw. It's fear.

A few seconds pass and I realise that she is not staring at me, but *through* me. I drop my hand slowly. Her face relaxes and melts into a sad frown. She lays back down, onto her side, raising her knees up into her chest as far as she can until the chains become taught, her eyes, never leaving mine. And slowly, she starts to cry.

"I'm sorry. I'm sorry. I'm sorry," she whimpers. Her voice trails off, gentle sobs flow out of her until all is silent again and she falls back into what appears to be a deep sleep.

I gently let out a long steady breath and crawl towards her bed, reaching for the flashlight. My face is merely inches away from hers and I dare not breathe or take my eyes off her, ready to rebound if she moves again. I study the curves of the bridge of her nose, the way it mounts to the tip and softly drops down to the grove of her upper lip. Her mouth, slightly parted.

My hands feel for the metal handle of the flashlight, and I tease it into the palm of my hand. I back away in one slight movement and sit back again. I wait and wait, but it seems like my patient's strange awakening has ended for tonight.

I rise, my back skimming up against the wall like a shadow, careful not to wake her.

Very quietly, I knock at the door again.

A moment later, I hear the distant jangle of keys. A pause, and then a key slots into the keyhole of the cell door. The latch turns and the door opens, shedding a slit of light across Patient A.

Nurse Weaver locks the door behind us and faces me.

"Are you alright?" she asks, gazing at me in concern. "You look like you've seen a ghost. Did anything happen in here?"

"I'm fine. I've noted down a few things, yes."

She leads me out of the secure block and as she unlocks the main door, through the darkness, Cleo's face appears between the bars of her cell, unnerving me.

"Told ya, didn't I?" she whispers with a glint in her eye.

Nurse Weaver quickly intervenes. "Cleo, go back to sleep," she says and Cleo's face slopes away into the shadow.

"May I ask why this process is necessary?"

"I'm sorry, I can't explain much at this time. But it has been a useful session. I'd like to come again."

"Of course. Book it in at reception in the morning and I'll make sure it's all prepared for you. Would you like something warm to drink? Bring some colour back to your cheeks?"

"Oh, that's very kind of you, thank you, but I ought to get back."

The gardens at night seem so different. Intermittently lit by the amber glow of elaborate streetlamps, emitting light through sculpted trees like silhouetted phantoms lurking in the grounds. After tonight, anything seems possible and the shadows look like they could be patients, lost and wandering from their beds, or worse still, they are their spectres – there's no way of leaving, not even through the passage of death. I feel a jolt of panic. I do not wish to linger and pace quickly down the path, waiting for the last tram home, eyes wide and alert.

Kirsty doesn't stop chattering the second I am in. I politely engage in the conversation although my thoughts cloud over her voice.

"Are you alright, Jane? You seem a little distant?"

I apologise and admit to feeling tired, but I don't mention anything about what happened in my patient's cell tonight. We talk for a little longer about small, mundane issues and Kirsty returns to her apartment, seemingly content and yawning. Jasper is fast asleep in his bed and I give him a kiss on the forehead.

I fall onto the couch and relish its soft velvet touch mould itself around me like a gentle embrace. Then, second by second, I recall my moments of tonight in the cell. My patient, coming to life in the darkness. Was she merely dreaming, or was she reliving a past memory? What was she so afraid of? Who was the person she was talking to? The shock of her speaking had gripped me so much that I had forgotten to write anything she said down. If only I had taken a tape recorder.

My eyes flow over the spines of books compactly nestled together in my bookcase, rows of novels I have picked up from charity shops that I have no time to read, some of Jasper's comics and on the top row, books on psychology and the mind that I've collected throughout my years of study and dreams of earning a doctorate. A thought kicks in. I jump up towards the bookcase and skim along the top shelf in search of one particular book.

'The Psychology of Sleep', a hardback, still in its glossy jacket though it had been well roughened at the edges. I take it off the shelf, skip to the chapter that describes how dreams reflect our thoughts – a cognitive way of consolidating our memories and resolving problems we encounter during our waking hours.

The patient was found naked at dawn with blood down her body. She was in so much trauma and shock, she lost the power to speak. Who did this to her? Why was she holding Gina's name written with blood in her hand?

I return to my own bed and stare up at the ceiling, deciding that I will do whatever it takes to help her to talk. Day and night, I'll be there.

CHAPTER

TEN

1952
Georgina

y monthly didn't come last month. When I told Charles he was beyond excited. Lillian flapped around us preparing all sorts of concoctions to make sure the baby, if there was one, would stick. I thought that God had finally answered our dreams. I had done everything right after all, everything that Charles had asked of me.

But it wasn't enough. The cramps began and I started bleeding on Monday. I hid in the bathroom for a good hour, praying for the bleeding to stop and my eyes became swollen from crying. Charles frantically knocked at the door, worrying something had happened to me. That was the problem – nothing was happening to me.

Drained of all tears, I eventually came to the door.

"Has your mother left?" I asked him.

"Mother? Yes, she's gone back home. Darling, what's the matter? You're really beginning to scare me now."

I slowly unlocked the door and opened it and his worried eyes fell on mine. My hand moved down to my belly, and I shook my head, collapsing into his arms.

"Why can't I conceive? What's wrong with me?" Fresh tears found their way up again.

He kissed the top of my head.

"Nothing darling, nothing is wrong with you." He held me for a long while and broke the silence. "Perhaps we should take you to the doctor. Some medical advice might help."

That night Charles told me that he had to leave for work again and wasn't sure when he would be back. It was as if there was no reason for him to stay at home anymore. I grew cross. I told him how the loneliness doesn't seem to shift and only gets worse with each day he isn't here. How I hated myself for falling for his promise of time with me. I could feel my sanity peeling away from its hinges. But it was all a plea for him to stay. For him to love me. Was he so blind to it? Was I asking for too much?

The next day, a man appeared in my kitchen when I came down for breakfast. Charles came in through the dining room.

"Darling, you're up! Come, I'd like you to meet someone." I reached the bottom of the stairs and entered the kitchen hesitantly. "This is Alexander. He's the superintendent of Beaumont Hospital."

"The Beaumont?" I said, recalling what the waitress in the coffee shop told me. "The mental hospital?" Once you're in, you're in for good.

Alexander cupped my hand. "Lovely to meet you, Georgina. You are as beautiful as Charles has been describing! If not more so!"

"Alexander has just come to see if he can help us."

"Help us?"

"Yes. Well, I told him about our troubles… as a married couple. In confidence of course. And he's suggested some options for you that might help."

"What kind of options?"

"Please, sit down with us."

"I'll stand for now, thank you. Are you here to help us conceive?"

He glanced over at Charles. "Not exactly, no… Charles tells me that you've been feeling unhappy lately?"

"Yes, I suppose he's right. But it's only because of our situation. I'm not crazy."

"I'm not implying that you are at all Georgina, of course not. But we know that all this upheaval cannot be good on your body, nor your… mental stability. There is medication that we are able to give you, to help steady the nerves. You'll feel much better for it."

"Wouldn't they be full of side effects and lower my chances of conception even more?"

"That's a very good question, Georgina. There's no evidence to say that any of the drugs would have an adverse effect on fertility. It could be advantageous for it even, we just don't know. But what's important for you now, and for your marriage, is to ensure that you are well, and most of all, happy."

I quietly studied him. His manner was calm, steady and strangely reassuring. I was unhappy and I didn't like who I was becoming, and maybe if I had help to change how I felt, Charles would want to spend more time with me again. Charles came to sit beside me and placed his hand on mine.

"If I agreed to the medication, would I have to stay at the hospital? I don't want that. I don't want to go there."

"I can prescribe you some medicine at the comfort of your own home and see how it helps. But the protocol is usually a visit to the Beaumont where we have all the tools to give you a full assessment." He smiles. "I assure you, you'll be well looked after there. A home from home, the people call it."

I look over to Charles who squeezes my hand, but he seems reluctant to meet my eyes with his own.

"Can I at least, have some time to think about it?" I ask.

"Of course, take all the time you need. We're only down the hill. I'll leave you in peace to have your breakfast now." He rose off his chair, put his hat on and nodded at Charles.

"Thank you for coming. I really appreciate it."

"Anytime Charles, and give my love to Lillian."

Charles walked him out into the hallway to the door and I heard their conversation continue, though their voices were muffled, and I was straining to listen.

"You could do with checking on her weight every week as well. She looks very frail. Do you know if she's eating properly?" Alexander asked.

"She doesn't have much appetite these days."

"Hmm, that is disconcerting and could be symptomatic of neurotic melancholia. Do keep an eye on that and feel free to call me if you need an opinion."

"I'll try and persuade her to come and see you. Thank you, Alexander." Charles closed the door, and I heard his footsteps come through. I rung the skirt of my dress in my hands, they were sticky with cold sweat. Charles paused at the kitchen door, his face, pale and serious and I bore my eyes into him.

"So, this is what you want for me now. Lock me away because I am no good to you anymore?"

"Don't be so absurd, Georgina…"

"Absurd! Now I'm absurd as well as crazy?"

I wanted more than anything to sit and talk through our concerns calmly, but our argument grew in intensity, and I threw a glass at him. It shattered all over the floor by his feet. He glared at me like I was some sort of wild animal.

"You see! This is what I mean! These violent outbursts that come from nowhere! You need help Georgina! Alexander's a good man – he can help!"

He stormed upstairs to the bedroom. I followed him, apologising as I ran, determined to make him listen, but he was stuffing clothes into an overnight bag.

"Where are you going?"

He steadied his gaze on me.

"I can't do this anymore."

"Do what? Me? You're leaving me?"

"I just need some space to think. You won't let me help you, so just let me be on my own for a while."

"Go then, do what you're best at. Leave!"

And leave he did. I couldn't watch. I ran outside, into my secret rose garden, pouring my anger out onto the flowers, tearing their buds out. Their scarlet petals scattered the ground, leaving their bare, thorny stems to cut the flesh of my palms open. When I came back in, he was gone. I don't know when he will return.

He told me he was tired of my guilt trips and that he couldn't handle all the pressure I put on him to fulfil my own happiness anymore, that I needed to take responsibility for it, myself. Take responsibility? For my own happiness? How does anyone do that when happiness is taken from them? I don't want to be here. I don't even want to live.

There was a knock on the door. It couldn't have been Lillian as she always used her key. I lifted the pen off my diary. My hands were shaking as they rested against its pages that were stained with tears and blood.

And there the knock was again.

CHAPTER

ELEVEN

1953
Jane

I walk past the cells of the secure block towards the meeting room and a piercing scream funnels down the aisle. A female attendant runs out of Cleo's cell, her hands covering her face. Her hair, wet, clinging to her scalp, acidic yellow liquid drips off her onto the floor.

"Help!" the attendant wails. "Take her away!"

Wicked cackling comes out of the cell.

Clive, the attendant, rushes out, pushing past me and almost knocks me over.

"What the heck is going on here today?!" he yells.

I stand frozen, unable to shift my eyes from the commotion. Dread seeps its way in as I wonder what Cleo has done. Two male guards rush into her cell and Cleo yells.

"No, no, no!!! Michael! Help me!"

In a matter of seconds, she is being hoisted out of the cell, carried by her underarms, her legs, kicking and flaying.

"Get her restrained! Where are the jackets?!"

Despite her bony frame, the strength of her resistance overpowers one of them and she manages to kick him in his groin, and he crumbles onto the floor, crying out in pain. She scratches the other guard across the face, scraping the surface of his eye and he loses his grip on her. She makes a run for it down the aisle flanked by cell doors and aims for the exit at the end, but she doesn't make it far before she is tackled to the ground. A huge thump to the hard floor of the corridor and she is silent. Blood flows from beneath her skull – and her body lies still.

I run over.

"Keep your distance, Mrs Galloway!" the guard shouts at me.

"Is she breathing?" I shout back.

He doesn't reply.

"Is she breathing?!" I push past him and brush Cleo's hair aside, revealing her pale face and I feel for a pulse in her neck. I see the gentle rise of her back and know she's drawing breath.

"Get medical assistance now!" I tell the guard. His expression, ambivalent. "Do you want this to get back to Sir Feyman?"

He rolls his eyes and nods to an attendant who runs out to get help. I stay to watch the attendant come back with a stretcher and they place her on to it with little grace or care. They take her out and I follow on.

"You are taking her to a hospital, aren't you?"

"We have nurses here, Miss," says the attendant, lifting one side of the stretcher.

"Do they treat head injuries?"

"They treat everything, Miss."

At that moment, Nurse Tolsy walks out through the doors of a dormitory.

"What happened here?" she says looking onto Cleo.

"She fell," the attendant says.

"You mean she was attacked," I interject.

"She threw her bucket of urine over an attendant's head."

I shake my head and turn to Tolsy. "Is this the sort of thing you allow to happen? Who's going to be treating her head wound?"

"Take her to the White Block, I'll head over shortly," she says to Clive and then looks me stark in the eyes. "Don't you have an appointment to get to, Mrs Galloway?"

I glance into the cell that Cleo left behind, the urine pooling out of the doorway.

"What's going to happen to Cleo?"

"She'll get treated for her wound, you don't need to worry about that. You deal with your patient, and I'll deal with mine."

A guard at the end of the corridor calls my name and I break from Nurse Tolsy's glare.

Rain beats heavily against the window of the meeting room and the downpour does not look like it will ease for the day, preventing me from taking the patient out for another walk. I have taken in with me some more personal times, things for her to see, touch, taste, smell – fabrics, books, chocolate, perfume, fruit, a mirror. I want to stimulate her other senses as much as possible, but my heart isn't really in it this time as my mind keeps wandering back to Cleo. Another session passes with a glazed look over my patient's eyes.

* * *

We invite Kirsty over for tea after school, and I prepare some basic food – small joint of ham, a potato salad and a new bottle of wine. The table is set with extra effort – a gesture to thank her for her help, in hope for it to lead on to more help in the evenings.

Kirsty arrives at my front door on time, wearing a blue and white gingham dress and presents to me a modest bouquet of tulips.

"Oh, these are wonderful Kirsty, thank you, you really didn't have to."

"I wanted to!" she says, handing them over and moving her cheek towards mine. I serve the food out and Jasper wolfs it down so he can continue playing with his metal cars. Kirsty tells him he'll get indigestion if he keeps eating like that and I smile at her efforts of discipline, thinking to myself that I should probably try harder to teach him better myself.

"And how is your job going, Jane?"

"Good, thank you. Actually, I wanted to tell you about a particular patient of mine at the moment. She is mute. But I have just discovered that she sleep-talks and I would like to monitor that a little."

I feel safe enough to open up to Kirsty. I have known her since I moved into the place when Jasper was only a baby. Throughout my ups and downs after Jasper's father left, Kirsty has always been the one entity that was constant, stable and reassuring. Her husband was much older and died from illness, but she has never spoken about it. She never had any children, nor did she get married again but she always possessed a nurturing quality that I admired. We just became two single women leaning on each other. There is no one of relevance that she could possibly share the information I had at work with, and I trust her not to gossip. Part of me wants to be able to tell somebody. To remind myself that I'm not going insane. That this really was happening.

"Sleep talking? And she's mute you say? Goodness," she says. "That is interesting! Did you want some extra help with Jasper?"

"Yes, I'll need it and I was wondering if it wasn't too much for you to take that on for a short while? I'll pay you, of course."

"I've known Jasper before he could even crawl. I'd be more than happy to help."

"You will let me pay you though, won't you? I won't accept your help unless you let me."

"Jane, please – you're both like family to me."

"No really, I just couldn't. It won't be much, unfortunately – just to say thank you."

Eventually, she accepts.

"Do tell me more about this patient. What kind of things is she saying in her sleep?" I offer her another glass of wine, but she waves her hand over her glass.

"Not much yet. But I'm hoping I will get to see more."

"I've always been fascinated with dreams and the mystical meanings behind them." She rests her cutlery against her plate for a moment with a whimsical smile, deep in thought. "Perhaps the stimulation you're giving her during the day filters into her mind and manifests through her dreams?"

I stop and stare at her and she becomes aware of my gaze.

"Sorry, just an idea. I should leave the professional things to–"

"No, no. Go on?"

She laughs and blushes.

"Well, I don't really know. But don't people say that our dreams are for working the things out that happen during the day? It's funny you should talk about it really – my sister used to sleep talk a lot when we were younger. She would have the worst nightmares and scream some awful things, almost like she was possessed by the devil! We shared a bedroom and it often woke me up, it was very frightening."

"I can imagine."

"But gradually, she managed to control them somehow and she was able to tell herself during these nightmares that it was only a dream. I rarely managed to get a full night's sleep with her either screaming or chattering. Sometimes, I would be so dazed, I would wake thinking that she was talking to me. So, I would ask her questions, and she would answer them, like she was awake!"

"What questions would you ask?"

"Oh, just things in response to what she was saying. 'Anna, where are you? What are you talking about?' She would answer me very clearly. A lot of the time it was nonsense and I'd go back to sleep myself. She never remembered our conversations in the morning."

Jasper interrupts us by telling us he has finished his food and wants to go and play and Kirsty diverts the conversation.

"Would you mind if I asked *you* something?" She eyes me carefully.

"Go ahead."

"How is… your friendship with the policeman?"

"The policeman? You mean Richard?"

She nods, looking eager for me to continue.

"Well. It's fine! Nothing is going on if that is what you're insinuating?"

"I insinuate nothing my dear! He just seems like a very nice young man, and we've seen you about with him and Jasper–"

"We? Who's we?"

"You know, just friends in town, neighbours."

"All of them?"

"No, no. Just a couple."

I shift uncomfortably around in my chair at the thought of us being the centre of Bramley's gossip and start clearing the plates as a distraction.

"Well, you can tell them that we are just friends!"

"Sure. Just know that there's nothing wrong with finding a new companion for yourself in life. We're here to support you. God knows that you deserve to be made an honest woman!"

"Kirsty! I don't need a man to make me honest. Look how that turned out last time I tried! And anyway, who made up these rules for women? It's ridiculous, *and* it ridicules us! Why should we be the ones that have to nest at home all day whilst the men have all the power and freedom! Give me rules and I will find a way around them. And I'm doing perfectly well looking after myself and my son, thank you very much. When he grows up, I'll make sure that he doesn't look down on anyone because they don't have a conventional family." I fluster as I try and stack the plates together. Kirsty reaches over and places her hand over mine.

"Of course, I don't mean to upset you. You know how proud of you I am, don't you? Really, I am. I'm sorry, I was just intrigued. You know me, love a bit of romance! Men like Richard don't appear at a woman's door very often!"

She helps me move the dishes to the sink and I'm aware that I may have been a little over the top in denying my fondness of Richard. My priority is my son, which also isn't easy for any man wanting a relationship. Richard's kind face crosses my mind, and a queue of young, much more attractive women than me come into the picture. I shake the silly thought of a relationship with him out of my head. Kirsty continues with other idle talk about the neighbours, but my attention falls short again at anything other than work.

During the middle of the night, I'm woken by the shrill ring of the telephone. I rush over to pick it up.

"Hello?"

I cradle the receiver against my ear. For a long second, no one answers.

"Jane Galloway?" A woman's voice speaks quietly on the other side.

"Yes?"

Another pause.

"Hello?" I say, thinking she can't hear me. "Hello, are you there? Who is this?"

I hear her breathing gently.

"Be careful," she whispers.

Then the sound of her unsettling breath is replaced by the dull continuous disconnected tone.

CHAPTER

TWELVE

1952
Alma

The bell of the door to the coffee shop rung and that was the first time I set eyes on her. She rushed in, holding her little handbag above her head that did little to protect herself from the downpour of rain. Her hair that was likely neatly positioned, now dishevelled, wet and flat, and her fur coat matted against its lining.

The place fell into silence as we watched the waitress show her to her table. She wasn't from around here, a new arrival perhaps. Her voice was delicate, like a young girl's. Southern too. Definitely not from here.

I take a drag of my cigarette.

"Another cup?" Vicky, my friend's voice distracted me from my trance, and I turned to see her clutching onto the handle of the teapot.

"No, thank you," and she carried on with our conversation. I laughed and smiled along on cue, but I wasn't really listening.

My attention was captured by the intriguing, nervous lady. By now, she had taken her coat off to reveal a silk dress and pearl beads draping around her neck and over her elegant frame.

"Alma?"

"Sorry?" My friends laughed and I widened my eyes with amusement. My cigarette, so short, it almost singed my fingers and I stubbed it out quickly on the ash tray. "What did I just miss?"

"Where did you go?"

"I was just – seeing if the rain had stopped."

They looked over their shoulders at the same time as the woman looked up. I exchanged a small smile with her. As lovely as she looked, there was a fragility in the way her fingers wavered whilst tucking the loose strands of her hair behind her ears and fiddled with the beads of her necklace.

"How's Howard these days? Alma?"

"Hmm? Oh yes, Howard. He's doing fine, thank you. He should be coming home at the weekend."

"Wonderful news! Poor old chap, there are so many like him. I do hope that the Beaumont are treating him well."

My memory flits to the day he admitted himself to the local mental hospital. After the War, he was never quite himself again. We never made love which I could just about cope with. Other friends seemed desperate to start their own families. It was not something I personally yearned for, it all seemed much too strenuous. I never seemed to have any affinity towards children either, but in Howard, I thought I would at least have a companion to grow old with. It was our friendship that I missed. We could not even make small chit-chat anymore. I tried my best to talk to him, distract him from his thoughts, but he regularly retreated into his own mind. And his nightmares from the battlefields woke him up too many times to count. It made him too afraid to come to bed and I would often leave him sitting in his armchair looking out onto the street. I went to sleep alone, and woke up alone.

One day at breakfast, he had his newspaper at the table, but I could tell by the vacancy in his eyes that he wasn't really reading it.

"Howard, everything alright?"

He glanced up at me and folded his newspaper together.

"I'm going to see a doctor at the Beaumont. I know you must be sick of seeing me like this."

"Will they treat you right? I've heard some awful stories about the patients in there."

"Nothing can possibly be as…" His voice trailed off and I knew his mind returned to the dark, cold place I could never reach. My heart ached for him.

"How long do you think they'll keep you there for?"

"As long as is necessary."

"If you think they'll be able to help you, I'll support that. But I want you back as soon as you can. You belong at home with me."

He placed his hand upon my knee for a short moment and lifted it away again. It was as much contact as he had given me in days, and I feigned a smile.

That was three years ago. And with each visit, he grew further away from reach.

My eyes panned back over to the woman who was now moving food around her plate and not really eating any of it. I could tell she was sighing by the way she heaved her shoulders and gazed out the window on to the street outside. Her eyes, wide and forlorn. She looked as lonely as I felt. Maybe I could introduce myself to her. Perhaps she could do with a little help if she was new in town.

When it was time for her to leave, I heard her ask the waitress about the Beaumont.

"Once you're in, you're in for good," the waitress replied, and a sharp feeling of deep shame entered me. How could I have let Howard go?

CHAPTER

THIRTEEN

1953
Jane
Night

onight, Patient A lays on her back. I place the flashlight carefully on the floor, directing its beam of light below her and it softly casts over the profile of her face, drawing attention to the curves of her skeletal frame. I press the red button on a new tape recorder I bought from the local electrical shop. The button clicks in the sparse room and I wince, hoping that the sound doesn't wake her. Her breathing is slow and rhythmic. Outside the cell, I hear the soft but discordant sound of Cleo humming. It's good to see her back. The wound on her head seems to have healed fully. There is a rustling and whispering from other patients and the occasional slamming of a door from a guard beyond the confines of the secure zone which emits continual activity during the night. But in this cell, all is silent apart from the gentle whir of the tape.

I take a note of the time. A quarter past eight. And I wait.

As if by intuition, I start to sink my breathing in with the patient's. It is slow and steady until her hand starts to move, and her long slender fingers curl and grip onto her blanket.

The breathing turns into short, sharp intakes. Her eyes dart around rapidly beneath their lids. I watch intently, mesmerised by their quick jolty movements for someone who hardly blinks during the day.

In the gloom, it happens.

First murmurs, nothing decipherable.

Then,

"Wait… "

I feel my ears prick and I strain every part of me to concentrate on hearing. Her voice, so subtle, it can be confused with a breath. Silence begins to instil itself again and I wonder if I had heard wrong.

She sucks the air in.

"Wait for me," she whispers, and I know that it is real.

Her head shakes from side to side. Her legs jolt and the chains clang. She starts to cry. Tears trickle down her temples.

"No!" she shouts, making me jump. The sound reverberates off the walls. Her eyes become wide open. "No, I can't leave him. Not yet. It would break his heart."

She kicks her cover off down onto the floor and it is as if she is running in her dreams. I worry that she might just try and get up altogether.

Her hands raise up to her hair and she tugs at it.

"No, no, no… Geor – gina."

Gina. The name written in blood that she clutched on to.

"Georgina, Georgina, Georgina… *please*…"

Her voice is so choked with emotion that I feel it myself, but I cannot see what she is seeing. I want to be part of it, part of her dream, or nightmare. She falls into silence, but her eyes remain moving within their sockets.

This is the moment I wait for.

"Who is Georgina?" I ask her, softly, so that my voice filters into her dream.

She does not reply.

"Who is Georgina?" I ask again, a little firmer.

Her mouth, gapes open slightly. An exhale.

"Georg-*ina*. Georgina…"

I take a deep breath in.

"Georgina. Is that your friend? Can you see her?"

She doesn't answer me and seems to be as unaware of my voice as she is during the day. I swallow, feeling foolish at how hopeful I felt that this would work.

She starts to shake her head from side to side again, rocking it against her hard pillow and then she speaks again.

"He'll find us," her voice pained as she digs her fingers into her own palms. I edge closer to her.

"Who is he? Are you in trouble?"

A long breath escapes her lips, and she starts to sob.

"It's Jane Galloway. I want to help you. Will you let me in?"

Her quiet cries continue.

"Too late…"

I stifle my gasp. She hears me.

"What has happened? You can trust me."

I wait for a response, watching for any further movements in her face. Her sobs percolate down to silence again and as the seconds pass, her muscles eventually relax, the chains from her ankles slacken and her eye movements come to a halt, sinking back deep into their sockets again. I know that I've lost her for tonight.

My heart races, the adrenaline still surging through me from seeing what I've just witnessed, and I stay in the darkness for some time until I feel my pulse settle. I draw the musty air slowly into my lungs, stop the tape, gather my things, and tap on the door.

Nurse Weaver lets me out.

"How did it go?" she asks, closing back the door to Patient A's cell.

"Uh – alright, I think," I say, as my eyes adjust to the light.

"May I ask if anything happened?"

I glance at her, wary and unsure if can trust her. If she is part of the institution, she might object to my practice and inform those who disagree, jeopardising my work.

No, it is not the right time yet. I do, however, think that it is time to come clean to Dr Blythe and I shall do this tomorrow, before my scheduled appointment with the patient. I clutch onto my tape recorder. Now that I have enough evidence, surely, he cannot refuse it. This new occurrence is something worth exploring, not only to help the patient, but on the grounds of medical science and experiment alone and I cannot help but feel a kick of excitement. I only hope that he will be understanding that I went against his authority.

* * *

The next morning, I clock in at reception and walk straight to Dr Blythe's office. My nerves are in the pit of my stomach. Each time I make my way through the dark Victorian corridors, under endless archways, passing doors that I have already passed a few seconds before, I feel as though the walls are slowly closing in on me. I am sure that it is the second right hand turning after the dining room, but I cannot find the dining room and instead come across another endless stretch of closed doors, much like the rest and Dr Blythe's office can be seen nowhere.

Until one of the doorknobs turn and the latch clicks. I stop in my tracks.

An attendant steps out of the room and stands partly into the corridor. She mutters something to somebody still inside. Then she turns, her front facing towards me and in an instant, I recognise it's Mary. She has her head lowered and walks towards me. I'm not sure why, but I feel as though I shouldn't be there, and I retreat into the turning under the safety of the shadow. Mary hasn't noticed me and continues to pass.

I start walking and just as I am about to make the turn, Nurse Tolsy appears. We both jump at the sudden appearance of one another.

"Goodness Mrs Galloway, are you creeping the corridors for a reason?" Her voice is loud, and I make a sideways glance to see if Mary has truly gone.

"Sorry, Nurse. I must have been daydreaming."

"In a world of your own," she says shaking her head and carries on.

I make my way towards the room that Mary left. The door is ajar, and I want to peek into it, but it suddenly opens, startling me and in the doorway, stands a man, tall as the door frame, wearing a taupe herringbone suit. His eyes mirror my surprise.

"I'm so sorry. I'm a little lost," I say. The man appears speechless at first, glaring at me as though I am an intruder.

"Excuse me," he says. His voice low and resonant. He steps out, his head towering above mine and I instinctively back away, regaining the distance between us. He looks along the length of the corridor where I have come from and locks the door. His eyes drift towards my visitor's badge.

"Jane Galloway, our new counsellor." It comes unexpectedly but he starts to smile and extends out a hand. "Alexander Feyman. I've been waiting to meet you. Have you come to see me?"

The superintendent who's back from his travels, I acknowledge internally.

"It's good to finally meet you, Sir Feyman." I have never shaken a man's hand before as it has never been offered until now. I place my hand into the palm of his hand and feel his long fingers wrap around mine. "Sorry, I'm trying to find Dr Blythe."

"Wrong wing! He's in the left. This is the right. But anyway, I'm glad you're here. Let's walk over there together and we can talk." His tone is clipped, impatient, like he is in a hurry to be somewhere.

Apprehensively, I follow his lead. As we walk down the infinite length of the corridor, I am conscious of how much smaller I am than him as I almost scurry to keep up alongside him.

"How are the sessions progressing with our quiet patient?"

He obviously knows what I have been employed here for, but no one apart from Nurse Weaver currently knows about my night visits, so I have to be careful with what I say. I don't want to arouse any suspicion.

"There's little response from her. I think she must have suffered a deep trauma and does not know how to come out of it."

"Hmm yes. So, you don't see any response reactions, not even reflexive?"

"No."

We stall when we reach the dining room and I finally recognise where I am.

"She is an interesting case for sure. Report to me if you do notice any differences?"

I nod, uncertain if that was an order rather than a request. He follows it up with a smile.

"We're here." He nods his head over to the door behind me, reaches over and gives it a knock.

"Come in," Dr Blythe's voice calls from inside.

Sir Feyman opens the door and Dr Blythe peers at us over his spectacles from behind his desk. He raises one eyebrow, a look of surprise to see both of us appearing together.

"I've brought Mrs Galloway here to you. She was lost, but now – she is found." He turns to me and gives me a subtle wink.

"Thank you, Alexander, that's very good of you," Dr Blythe says. "Come in Jane!"

"I asked her to report to me any changes she sees in Patient A. You'd be alright with that, wouldn't you, Robert?"

"Of course."

Sir Feyman bows his head and closes the door behind me.

"Good to see you again. Please, take a seat. How have you been?"

He offers me tea from a delicate China pot he has on the side of his desk. I politely decline and he makes a light-hearted remark about how I made the right choice as it's already turned cold.

"And how was your last appointment with your patient?"

"As before. No progression."

"Hmm," he hums, tapping his fingers against the table. I face him, cross-legged and choose my next words very carefully. I look back towards the door, checking that it is firmly closed.

"No progression during the day, that is."

I've got his attention, and he peers at me through his glasses with curiosity.

"Dr Blythe. I want to explain something to you, but I hope that you won't feel… like I have gone against you."

"Oh dear," he says, taking his glasses off and settling his elbows onto the arms of his chair. "I'm all ears."

"I came one evening to assess her whilst she was sleeping."

He momentarily closes his eyes and shakes his head.

"Oh Jane," he sighs.

"I know, I'm sorry. I really am. It wasn't intentional. The… opportunity arrived and so I, I just followed my instinct."

"And who gave you this opportunity?"

"The charge nurse at the time allowed me in. She wasn't aware that it wasn't authorised."

"Who is..?"

I dare not say her name and get her into trouble.

"I don't want them to be disciplined in any way Dr, it was my fault. I agree that you feel it may have put me into harm's way, but I was very careful. And I'm here now because I want to share with you my findings."

He rubs the bridge of his nose as if to soothe away some agitation and extends out the palm of his hand.

"Go on?"

"Well. Our patient spoke. Quite a bit."

My statement makes him shift in his chair.

"And?"

"She has mentioned the name Georgina as a friend. Gina is the name that is written on the piece of cloth she held when you found her. And she mentions someone male – about needing to escape from *him*."

His fingers tap again, this time against the end of the arm rests.

"I see," he says.

"Not only that. I spoke to her once she had entered a calmer dream state… Dr Blythe, she understood what I said and she answered."

His eyes widen.

"I have a recording. Do you wish me to play it for you?"

"Please," he says.

I take the tape recorder out of my bag and play the evidence to him whilst I watch his reaction. He tilts one ear to the side and his forehead pinches in concentration. When the recording ends, he shakes his head and raises his hands to the air, bewildered.

"This is… revolutionary. This other man… she didn't say his name?"

I shake my head.

"I know that she was very frightened of him. Do you think perhaps… the body?"

He takes time to think, and his gaze becomes serious. I am not sure if I am to be removed off the mission because although I have found something incredible, it was against his authority.

"How can we know for certain that what she is saying is not just something conjured from her dreams? Her dreams could only be an expression of her emotional distress – what if there is no such man? Or perhaps this male figure isn't a man at all, and is a monster."

"I understand. But I think for now, the miracle is that she *can* speak. She *is* speaking. And moving! She can turn in her sleep. I'm sure if her shackles were removed, she'd be able to get up and walk. I do believe that in time, she'll be able to say much, much more."

He is quiet for a moment, and I let myself sit under his calm scrutiny.

"I do not appreciate my orders not being followed Jane. I restricted you for a good reason – for your own safety."

My heart starts to sink.

"But," he says.

"I'll allow you to continue this experiment. I may need to organise for an extra guard or attendant to stand duty the nights you visit but I need some time to figure out who. You can tell me the name of the charge nurse, she won't be sanctioned in any way."

A giant weight lifts off my chest and I clench my fists in eagerness.

"And please listen to me when I say that you must be careful Jane. You might not know who you're dealing with and what you might uncover."

I nod enthusiastically.

"Will you still continue your daytime appointments with her?"

"Yes, Doctor."

"Good. One more thing. Let's not advertise this to everyone here. The man who walked you to this room is not so accepting of new… treatments. Not of this sort anyway. He prefers medication and surgery. I had a difficult time trying to enrol your help especially since you are a woman, but it was a little easier to do so whilst he's been away. I thought if she was under any danger then it would be better if we enrolled a female counsellor, someone she could trust with a softer touch, to coax her out."

I try not to blink at the word 'woman' and the way his eyes wash over me from head to toe.

He continues. "He and many members of the staff think talking about your problems is unorthodox, improper even – too Freudian! But if anyone says anything, let me deal with it." The faces of those he might be talking about come into mind and Nurse Tolsy is at the forefront.

"What about Nurse Weaver? She is the charge nurse in the evenings. Although I didn't give anything that happened inside the cell away."

"The fewer who know, the better. Keep it quiet for now. And for goodness sake, keep those shackles on her, she may be unpredictable and I can't have you being hurt."

He places his spectacles back over the bridge of his nose and takes hold of his pencil to start writing in his notes as in signal for me to leave.

"Dr Blythe?"

He lifts his eyes to meet me.

"Thank you. Thank you so much."

He nods in acknowledgement. Relief washes through me as I leave the room, thankful for having one less person to deceive.

CHAPTER
FOURTEEN

1952
Georgina's Diary Entry

I'm sorry it's been so long since I've written to you. I'm starting to feel as though I'm neglecting you. I know it's silly – after all, you are just a book of blank pages until I fill you with my thoughts. But then I think that you've been my saving grace for all these weeks. Everything I've felt, you feel. All my burdens, you carry too and you now hold a part of me.

I have some news – I've met a new friend!

Her name is Alma.

She appeared at my door at my lowest point with a bouquet of flowers and I was struck by her bright smile. She recognised me from the coffee shop the other week and wanted to introduce herself, although I couldn't say that I remembered her.

I was conscious of how red my eyes must have appeared from crying and saw her look of shock when the direction of her eyes fell onto the mauled skin on my hands. I apologised and made a little joke out of fighting with a rose bush, and she laughed which put me at ease.

She had this expectant look on her face and it felt rude to not invite her in, so I asked if she wanted a cup of tea. She seemed in awe of the house as soon as she walked in, and I told her to make herself at home whilst I went into the bathroom and fixed my face and hair. I tugged the ends of the sleeves of my cardigan down so the cuts wouldn't draw her attention again. I must have looked quite unwell, and I hoped that she was not just another busy body wanting to know my business.

It turned out we have a lot in common. We're similar in age, also married to husbands who travel a lot – I didn't want to tell her that Charles and I had an argument and I didn't know when he would return. She lives in the white house at the top of the hill behind the Beaumont, so we both feel a little detached from the rest of the town. I felt an instant warmth towards her, and we have met up a few times since then for walks in the countryside – I'm getting to know her quite well and I feel secure in her company. I'm starting to laugh more and catch myself smiling even when I'm on my own.

There's something about Alma that I am quite intrigued by. It must be because she is so different to me, it's like breathing in fresh forest air. She possesses a wild and almost capricious way. Her hair, the colour of honey, is always loose and untidy with just a simple hairpin to hold part of it in place. She rests a cigarette between her fingers like she had never existed without one, her nails cut so short, down to the skin like she bites them. And she walks like a dancer would, nimble and light. I gazed at myself in the mirror this morning for a long while, wondering what it would be like to be her. I think I envy her – I wish I could be that free.

CHAPTER

FIFTEEN

1953
Jane
Day

hank you, Mary, I'll take it from here," I say, after Mary helps my patient into her wheelchair and places a blanket over her. She watches me as I push the patient into the gardens, and I try to ignore the feeling of her eyes on the back of my head. I deliberately take the long, winding path down so her gaze cannot follow us.

As before, I make a commentary on our journey, but my intentions today, are clear. I describe how blue and crisp the sky is that morning, not a cloud in the sky. How the cold air stings my cheeks and the breeze makes my eyes water. We stop at a bench, and I bend down to level my eyes with hers. She is so still, despite the wind flicking her hair around her face, bringing colour to her cool palette. She must be feeling the cold as much as I am. I take my woollen hat off and show it to her.

"This is my hat, it was made by my nan. It's very precious to me. Do you see how soft it is? And how colourful? My nan loved all the colours," I smile as I admire it and carefully take hold of her hand, tracing her fingers along its top so she can feel the bobbly surface of the crocheted wool, threads that have frayed over its surface into a fine layer of fluff from years of use. They stiffly glide over the hat and fall back on to her lap. Her eyes are looking elsewhere, and nowhere.

"It's getting very cold, so I'm going to lend you it. I'll place it over your head to keep it warm." I pull the bottom of the hat down over her ears. In an instant, she appears like any other normal civilian, not a prisoner inside an asylum, or inside herself. "Is that better?" I smile. "It suits you. You look really lovely. If only I could hold up a mirror to show you… I wish I knew your name."

I look for any change in the size of her pupils at the sound of my voice, but I do not see a thing. The hospital building spans out behind her and stretches through the view like an impenetrable wall. And I am sure that through one of the doors, Mary stands on guard waiting for our return.

"Let's go a bit further afield, shall we?" I say to my patient.

We wander off the main campus, across the lane and pass the church. The wheelchair bumps along the path down the graveyard, beyond rows of headstones, some weathered and centuries old, and some nearly new and polished. The patient is unable to keep her body straight and her head lolls to the side, so I pause a couple of times to reposition her.

We arrive at a memorial garden where men from Crowbeck who lost their lives in the War lie at rest. We stroll along the headstones, and I take in all the names and the years they were born not nearly enough decades ago, and a sharp pang of sadness cuts me as the memory of the War is still fresh in my mind. Somewhere along the path I forget to speak, and my ongoing explanations stop as I wonder to myself where my patient was during the times of War. Did she work? Did she have family or friends she lived with? Perhaps she is widowed like so many of the women are today.

Towards the end I see what looks like an open lawn, overgrown grass stretching for about half a mile wide and deep, maybe more. About two thirds of the way along are rectangular mounds of soil where the earth has been disturbed in a succinct and methodical line. In the centre of it all, sits one stone pillar. Intrigued, I walk across the lawn, using more force to roll her chair against the wet blades of grass that catch in the wheels. Upon the pillar, an engraving.

In memory of the lost souls. May they rest in peace in the arms of God.

It only occurs to me now, that I stand upon the graves of the dead, the ones that passed away in the Beaumont, the ones whose families did not come to bury or claim as their own. The lost souls, without even headstones to mark their existence.

I turn to my own patient who is still very much alive, but whose eyes are like glass marbles, vacant, glazed, and now fixed on the tips of the grass by her feet. Please God, I pray that she does not become one of these souls. I place my hand over hers.

"My dear. Can you hear me?" I receive nothing in return and envelop her cold hand in my own. "It's Jane. Listen to my voice. Feel my touch." Then, like a flicker of light, the pupils of her eyes

121

contract ever so slightly. I am sure that I did not imagine it. A split second of response, but it meant everything. Just to be away from the prying eyes of the institute may have sparked the change.

"What you do in your sleep, when you talk – I need you to do that when you are awake with me. When the sun is up, and I am here to see you. We don't have to tell anybody. It can be just between you and me. A secret. I will protect you."

Her other hand that rests on her lap, slips down to the side of her thigh. I fold her blanket over it to keep her warm. Perhaps taking her to other places may encourage her further, places she may have been to before, places that herself and Georgina might have been.

I take in the view of the hills around us, a patchwork of greens and browns, sewn together by limestone walls. I did not realise how close we were to the moorland. Around the perimeter of the unmarked graves, I spot the railway line. After that, is the first hillside with trees defining its top, their branches still mostly bare, with just a few green shoots. And near the hill's peak, a distinctive, white cottage set upon it.

As I wheel her back into the premises, I smile inwardly at the progress we are making. Just a little flicker, but I know that in the depths of her mind, it means much more. I think towards this evening and what she might reveal to me. Mary has not moved from her position by the door except that Nurse Tolsy has joined her. Her hard glare penetrates the distance between us, her arms cross over her chest.

I lower my head down to the patient's ear.

"See you tonight," I whisper.

Without a glance from Mary, she wheels my patient inside.

"You're not supposed to take patients away from the hospital grounds," says Tolsy.

"I have permission from Dr Blythe."

"Still, you have made her late for her wash and we have a strict timetable for the use of the bathroom facilities."

I sigh. "I'm very sorry. I'll keep an eye on the time during the next appointment."

Tolsy stands as solid as a boulder.

"Nurse Tolsy, is there something you'd like to say to me? Do you disagree with the way I practice?"

"You may not respect it Mrs Galloway, but everyone here must follow the rules. We are all here for one thing, and that's to take care of our patients."

"As am I."

"When I see it, I'll believe it." She struts away from me. I shake my head in disbelief.

"If you think I'm bad now, wait 'til the sun goes down," I mutter under my breath.

* * *

Night

When the clock strikes eight at night and my tram arrives at the Beaumont, the deadly quiet entrance never ceases to unnerve me. As the wind pushes past treetops, making their branches sway like arms of gangly ghouls, I cling onto the feeling of Jasper as my beacon of comfort. His hair, damp, and his skin still blush from his warm bath. The soft wetness of his lips from his goodnight kiss and his sweet giggle.

The large hospital doors open, and a familiar hall porter lets me inside.

"Where is Nurse Weaver?" I ask him.

"She's just with a patient. I'm Raymond."

"Yes, I think we've met."

He nods. "I'll let you into Unit 1," he says, walking me though to Patient A's cell.

"Nurse Weaver told you about my visit?"

"Dr Blythe did. I know it's confidential, don't worry Mrs Galloway, I won't say a word to anyone. Been here long enough to know who to talk to and who not to talk to. The walls here have ears too so be careful with what you say, even to the people you like."

"And who do you like?"

"Oh, I just keep to myself. Easier that way. People come and go, you don't get 'chance to get attached."

I suppose if Dr Blythe can trust Raymond, then so must I, but from first appearances, he seems like quite an uncomplicated and straightforward man. We reach the isolated cells lining the dark corridor of the secure block, lit only by the dull orange glow. He holds open the door.

"I'll be right outside when you need me. Just tap on the door or call my name."

"You can tap on my door anytime, Raymond," Cleo's voice rings out from her cell.

"Get back to bed!" He rolls his eyes and sighs. I hear her distant chuckle as I enter Patient A's cell.

At a quarter past eight, a ritual is taking shape. I set up the tape recorder by my side, take out my flashlight, notebook and pen, and settle onto the floor opposite the length of her bed. I press the record button and sit silently, watching her breathe.

Right at the time I expect, she starts to stir, and in the dimness, a moan drifts out of her.

"Hmm… No…"

She begins to shuffle, her breathing hitches.

"Georgina…"

I sit upright with all my focus on her.

She slowly exhales.

"I'm sorry…" she whispers. "You shouldn't be here. It was a mistake." Her voice is as clear as though she is speaking consciously to me now.

A pause.

"Quickly, you must go!"

"Where to?" I ask.

"It doesn't matter now, I'll find you." She's talking directly at me, but her eyes are closed. "There's no time. He will kill us."

She tugs at her blanket and her legs jerk, needing to run, but she cannot because she is tied to the end of the bed. The chains scrape and clang against the metal railings. I fear that the noise of it will wake her, but I do not realise what is to come.

A deafening shriek escapes from her lips.

"Go!!!" she screams. "Now!!!"

I jump and hear a groan come out from another patient's cell.

The latch clicks and the door is ajar. Raymond's silhouette stands in the gap. The patient is still kicking and yanking at her blanket. I raise my palm towards him, and slowly beckon him away, a signal to ask him to stay outside, and a nod to let him know I am well. He closes the door until it clicks shut and I turn back to the patient, who by now is in tears.

"NO!! Why?" she cries. "Georgina, why?"

Her panic rises. I suppress the urge to hold her hand. I want her to feel my touch to reassure her that she is safe, but I don't want to risk waking her. I don't want her to fall out of this trance. I want to take this further.

"Can you tell me what you see?"

"Blood… So. Much. Blood…" She turns her face towards me, her eyes darken with anguish, paralysing me under her gaze.

"Whose blood?" I ask.

A pause as her stare deepens and she opens her lips again.

"What did you do?" she hisses. "Have you killed her?"

Fear creeps into me and I struggle to keep hold of my pen as my palms start to sweat. I am trapped inside her dream but I'm not sure who I am to her. How do I get out of this? I am in too deep. I swallow down my nerves and play the role she casts me, whoever it may be.

"Is it Georgina?"

She exhales. "Yes…"

"Is she alive?"

A tear rolls down her cheek. "I don't know."

"Are you safe?"

"No…" Her breath quickens. "I'm sorry Georgie… my Gina." Her legs start kicking as though she is running.

Another deathly scream follows, her face contorts into terror. I raise my hands to my ears reflexively and squeeze my eyes shut because I cannot bare her stare any longer. And then… Silence. Her kicking slows until it stops completely, and her eyes eventually close. I sigh a long single breath. I have failed again, unable to move the patient past this point and calm her from her fear. How do I get her to tell me her name? Who is this other person who she's terrified of and where is Georgina now, if not already buried underground?

I tap on the door so Raymond can let me out and the hinges of the door creak as it opens. My joints feel stiff as I rise off the floor and see his face which is a welcoming sight, sane, real and human.

"That was quite something," he whispers, wide eyed. I make a point of looking into Cleo's cell as we walk past it, but she is already there, her eyes full of knowing. I furrow my eyebrows, wondering if she knows more than I do.

When Raymond locks the door to the secure zone behind us, I turn to him.

"You won't say anything about tonight? Nobody is to know, not the superintendent, no guards, attendants, nurses or patients."

"I know the rules, Mrs Galloway," he assures me.

At the other end of the corridor, a door opens and Nurse Weaver walks through it as if able to hear the mention of a nurse through solid walls. Raymond disappears through another door, and we are on our own.

"Would you like a cup of tea before you head back?" she asks.

I check my watch and there is still time before the next tram arrives. I follow her to the staff kitchen where I take a seat on a standard hospital chair. Everything is pale blue and white, lit by one harsh florescent tube.

"Just call me Serene. You don't have to be formal around me. Especially during these hours. I've seen you here day and night," she says as she fills the kettle. "How did it go?" She takes two cups out of the cupboard and places a tea bag in each. "Milk and sugar?"

"Just half a spoonful and some milk please. You can call me Jane as well."

She hands the tea over to me and we sit in silence for a while.

"Are you tired?" she asks.

"No, I'm fine." I smile, although a dull ache's reaching my head. I am unable to tear my thoughts away from Patient A's scrambled dream.

"How long have you worked here?" I ask.

"Oh, uh, probably about five years I'd say. Kind of lose track."

"You must be able to get to know the patients well."

"I guess you could say that, yes."

"What about the people of Crowbeck?"

She shakes her head. "I don't venture out into town much, only on a Wednesday, my day off."

"The murder," I begin saying, "of the woman that Patient A is associated with. Did you hear anything about that?"

Her blue eyes rest on mine and she takes a deep breath.

"That was a hard day. Shocked us all. Poor soul." She gets up and busies herself with tidying the countertop. "No one knew who she was or dared to really talk about it."

"Can you tell me exactly where the body was found?"

"Near Chalk House at the top of the hill behind the railway line." Her expression becomes more serious. "Why?"

I take a few more sips of tea, borrowing a few seconds to formulate a careful reply.

"I – was just wondering what really happened." I divert the conversation back to her. "It mustn't be easy. Living here as well as working here?"

"No, there's no getting away from it, that's for sure! Beats being poor though. My husband died a few years ago."

"Oh, I'm so sorry. In the War?"

"No no, he was poorly. These things happen. Got to look on the bright side – I have the freedom now to help during the hours everyone else wants to be at home with their families. They don't pay me too badly. Still, I shan't stay for that long. Another year or two maybe. How about yourself? Will you stay once you've finished treating your patient?"

"I'm not sure how long it will take for my patient to recover. She may never fully recover. And I may not have a say in how long I wish to stay for."

"Oh? Why's that?"

"It seems that Dr Blythe has a different method of running the place compared to Sir Feyman?"

"I have noticed some contradictions, yes. They both have a unconventional rule book of their own."

I raise an eyebrow. "How do you mean?"

"Well, call me ignorant, but I have worked here a fair while and I've never seen a counsellor working so closely with a patient before, taking on responsibilities that a doctor normally would?"

I lower my eyes from her gaze and smile. Serene had a keener eye than I had assumed.

"I'd appreciate it if you didn't discuss my role with the patient with others in the hospital. Dr Blythe and I solely just want to help the patient."

"I understand. To be honest, I admire you. And I envy you too. It's not common to see another woman trying to reach for more than they are given, is it? And to have a male doctor to back your decisions is something we could all do with having." She changes the tone of our conversation. "Another cup of tea?"

Our exchange over the two leaders doesn't go much further and we end up amusing ourselves with talk about Tolsy and some of the attendants. In the midst of stifling our own laughter, something out in the corridor catches my eye. We still our voices and I hear a shuffling of footsteps. A figure in white walks past the staff room, casting a ghostly shadow along the side wall.

"Evelyn?" Nurse Weaver calls. The corridor is silent. I wonder how she knows who's shadow it belongs to. "Evelyn, are you up again?" A woman in a long nightgown shuffles to the doorway.

"I need the toilet, Nurse."

"They aren't that way, Evelyn. Where is Harold?"

Evelyn shrugs and Serene rolls her eyes up.

"Asleep on the job, probably!" she scowls to herself. Then she turns to me.

"I'm going to have to love you and leave you now. Thanks for the chat, it's nice to hear some laughter! Will you be alright getting home?"

I look at my watch and drink the rest of my tea.

"Yes, thank you Nurse Weaver."

"Just leave the cup there, I'll sort it out. And call me Serene," she calls back to me as she wanders off down the corridor.

CHAPTER
SIXTEEN

1952
A letter to Alma
18th May, 1952

Dear Alma,

I hope you are well?

Thank you for inviting me over for dinner on Thursday night. What a wonderful, charming house you have. Thank you also for the delicious meal. You are truly so talented in the kitchen!

You must come round so I can return the effort! Shall we say next week Monday? Come and stay the night. There's so much room, it would be nice to fill it a bit. I will prepare the spare bedroom and we can take Charles's car, drive into town and watch a film together! Have you seen the new Gene Kelly film – Singing in the Rain? I love Gene but really I'm a bigger fan of Jean Hagen. If only I had half her elegance and grace. We could see that and then go for some dinner. A new restaurant called "Fine and Pheasant" opened just last month and I have been dying to try it but with Charles always away, there has never been an opportunity. I may be old and grey by the time he is able to join me. Would you like to go? I'll book the tickets and make reservations – My treat!

Lately, I've been enjoying my walks. They are in solitude, but I feel that they clear my muddied mind and shifts my melancholy a little. Lillian pops in and out as she pleases. I do sometimes enjoy her company, but we really don't have much in common. Perhaps I'm being unfair on her. She's never done anything unkind. I just find the way she fusses over everything agitating!

I didn't feel like it was a good time to share this when we saw you. But Charles and I have been trying for a baby – for quite some time. Things used to be good between us – really good. Now Charles and I hardly see each other and when we do, we can't help but argue. Our last fight was so bad that he left for days.

Charles' cigar business has been expanding and they keep employing new people. The new shop in Leeds has just opened and I was invited to the lavish opening ceremony where I helped Charles cut the big, bowed ribbon at the door before everyone came in. The place was astounding! They must have clearly spent a lot of money doing up the place, so rich with decorative panelling, burgundy velvet stools, leather armchairs, crystal chandeliers and endless rows of glass cabinets full of cigars from all over the world. I'm sure that they even have gold on the walls! I was a proud wife that day.

I met a lot of his new co-workers too. His friend, Alexander was there, the one who owns or manages the Beaumont. The way he addresses me makes me feel dreadfully uncomfortable. I'm not sure why Charles had to invite him, but it seems like he highly respects him, to the point where he almost looks intimidated.

There were a surprising number of women too – very young and attractive ones! I distinctly remember one called Cassandra because she acted like she had known Charles for a much longer time. I asked Charles about her, but he just brushed it off and told me that she was just the company's secretary and had been working for them for many years.

I've been trying to accept that but then he's started to come home increasingly late from work. Missing tea and supper most nights. I suggested that I could go and help him at the shop – it's not as if I'm busy and it would be a nice way for us to spend more time together, but he strongly disagreed and told me that I was still looking frail, and that my health comes first. I'm sure it is because he means well.

I'm so sorry, I've just drivelled on. I do hope that all is well with yourself and Howard?

I heard that there is a lovely walk by the River Wharfe. Would you like to join me for a walk one day when the skies are brighter? We could take a picnic. Not so big that it would hinder our walking.

I'm looking forward to seeing you and some company so much, I could jive on the spot! Why is it always so grey here? It's meant to be Summer now – I long for the sun!

Yours truly,

Georgina

CHAPTER

SEVENTEEN

1953
Jane
Day

I sit across the table from Dr Blythe as he listens to the recording from last night and he rubs his brow in concentration. The patient's eerie calls through the small speaker are interfered by crackles and the droning of the machine. He looks up at me after the patient appears to enter back into a deep sleep.

"We need to move her past her point of despair," he says.

"I'm not sure how. If I force my way in, there's a huge risk that she'll just regress."

"Then make her feel at ease. If you are able to guide her through her visions, her dreams, then take her to the places where she was happy before she lost her voice. Then, when she is more comfortable, bring her back to that night. We want to find out what happened."

"I thought I wasn't meant to be getting involved with any detective work and that I was just employed to help the patient gain her voice again?"

He sighs and closes the patient's file. "No, you're right Jane, sorry. There's been pressure put on me about this whole situation and my employment of you. Whether you are able to help her talk or not will affect her future very soon. She doesn't talk when the sun is out and everyone else is listening. So, make her talk under the cover of the moonlight. Keep up the work during the day too. Tease her senses out. Time's ticking. She'll be scheduled for a lobotomy before the year's out and you know she won't be the same person after that."

"Who'll scheduled it?" I gasp.

He holds his hands up. "Take a guess."

"Sir Feyman? Why?"

"Because he's returned from his travels and has decided that certain changes need to be made. He's applying his decision with a broad stroke of the brush. He doesn't care about the people and their own individual needs like you and I do. Another batch of new, untested drugs have arrived. He's already warned me that he'll be selecting some patients for a medical review and lobotomies over the month. And on top of that, she might still be convicted of murder. Do you see now why we need to act fast?"

Nausea rises from my stomach. Having to push my patient to speak to stop her brain from being mutilated and clear her name of murder was all too overwhelming.

"I – I don't know if I can do this, Dr Blythe," I choke. "I know you've taken a risk with me and I'm so grateful for everything you've done, but this – this is far more than I can handle."

"Jane, please. There's no one else. Only you can do this."

I'm with my patient in the same meeting room again, staring into her quiet face, wondering what I'm to do.

From my bag, I take out my tape recorder and place it on the table in front of her. I pay a glance towards the door to check no one is there listening, and I play one of her night sessions back to her, watching her carefully for any reaction.

"Can you hear that? It's you. It's your voice. You're talking."

The patient rests her eyes blankly at the table before her.

"You're reliving the same nightmare over and over again, each time, the same thing happens to you. What you're going through in your sleep – did this really happen to you? Was this your last night with Georgina? Can you close your eyes or blink or nod? Show me any sign that you understand what I'm saying?" She gives me nothing in return and I sigh, reverting back to another new set of materials I bring to the table for her to feel, see, smell.

When I return home with Jasper, I plate up a sandwich for him to eat whilst I pick up the phone and try to call Richard.

"Hello?"

"Richard, hello. It's Jane. I wasn't sure you'd be in."

"Been in all day – heading out for the night shift in a couple of hours. How are you?"

"I'm fine thank you, I just wanted to check with you on something. Do you remember the patient I'm treating at the Beaumont? My manager tells me that she might still be prosecuted for the murder?"

I hear him sigh. "Yes, it seems that they're not going to pass it off as an accident. The sergeant thinks some evidence has come in to suggest that there could be a link between the death of that woman and your patient. He didn't tell me what it was."

"I see. Do you think you could find out?"

"For you? Jane – you know I like you but that might be crossing the line."

"Sorry, I know I'm asking for too much. I'm just worried about my patient. It seems hardly fair if she can't defend herself."

"I can understand that." He pauses and I think that might be the end of our conversation, but he adds, "I'll see what I can do."

I thank him, not expecting much to come of it but pleased that he'll at least try, and I put the phone down to see that Jasper has finished his meal and starts to play with the tape recorder I left on the dining table.

"Jay, no! You can't use Mama's things without asking!"

"Sorry! I was just looking! What is this?" he says.

"It's a tape recorder, and it's for work. Not a toy!"

"Oh, what about the flashlight. Can I just look at that, please?"

"Alright, fine. Just until Kirsty comes over, alright?"

He nods as he flicks the flashlight on and shines it through one of his toy cars.

Night

I am in the hospital so often now that its dulled, magnolia walls, green tiles and iron gates feel more familiar to me than my own home. Kirsty must be in my apartment more than me and there is a growing ache in my heart when I think of Jasper. He's starting to get tearful when I say goodnight to him after his bath, asking why I must leave and why I never read his bedtime stories anymore. I can feel the anxiety building within him. I tell him that it's work, that it won't be for much longer.

It's a quarter past eight. I'm on the floor of Patient A's cell, setting up to record what she might reveal, hoping that one night she will say something I haven't heard of yet. But it is always the same. "Georgina, no, Georgina." Over and over like she is stuck in the same loop of events, every night, unable to move backwards or forwards from that single moment in time. I could replay last night's tape and it would be no different to the recording from the night before, or the night three weeks ago.

I still don't know her name.

I miss spending time with Jasper, holding his body close into mine for one final hug before he falls asleep. The room feels darker than usual, jogging my memory that I'd left my flashlight with Jasper to play with at home. No matter, I think. The dull orange light is enough for me to see what I need.

"NO!" she screams again. "Georgina! Stop!"

She sits upright, heaving short breaths in and out. The sounds of her staccato panting fill the cell, her chest rises and falls in quick succession. Her dark eyes like black holes stare at the wall opposite her. I dare to stand up, stalk around the bed and meet her, see the trauma sketched all over the contorted lines of her face. I am hardly breathing as I watch. Do I try and intervene? I feel the pressure of Dr Blythe's words deepening.

I do something I've not done before and sit down beside her bed, close enough for me to touch her. I reach my hand and place it over her shoulder. Her gasps subside.

"This is Jane, your counsellor. You're safe. Where are you? Tell me what you see?" I ask.

There is a delay before she speaks, like my words travel some distance to reach her. Her lips open apart, but nothing comes out.

"Tell me what you see," I say more firmly. It's a command more than a question.

"Fire!" she whispers.

Fire? She's never mentioned this before.

"Where is the fire?"

"The car! It's burning hot!" Her eyes lower to her hands and pan up her sleeves. "There is oil, all over. It stings. I have to get it off! It needs to come off! Off! Off! Off!" Her hands grip hold of her gown, tugging it from her skin and I jump away from her. She shuffles her bottom on the bed until she manages to drag the gown off her entire body, and she throws it at my feet. I feel its fabric draping over my skin, warm from her own heat. Her small breasts hang down against her bony chest, a distressing sight in its stark bare form in front of me.

"Talk me through what's happening now." I manage to say, narrowly keeping my fear at bay.

She slowly turns her eyes towards me, and I am trapped, hypnotised by her gaze.

"Run!" she breathes.

Suddenly her face disappears. A loud click sounds from the hospital somewhere in the distance and we plummet into darkness. A black out. I now kick myself for forgetting my flashlight tonight out of all nights.

I stand in my spot, able only to rely on my hearing and my sense of touch heightens so much, the tips of my fingers tingle and the fine hairs of my skin stand on end. The sound of heavily ladened breathing comes from my patient in her bed.

But without warning, her breathing stops. I cannot see her; I cannot hear her.

An electric buzz resonates in the air as light snaps back on like a flash but is unable to sustain itself. It flickers on and off and during the sparks, I see her silhouette appear like a pulse. Her long hair, now cloaking her face. I keep my eyes fixed on her position as I reach my hands back and feel the coolness of the wall behind me. I use my hands as a guide as I skirt my way towards the door, feeling her gown fall off my feet. I know that her ankles are chained to the bed, she cannot possibly move, but in her cell, fear begins to stretch its icy claws around me.

I nearly reach the door when we are submerged into the pitch black once more. I hear a faint voice in the distance, a male voice calling for help. I think it must be a guard or an attendant. Someone close by to let me out.

My eyes have to adjust to the complete absence of light again, and I search the room for her figure. She does not seem to be sitting on her bed any longer. Has she managed to break free?

"Where are you?" I whisper into the dark. My hand reaches for the door, and I peel myself away from the wall. Strange, moist air brushes the back of my neck. It is her breath.

"Here!" she whispers back. Her stony hand smothers my mouth, pulling me back as I scream into it. I grab hold of her arm and try to drag it down, but her strength is overpowering. My cries are muffled. She starts to laugh in my ear, a loud, sinister shrill that I recognise from someplace else. This isn't her. It can't be!

"Cleo!" Raymond's low, urgent voice suddenly extends into the room. His flashlight beams through the space and frantically darts around as he struggles to get the woman off me. I catch the shadow of my patient's body lying still on her mattress, curled and naked. There is a thud as Raymond takes Cleo to the ground. He drags her back up, pulls her back into her cell and pulls out his keys to lock her door.

"Who the hell left her cell unlocked?!" he shouted, whilst I'm still heaving air back into my lungs.

As if to mock us, the lights come back on, and the block is rendered under the orange glow once more.

Raymond walks over to my patient's cell, checks she is there and locks her door. He rests his eyes on me.

"Are you alright Mrs Galloway?"

I manage a nod.

"How did she get undressed?" he asked.

My cheek stings with pain. I bring my fingers to it, tentatively feeling the dampness on them and my own blood comes into focus.

"She's got some sharp nails. You'd better get some antiseptic on that, don't know where her hands might have been," he says. "Come on, let's get you some first aid."

"Wait, what about the patient's gown?"

"She'll be alright until the morning," he says, unfazed. I disregard him and drape her blanket over her as best I can before I follow him to Serene's room and he knocks on her door.

"Hello?" I hear her voice ring from inside. Raymond swings the door open, and Serene is at her desk with spectacles on and an open pile of folders. She looks up with a smile. "Everything alright? Nothing went wrong in the black out?"

"Well, not quite Nurse Weaver," Raymond says. "Someone forgot to lock Cleo's door, so she took the opportunity to escape into Patient A's cell where Mrs Galloway was. Scared the life out of her and scratched her face."

Serene's concerned eyes scanned over my raw cheek.

"Ouch. Let's get that seen to."

"I'll leave you to it," Raymond says, giving me a nod and closing the door behind him.

"Come, sit down. Quite the evening huh?" Her voice is soft and comforting. "That really shouldn't have happened to you. Useless attendants."

I look around the room. There is a single bed in the corner. A patchwork quilt spread neatly over it. A small chest of drawers and a freestanding wardrobe in dark stained rosewood. There is a sink on the side with a small, mirrored cabinet above it.

"This is your room?" I ask.

"It is indeed. Welcome to my home!" she says with a sparkle in her eye. "Would you like a tour?"

I manage a small laugh. "It's nice," I say.

"It's simple and comfortable. We don't need much else." She heads to the cabinet and takes out a small, red medical kit. "Let's take a look at this. Doesn't look like you need stitches. Just a clean-up should fix it."

She pours some antiseptic solution onto cotton wool and wipes it against my skin. The cool liquid burns against the wound.

"Little live wire, Cleo can be," she says. "Been here for most of her years I think and all she's seen are the walls of this institute. Probably doesn't remember what life was like outside of it."

"I suppose she was just trying to have some fun." I think back to her blood-curdling laugh tonight.

"Not much fun for you though," Serene says, with a sympathetic gaze.

"Tea?"

I feel another ache in my head settling in. "I think I'd rather just head home thank you."

She nods and rises to open the door for me, stopping just short of it.

"Oh, it's the Queen's coronation tomorrow! We're having a dance in the evening. Will you be joining us?"

Of course, I had completely forgotten the biggest national occasion there ever was taking place in just a few hours' time. I remember that there won't be any appointments with my patient tomorrow but I'm faintly glad for it after tonight's upheaval.

"Um. I'm not sure. My neighbour says there's a street party and my son will want me there."

"Come after the party! Bring your son! It will be fun! Have a night off, you look like you need one."

I hesitate and think that the last place I would choose to have a night off with my son to celebrate anything, would be here, but I'm careful not to be appear snotty, seeing the amount of enthusiasm on Serene's face.

"Perhaps. I'll have to see." I smile, grateful for her invitation. It has been a very long time since anyone apart from Kirsty has wanted to include me in anything.

"I'll take that as a yes! No cancelling!" she grins.

Kirsty sits on the small armchair, working on her knitting when I return. Her hands work nimbly over what looks like an intricate fair isle pattern for a top, possibly a cardigan, in cream, brown and blue and I surmise that there's nothing she can't do. She beams a smile over to me.

"You're back! How was it?"

I let out a sigh of relief, grateful to be home. "More eventful than I had planned."

"Oh dear! You're hurt! What happened?"

"Long story. Another patient." I dig into my bag for my purse and hold out some money for her.

"Oh, I really don't like to take anything from you."

"Please Kirsty," and she reluctantly collects it into the pocket of her skirt.

I poke my head into Jasper's room and see him snoring quietly with his face almost hidden under his cover. My headache had fully set in during the tram ride home. I grab the painkillers from the cupboard and swallow them down with a glass of water. Then pull the half-opened bottle of wine on the kitchen counter towards me.

"Would you like some?" I ask Kirsty.

"No, no – it's only Monday night. I have to be up early tomorrow. There's a parish meeting before the coronation."

I don't reply and help myself to one. I drink it quickly. Kirsty's eyes never leave me and then I see them flit to an empty bottle by the bin.

"Maybe you should come with me, I know some people would love to see you."

"Come with you where?"

"The parish meeting."

"Oh gosh no. I wouldn't feel comfortable. I'm not religious."

"They… might be able to give you some comfort."

"Comfort?"

"Well, this is difficult for me to say, but it's only because I care. Really care. I think you've been drinking perhaps a little too excessively recently."

"Oh, come on Kirsty, you are joking. A little wine won't do me any harm. I've had a really, really tough day."

"But, should you be drinking with painkillers?"

I grip onto the kitchen counter and take a deep breath in to suppress it, but my exhausted self lets the next words snap out of me.

"It's fine, Kirsty."

She steps back.

"I'm sorry," I say, shaking my head. "I just have a splitting headache. There's a lot going on with work, but I am fine I promise. Thank you for looking after Jay again, you should go back and rest." Kirsty's gaze is gentle. I know she only means well. I walk over and place my hand over hers softly. "I'm alright, really."

She smiles and gathers her things, but I can tell that I've upset her.

"You know you can talk to me anytime you like, Jane. I'm a good listener as well as a babysitter." Her comment pulls at me, and I feel like I have been taking advantage of her kindness and free time.

"I know Kirsty. I appreciate it."

Once she leaves, I sit and consider hiring a proper nanny in to look after Jasper. As much as I could trust her, I did not need a neighbour prying too much into my personal life or counting the amount of wine I consume. Then guilt and self-doubt start to make their way through. Maybe I should give Kirsty a knock now and apologise for snapping at her. I shouldn't have taken my frustrations out on her. I take a look at my half-drunk glass of wine, and it doesn't look that appealing anymore. Down the kitchen sink it goes and I rest my hands on the kitchen counter, staring at the red liquid pooling down the sink hole, looking so much like blood. I close my eyes and inhale deeply, overwhelmed, I start to tremble, trying my best to hold back tears.

I am beginning to lose a sense of who I am and what my purpose is. I can't tell if I am helping my patient or sending her into a new deeper level of terror. I could have gotten myself really hurt tonight. What am I thinking, trapping myself in a cell each night with secure block patients? I'm a mother!

The phone rings and I stare at it for a moment. I don't want it to wake Jasper, but I'm worried it might be another call from the anonymous woman who hung up on me last time. With trepidation, I hold the receiver to my ear and wait without saying a word. The silence suspends time between the caller and I.

"Hello?" Richard's soft voice is on the other end of the line. Somehow, I feel both disappointment and relief.

"Hi Richard, sorry, I – was distracted for a moment."

"Jane! I'm impressed that you recognise my voice from just a word!"

I laugh, but it comes out nervously as only seconds before his call, I was trembling by the kitchen sink. "Believe it or not, there aren't many men that call me at home."

"I don't I'm afraid. I bet they're all queuing outside your door right now. In fact, I should probably come and help you fend yourself off them." Another tired laugh escapes my lips. His call, in fact, could not have come at a better time. "Sorry for the late call. I remember you saying that you work nights so I thought you wouldn't be back until around now. I've not woken Jasper up, have I?"

I crook my neck to look round the corner and check that he hasn't stirred.

"No, he's fast asleep. Are you alright?"

"Good. Yes, I've only just finished work myself and I just thought I'd check up on you." I smile even though I know he can't see me. "I also wanted to let you know that I asked the sergeant about that woman's body." My interest peaks and I stand up straight to listen. "They did a wider search on the area where they found her. There was an empty gas can and a torn-up gown in a wheat field not far from the car. There was blood on the gown, and more significantly, it was covered in gas. It wasn't an accident, and…Well, your patient was found naked, wasn't she?"

"Yes." I hold my breath, knowing that the gown must have been hers, the strip of cloth with the name, Gina, scrawled on it must have been from that gown, and that the same gas that covered the gown could have been what also set the car alight.

How strange it is that it was tonight that my patient dreamed of a fire. It was like she was sending me a message… a warning.

"I'm sorry, Jane. Looks like the investigation will have to continue. Crowbeck isn't in my section though. I won't be close to it, but if anything comes up that I'm able to say, I'll let you know."

"Thank you. I really appreciate it, Richard. I'm worried for my patient. I know she can't speak, and I have no proof that she didn't do it, but I just have this feeling. It sounds silly I know."

"It's not silly. If you need a friend, you know where I am."

I pause.

"Are you doing anything tomorrow?"

"Tomorrow? It's the Queen's coronation. I'll be working for most of the day. Celebrations often erupt into chaos."

"That's a shame. I wondered if you were going to join us at the street party." I stretch the telephone wire over to the armchair and nestle myself into it.

"Ah, no. Unfortunately not. If you're free in the evening though?"

"I said I'd attend the dance at the hospital tomorrow night. They're celebrating too."

"I see. Never mind, another time?"

"Would you like to come?"

"To the dance?"

"Yes, I mean I can't imagine that it will be like your normal kind of dance, so don't feel like you have to say yes."

"I'm intrigued. But more than anything, I'd like to spend some time with you."

I press the handset into my ear to savour his deep, resonant voice. It calms me after the incident tonight and I feel my headache subside.

We speak for over two hours about anything and nothing. It's nearly midnight. My eyelids grow heavy, and I stifle a yawn. I don't want to hang up, but I think he hears my exhaustion.

"It's late, I should let you get to bed. Big day tomorrow. I need to be up in a few hours too."

"Yes, I should let you go too. It's been nice speaking to you."

"Funny how you're just a few houses away."

I wanted to tell him that he should come over next time instead, but I stop the thought before I run away with it. It wouldn't be a good idea.

I slump into bed, smiling to myself before I enter a disturbed sleep, not deep enough to be restful, but deep enough to dream harrowing dreams of the Beaumont.

CHAPTER
EIGHTEEN

A   *lma called round as soon as she received my letter. After telling her about our marital problems, I felt a deep sense of regret and guilt – I had betrayed Charles with our secrets. It's been so long since I've had any real girlfriends, that I've forgotten how I should be interacting with them. But she was so kind and understanding. She has a way of making heavy feelings feel lighter.*

She revealed to me her own problems with Howard over tea – about how distant he seems now since returning from the war. He was one of the prisoners held in the camps in Thailand by the Japanese, poor soul. He won't talk about it with her, she can only imagine how much he has suffered and sits silently with him. He leaves home for work for days too, so we have quite a bit in common. We talked until Lillian turned up. You should have seen the surprise on Lillian's face! Completely floored by seeing me with company. She had carried over boiled beef and dumplings for dinner but didn't realise I had a guest, or she would have made more. Alma was very polite and said she wasn't meant to be staying for so long anyway.

Lillian busied herself around the house, doing all the jobs that didn't require doing, sending Alma off sooner than I wanted. Alma started to head to the door. Once we were out of ear shot, I asked her how long Howard was going to be away for. She said that he wasn't going to be back for quite a few days and I asked her to come round to stay for the night on Saturday. Lillian helps with the village dance at the Hall every last Saturday of the month so I know the house will be free.

Her smile widened and she threw her arms up in excitement, wrapping them around me. Having anyone touch me like that was a shock, but I found it so refreshing! It seems like she has no boundaries, no fences built around her. So ready to let me in to her world. I watched her drive out of the grounds in her Morris Minor and felt a buzz of excitement in my gut.

I could not wait for Saturday to come! I spent most of the morning tidying the house, preparing a salad and measuring the ingredients for a sponge cake, putting pretty decorations up, and making sure we had enough drinks in.

She showed up at the door and flew into my arms as though we had always been best friends. I wondered if she had brought her overnight bag. She merely held up her small clutch bag and said "cigarettes" with a grin. I asked her if she wanted any tea. She laughed and asked if I had anything stronger, so I made us both a glass of gin fizz with a couple of olives in each, a recipe I had followed from the Good Housekeeping book I bought over from London. I gave her the grand tour of the garden and the house, showing off the new washing machine and fridge that Charles had bought. She seemed in awe of everything.

We had a good natter in the living room, and I made us another drink whilst I put the cake in the oven. She grabbed my hand and pulled me away, asking me to show her the upstairs too. I passed the little room that was empty and only stored boxes. I didn't tell her that our hopes and dreams of a family lay in that room. Instead, I showed her the guest room first where she would be staying. It had a large four poster bed in it. She 'ooooh'ed and asked me what was next.

I led her into mine and Charles' room. She admired the shade of green I chose for the wall and said that it was so different to what one would normally see – like an emerald from a peacock's feather. I took hold of her hand.

"This is the most exciting place of the house!" I said, opening the door to my side of the bed, which opened into my exquisite display of clothing. On the side wall were two rows of Charles' suits and shirts for every occasion. On the rear wall, were my dresses ranging from more simple day wear to evening frocks for cocktails and dancing.

I took out the dress that I intend to wear to Charles' business ball, and she loved it although she seemed to show more fascination towards his side of the dressing room, running her fingers across the sleeves of his suit jackets that were all hung neatly in a line. I did wonder at that point, whether she had taken an interest in my husband and a peculiar feeling crept in – what was it? Jealousy? I'm not sure.

I asked about Howard, bringing her husband back into conversation. She didn't seem to show any change in her. Her smile as effervescent as ever and she nonchalantly explained that Howard likes to keep busy in his allotment and doesn't mind if she leaves to *see friends. I found that strange as the last time she was here, she said that he was away for many days, but I didn't want to question her any further.*

She placed her hands over my arms and clutched them, her grin broad and beaming. "I'm so glad to have met you!" and planted a firm kiss on the tip of my nose and I caught the scent of her sweet, floral perfume. I blinked in amusement and in that moment, she asked what that smell was. It took a minute for me to realise that the cake had been in the oven for about an hour more than it should have been. I ran downstairs in panic, grabbed the oven gloves, flung the oven door open and choked on the black smoke that was steaming out from a hardened burnt cake.

I heard Alma's laugh behind me. I was never much of a cook and should have never pretended I was anything else! Instead, we made some more drinks and headed to the rose garden. The night air was still and warm, and the sky was clear, with stars like diamonds scattered across it. The gin made us heady, and she lay her head on my lap, playing with one of the roses she had picked off the wall. She put it to her nose, deeply breathed its scent in and plucked each petal away, one by one as I played with the waves of her soft hair, twiddling them around with my fingers.

Eventually, we fell asleep in my bed wearing the same clothes. I woke up next to her completely dishevelled, but she was still as beautiful as ever. How I adore her! I've only known her for such a short space of time, but it feels like I've known her all my life. How strange it is that the stronger this feeling for her grows, the more fearful I am of her. I think if Charles ever met her, he'd be completely beguiled by her bizarre and alluring ways too. I don't want him to meet her. I want to keep her all to myself.

CHAPTER
NINETEEN

2 June 1953
Jane

*B*unting stretches across the street from post to pillar and small camping tables line up the entire length of it with three tired plate settings, cakes, scones, sandwiches and jugs filled with fruit punch, Queen Elizabeth II's crowned portrait stuck on every banner, poster, paper plate and cup. I'm wearing my favourite black shirt dress with a daisy print and a light cardigan over it. It's June but there is a cool breeze in the air.

All the children are dressed up in the smartest little suits and frilly dresses with paper hats decorated with plastic jewels, waving about the British flag on wooden sticks. There is joy and hope in the air as people play games, dance and sing.

Kirsty approaches me with a tray of small delights wearing a lovely frock that I'd never seen before and a fancy, green headband with a bow on the side.

"Coronation cracker, Jane?"

"Oh, thank you." I try and pick one up as delicately as I can with two fingers. "We're so lucky with the weather today! You look fabulous too!"

"Oh, thank you! I thought I'd make an effort. It's not often we get a good excuse like this to dress up!" She smiles at me proudly. "It's good to see you in a social setting! Why don't you come and join me and Valerie at a table?"

"Oh, I won't thank you. I can't stay for long." I still don't feel comfortable mingling with other neighbours. They all smile politely at me from a distance, but I still feel their judgement over my situation with Jasper. "Jay especially has been very excited about today. He couldn't wait to get dressed up!" We glance over at him in his knight costume playing hopscotch with a few of the other boys.

"He's such a happy boy, bless him. You'll be leaving him with me tonight, won't you?"

"Ah no, actually, I'm taking him to the dance at the hospital."

"Oh! How lovely!" she says.

"Jay, it's nearly time to go. The dance at the Beaumont starts soon."

"Mama, no I don't want to go. My friends are all here!"

"But I promised the Nurse that we would. I can't let them down."

"Please Mama, can't I stay? Kirsty, will you look after me?"

"Jasper! That's rude!"

"It's alright, I can look after him if you like, Jane," Kirsty laughs.

"I couldn't – you already do so much for us!"

"It's lovely seeing them all play together, really, it's no trouble. There are loads of us around to watch him. You have fun – he can stay the night with me! I have room."

"Yes!! Please, Mama, can I stay with Kirsty? Can I?!" He tugs my hand, pleading me.

I sigh whilst Kirsty chuckles at the sight. "Oh alright!" I turn to Kirsty. "Are you sure you're alright with this?"

"Yes! Positive! We'll make sure you're well looked after, won't we Jasper?"

Jasper pulls my head towards him for a kiss and runs off with his friends to play tag. I marvel at how he usually hates me leaving without him, but I'm also inwardly relieved that he won't see the hospital tonight.

The usual tram takes me up to the hospital to join in with the next phase of celebrations. I did not even consider myself a royalist and here I am attending two parties for the Queen in one day. The first one was out of courtesy, and the second, more out of curiosity on how they will manage to turn the sterile, soulless place into something else other than that.

The coronation party at the Beaumont, it turns out, is really quite different to any other normal day. The grounds have been decorated with more bunting and flags and as I go into the dining room, a large poster of Queen Elizabeth is hanging against the wall with bouquets of flowers around it. The long curtain drapes have been drawn so the only light coming in was from the glass dome in the ceiling. An attendant brings in old decorations he salvaged from his mother's loft, a large grin fills his face. The walls of the hall are lined with seats with the rest of space left empty, presumably for dancing.

The patients are led into the room and music starts playing. It is fast paced with a brass band leading into a chorus, an ironic contradiction to the tone that the audience is projecting. And then one elderly man slowly rises out of his chair and shuffles to some sort of rhythm along the floor to another woman. He holds out his hand and bows his head and the lady's cheeks turn crimson as she wafts at the air in bashfulness. In shy reluctance, she takes his hand, and he leads her into the middle of the room. They bob their knees up and down, not in sync but with no care in the world as if they were the only two in the room. Some of the other patients clap along and start tapping their feet against the beat.

Neither Dr Blythe nor Sir Feyman are around. I see Tolsy on the other side watching with her sustained straight face, but the corner of her mouth raises a little. Maybe when she is not a nurse, she can take a minute bit of pleasure out of life. Maybe Minerva can feel good emotions. I wonder if she dances?

As daylight fades, the dome fills with darkness and the faint hint of stars. Cigarette smoke fills the room and coloured lights filter through it. Serene approaches me with a smile and two plastic cups of punch in her hand.

"Oh no, I won't, thank you."

"There's no alcohol in it."

I watch all the patients interact with the staff. It is the first time that I have seen all the patients from the men's ward in one room, interspersed between the women. A lot do not acknowledge each other and do not seem to know that they are there.

I scan the room for my patient. She is not there.

"She's still in her room," Serene says as if hearing my thoughts.

"She won't be coming?" I ask.

"Not sure. We don't usually let the patients from the secure blocks out for social events in case it gets out of hand. But I think it'll be different for Patient A since she can't actually move very well."

As if on cue, Mary appears pushing a wheelchair with my patient sitting in it. I watch closely, waiting to see where they will stop. I have an overwhelming urge to walk straight over to them and see how she is, to embrace her, telling her how sorry I am for leaving her in that state last night. I want to know who found her in the morning, and how she was, if someone had the decency to dress her back in her gown again and make sure she was warm enough. I start to make my way over when someone steps in my way.

"Pull my cracker?" one of the male attendants says, startling me.

He stands just a few inches away from me, looking at me expectantly with the cracker. If it weren't for his uniform, I would have easily confused him for a patient.

"Oh, no, thank you," I smile politely at him. He shrugs and reaches past me to grab a cocktail sausage from the table and shoves it in his mouth.

"It's been nice seeing you around here," he says whilst negotiating the meat around his mouth. "Refreshing change." I look at him and have no idea who he is. Behind him, I see Serene a few feet away and raise my eyebrows at her. I mouth the words

"Save me." She looks around her as if I would be talking to someone else and makes her way over.

"Please excuse me Stanley, could I take our counsellor away from you for a few minutes?" She turns to me and asks, "Would you like to dance Mrs Galloway?"

"Yes, I would love to!"

We start off with small side-to-side steps, moving awkwardly to a song I would not normally have danced to and as we start feeling the rhythm take over our limbs, we begin to laugh and for a moment, I feel a spark of joy.

When the music changes to another song, we walk back to the tables. My attention is drawn towards where my patient is, but I do not look at her. Instead, I find myself caught under Mary's gaze. I see straight away that it is not a friendly look. It is a cold, hard, stare. So penetrating that I find myself needing to look away and questioning why she was showing me such animosity.

"Something wrong?" Serene pulls me out of her trance.

"Nothing," I smile.

The music stops and a high-pitched frequency rings through the speakers whilst an attendant on stage adjusts his microphone. We all turn to face him.

"Uh-hem, sorry about that. Ladies and Gentlemen, please welcome our very own, immensely talented hospital band!"

Only the staff clap enthusiastically. Against the wall, there are some instruments and a piano near the centre as the musicians take their positions. Cleo is one of them. She is a very different sight to the one that went for me last night. Her eyes, calm and subdued, not crazed and frightening. She makes her way to the cello, and I am eager to listen to her play. She places her bow over the strings of the cello and starts the music off with a solo performance. Her fingers dance across the strings as she moves her bow back and forth and I am entranced by her talent that I never knew she had. But her head sags to one shoulder, her eyes glazed like she's not in the room even though her hands play effortlessly, and I think that she may be suffering from any sedatives they have given her. Or perhaps they gave her another dose, knowing that she had to be in a crowd of people tonight.

When the rest of the musicians join in, I make a beeline towards my patient. Mary's hard glare does not leave my face as I get closer. At the same time, I hear someone calling out.

"My love, my love, my love!" A male patient cuts across me. I turn to see his arms wide open. From his erratic energy, it's difficult to gauge whether or not he's being welcoming or threatening but it's alarmingly clear that this man thinks he knows my patient or Mary, and is charging straight for them. Mary's face is filled with fear, but he does not get the chance to get close, as a much larger attendant grabs hold of him, stopping him a few feet away from my patient. A guard soon joins them and hoists him away quickly. His shouts are drowned out by the orchestral music playing. I stare after them in dismay. When I turn back to see my patient, Mary is already wheeling her away. I run after them through the crowd of patients.

"Mary? Did you know that man?"

"Just another patient," she mumbles, now hardly throwing a glance in my direction.

"Is everything alright?" I ask her, but my eyes are only on Patient A. Suddenly, I see it happening. Her fingers, they're flickering. And not at random, but in time with the music. Music! The one thing I had not thought of to bring to our sessions. I look up at Mary who sees what I see and a softened expression I have never seen before, reaches her eyes.

But then, one of the other patients starts jeering in the middle of the room and it turns into full blown laughter. Others start to join in, and Mary and I are pushed to face the crowd of patients gathering around the stage. Cleo rises to her feet, bow in hand. In a slow and steady pace with no feeling from her eyes, she comes off the stage, walks up to the patient who started the commotion, and thrusts her bow into the patient's chest, pushing him over. He cries out in pain.

The laughing stops and is replaced by gasps. She raises her cello above her head and looks as though she is about to smash it into the man when a guard rushes over and intervenes just in time. Others start running in panic. One pushes me over and I cut my wrist on something sharp at the corner of the table.

Serene sees me. "You're hurt! Follow me." I leave the room with one last glance at my patient. She is still again. I go with Serene into the first aid room, and she pulls down boxes of bandages and antiseptic water.

"You're making a bit of a habit out of this, aren't you?" Serene said in jest. "I only stepped out for a minute. How did that happen this time?"

"I'm not sure. I think the table must have been broken somehow."

"Oh, so no one attacked you tonight at least?"

"No. One of the patients aggravated Cleo.'

"Cleo again? That's not good news." She inspects my wound. "It's a deep cut. You may need stitches."

"Can you do that here?"

She shakes her head. "Tolsy might be able to source the materials from the operating theatre."

"I'd rather not have to speak to her. Can you just see what you can do with a dressing?"

She lays my forearm onto her lap, and she places the wet cotton wool into my wound. It stings as the cold dampness seeps in and blends with my blood. The cotton wool slowly turns red, and she replaces it with another. She rests her eyes on mine as she does this. Taking the dressing, she places it on the gash and wraps a gauze around my wrist, expertly tying the end into a knot and cutting the end.

"There, how does that feel?"

I lift my hand off her thigh and flex my fingers.

"Good. Thank you." I sigh. "I'm so glad I didn't bring Jasper."

The door opens. It's Tolsy.

"I'm clocking off now, Sister Weaver."

"Sure, see you in the morning."

Tolsy's eyes meet mine and then travel down to my arm.

"What happened?" she asked.

"Just a little fight with a table. Table won."

"Make sure you fill in an accident form, I'll get Clive to get rid of the table," she says coldly and closes the door behind her.

I clear my throat. "Why is she like that?" I ask.

"Like what?"

"So unfriendly."

Serene frowns. "She was formally trained as a nurse for the war veterans. She looks down on us nurses that are only trained for psychiatric care. We're not proper nurses to her. I used to do the day shifts with her. I'm glad I don't have to be around her every minute of the day anymore."

"I can't imagine being so miserable all the time."

"Maybe she's just sick of being here. We all feel trapped in one way or another."

I feel a little sad for them both at this point. Was there really no other option for either of them but a form of self-chosen incarceration? Trapped is not what I want my patient to be.

"I saw my patient move at the party," I say.

"What, Patient A – move? In what way?"

"Her fingers tapped along to the music. She's becoming responsive to me. I can feel it."

Serene stops in her tracks and stares at me like she is dumbfounded. I want to share my night visits with her and everything that the patient has been telling me during her sleep, but I know I mustn't, not yet. Before she can say anything, I turn to a familiar voice behind me.

"Jane?"

"Richard, you came!" He's standing in front of me in a navy blue suit and slim tie to match.

"Sorry I'm so late. One of the attendant's said you'd be over here." He nods at Serene who smiles back at him. "I wasn't interrupting anything, was I?"

"No, I was just leaving." I turn to give Serene one last look and she nods at me before I close her door behind us.

"Where is everyone? Has it finished already?" Richard's eyes fall to my arm. "You're hurt – what happened?"

"Just a little accident. I'm fine. There was a little disruption. Sorry you came all this way for nothing. You look very smart."

"Thought I'd dress for the occasion. See what I mean about parties! Something always happens!" he says, "Are you ready to go?"

We pass the dining room and I see all the attendants tidying discarded plastic cups and plates away into bin liners. One is up on a ladder taking the paper decorations down from the walls and I feel the pity that the dance didn't end well. Richard takes me back home, turns the engine off and climbs out of his car seat before I do, to open the door for me.

"Let me walk you back in."

We reach the top of the stairs and stop at my door.

"Do you want to come in for a night cap?"

He stands so close to me that I feel my arm brush against his jacket and smell the scent of his aftershave linger in the air between us. I open the door.

"Where's Jasper?" he asks, removing his hat. I hang it up for him on one of the hooks by the door.

"He's next door with Kirsty. Hopefully fast asleep! Drink? I only have wine."

"Wine's great!"

I pull a couple of glasses from the cupboard and pour some wine into both. I turn around, placing a glass in his hand; we clink them together.

"It's been an eventful evening anyway," I say, taking a drink.

"You seem to be a bit of a target for accidents this week, that's for sure." He touches my bandage lightly with his finger. "You alright?"

I nod slowly, feeling nervous under his intense gaze. He lifts his hand to my cheek and strokes the curve of my cheek bone, tucking a loose strand of hair behind my ear. I feel myself freeze in one spot, nervous but wanting him to go further. He leans in closer, slowly, and plants a kiss on the same cheek, so slight, it feels like a feather brushing against it. He moves away to see the look in my eyes. They're wide, beckoning him to do it again.

I feel his shirt collar between my fingertips and pull his tie closer to my chest. His eyes, kind and hesitant, look down towards me. Slowly, he lowers his face towards me. It has been so long since I've felt the touch of a man, my heart's beating double time as the warmth of his lips linger against mine. My fingers grip on to his jacket. He moves away to focus on me again and I wait, my breath baited.

Then, the feeling of gravity takes over, drawing me towards him and I lose myself within his kiss. His hands grasp onto my waist as I wrap my arms around his shoulders, pulling him closer.

Eventually our kiss slows and we pull away from each other. He chuckles under his breath.

"I'd better stop before I lose control. You're too much to handle."

I grin, shyly diverting my eyes to the floor, trying to slow my breathing down. He starts to back away and I feel a yearning, wishing he would stay but knowing that it would be wiser for him not to.

"I should go. I'll take a rain check on the wine if that's alright?"

I smile and nod at him. He grabs his hat and places it back on his head, slipping away quietly.

CHAPTER
TWENTY

1952
Georgina's Diary Entry

*T*oday was a hot and sticky day! Alma and I thought we would head to Semerwater to take a picnic and cool ourselves down by the lake. We thought it would be fun to take one of the boats out but neither of us could actually row the damn thing, and we ended up drifting towards the middle of the lake, losing one of the oars along the way! Alma seemed not to care as long as she had hold of her cigarette!

I leant over the side of the boat to try and retrieve it. Of course, the boat would topple over and we capsized! Alma swam to retrieve our remaining oar and we clambered back into the boat, drenched, our dresses clinging to our skin. We looked at the sorry state of ourselves and bent double with laughter. We laughed so hard, we butted heads which only made us laugh more. But at some point during the moment of our silliness, she stilled and the laughter fizzled, ending with us existing in a moment of quietness. She looked at me in a strange sort of unsettling way and said something about needing to get home.

We rowed back towards the shore with just one oar, and it took ages and time passed even more slowly as we didn't say another word to one another. The air hung strangely between us, but I had no idea why.

As Alma drove us back home, we had our windows down and I glanced over towards her, her hair billowing around her gentle face but she hid her eyes behind her sunglasses so I couldn't gauge what she might have been feeling. All I remember thinking was how I wished our awkward moment hadn't occurred so we could laugh like nothing mattered again. Had I done something wrong? I couldn't bear to lose our friendship now.

CHAPTER

TWENTY-ONE

I know you can hear me. I know you heard that music and you felt something. Are you afraid to show it? You can trust me. I only have a few weeks left with you and I'm desperate to help you, to help you find out who you are, where you belong. You do not belong here, but if you don't speak to me, you'll stay here until you die, do you understand?" I am met only with the usual blank stare into the room. And I feel guilty for being so abrupt with my statement, for wanting to shock her into speaking like she isn't suffering from shock enough.

"I'm playing some music for you today," I say, pointing towards the phonograph in the middle of the table. "It's Bach. Are you familiar with him?" I place the needle on the groove of the vinyl and crank the motor. The music of woodwind and brass instruments fill the room and I study her whole body, mentally willing her to react. I pay particular attention to her hands and her eyes but there is not the slightest bit of movement in them.

"Do you like other music? Let's see... I have The Hills Brothers or… Why don't you believe me? By Margaret Whiting?" I shuffle through a short stack of vinyls. I gently stop Bach from playing and place the next vinyl and needle back in position.

The catchy rhythm of the record is infectious, and I start to grin, tapping the palm of my hand on my thigh. Intuitively, I grab hold of her hands and start swaying them from side to side along with the music. It is as close to a dance as we can get when an attendant opens the door and Mary comes back in. Her face is filled with shock, but I act like nothing out of the ordinary is happening. I look at the clock, an hour had passed already!

"Hello, Mary. I thought I'd continue with the celebrations from last night. Would you like to join us for a dance?" I smile, knowing she would say no. "You saw it too last night, didn't you? She moved her fingers to the music of the orchestra." I let go of her hands and gently placed them back on her thighs where they are deathly still once more.

"Yes," Mary says without a smile. She says it quietly, and only once, but once is all I need to validate that it happened, and I didn't imagine it.

I lean into the patient's ear, and I whisper softly, "See you tonight."

Night

A few nights pass and a change is happening. The evening sessions are as contrasting as the moon is to the sun. When I am in with her, the space between us is sacred. I take on the role of the person in her dream and I believe that is Georgina. The panic she displayed when we first began has subsided. I am able to calm her, and we have full conversations as if she were awake. It is as though she is learning and building up a memory of our connection.

"Georgina," the patient begins. Already, her eyes are open, staring up to the ceiling. Her voice sounds lighter tonight, unburdened.

"Yes?" I say.

"Are you happy?"

I take a deep breath in, and will myself to immerse into her dreamworld.

"Yes, I am. Are you?"

"Always, when you're near."

"Where are we?"

"In our favourite spot, by the waterfall. It's quiet here, no one can see us. No one can hear us."

I ready my pen over the notepad.

"Which waterfall is this?"

"Cauldron."

Cauldron Falls? West Burton, I scribble.

"Why do we hide from people?"

"Because it's wrong. Except it doesn't feel wrong."

"What are we doing?"

She turns to me, her eyes are soft… tender.

"Just being happy."

I see her features working into a gentle smile in the dim moonlight filtering in through the barred window and her eyes glisten through the darkness. For once, her dreams do not start with fear.

"Describe to me what you see now."

"Lavender. The scent is so strong. I run their soft tips through my fingers. So many… a field of purple. And you. Wonderful you." It feels like we have jumped through time.

"What are we doing there?"

"Running," she laughs again. "I feel free."

"Is this a memory?"

"Not sure. You're blowing dandelion seeds everywhere. Making a wish."

"I'd like you to hold on to this thought. This happiness. When you wake, you will be this happy."

She holds on to her smile for a second longer, but it fades. A single tear rolls down her temple. She shuts her eyes, and her head starts to shake, unwilling to accept my words.

"What's wrong?" I frown.

"Impossible."

"Why?"

"My husband," she whimpers.

"Your husband?"

"Yes."

"Did – your husband hurt you?"

She shakes her head again. "I cannot leave him for you. He needs me."

"Leave him for me?" I ask. "Why would you need to do that?"

"Secret. It stays a secret."

"I won't tell anyone."

"You know already… Georgina."

I want to draw out some more information, but it is difficult when she thinks I already know everything, especially if she is desperate for it to stay hidden. I need to talk to someone else she knows, someone who may still be alive.

"Can you tell me who your husband is? Where he is?"

"He… he isn't with us anymore."

"Why, what happened?"

"Secret. Secret… Secret…"

Her voice trails off, her breathing slows, and our session ends once more.

I tap gently at the door and wait for the lock to turn. The door creaks as Raymond opens it. I thank him and he leads me out of the secure block, into a corridor where Serene walks down and greets me warmly. Raymond says goodnight, I thank him and continue to walk with Serene.

"Would you like a cup of tea before you go?" she asks. I glance at my watch, there's still a little time before the last tram is here so I accept her kind gesture. The night sessions drain me, and I could do with warming up.

In her room, Serene passes me the hot cup of tea.

"How are the night visits going?"

"Alright, thank you. Just stable… Last night," I say, wanting to take control of the line of questioning as she still wasn't meant to know about the sleep talking, "there was a patient, a man who charged up towards Mary. He was shouting 'My love!' or 'My darling!' Did you see it? They dragged him away before anyone could speak to him. Do you think it's possible that he knew her?"

"Knew her? I don't know – I must have missed all of that! But perhaps it could be possible. Crowbeck is not a big town, they might have been acquainted before."

"He acted like he was much more than acquainted. Mary couldn't get away fast enough! Could I find out who he is? How many wards and blocks are there?"

Serene puffs up her face and blows air out through her mouth. "Too many to count. They're all coded in colours, apart from the secure block. I only deal with the orange and sage ward, the easier of the females. Don't know much about the others I'm afraid. I could ask Nurse Tolsy or Sir Fey–"

"No. I wouldn't want to bother them with this." I look at my watch. "Goodness, the time! I'd better go, or I'll miss the tram! Thank you for the tea, Serene. Perhaps I'll see you tomorrow?"

I march out of the front door and race to the tram stop. A couple of minutes pass but I am too late, left in the dull gloom of a single streetlight. I curse under my breath. A night owl hoots, the breeze brings its haunting call nearer towards me and I shudder. Fog rises over the top of the road, spreading its reach across the surface of the lawns and I stare into the distance where there is nothing but darkness. I try not to panic over feeling so vulnerable to the night and resign myself to the fact that I'll have to walk back inside and ask to use the telephone and call for a taxi.

I start walking up the hill again but a vehicle's full beams shine from the end of the road through the darkness. The rattling of its engine draws near. Who is it wanting to visit the hospital at this hour?

It stops at the junction and instead of turning towards the hospital entrance, it drives towards me and slows to a halt. The side window winds down.

"Jane!"

"Richard?" His familiar face peeks out from the driver's seat. "What are you doing here?"

"I rang your home and Kirsty answered. She said she was worried and that you should be home by now, so I came to find you." I'm astounded by his kindness and unable to find the words. "Come on, I'll give you a lift home."

Relief fills me as we drive away from the hospital, and I am sitting in the warmth of the car.

"Thank you for coming to get me. I ran late and wasn't aware of the time."

"It's no problem, Jane. Still working with the mute woman?"

"Yes... Although..."

"Are you alright?" Richard asks.

"Sorry... Just tired. Thank you for picking me up."

He smiles. "Any time. It's nice to have some company from someone who isn't in the police or a criminal. How is it going with her?"

I feel the tension in my face from constantly frowning and sigh. "I'm not sure I can tell you."

"I might be able help?"

"Can I trust that you won't tell anyone until I'm ready for you to?"

He glances at me. "Is it about the body?"

"No. Definitely not. But it is about my patient and her progress. I want to make sure she's protected because she's still innocent to me. Can you promise not to share it?"

"Promise," he nods.

"She has these reoccurring nightmares in her sleep, they happen at the same time every night, and during these episodes, she talks. I've been coming every night to monitor her, and I've discovered that if I start asking her questions, she can quite often respond to them. Don't get me wrong, the conversations are – disjointed. I can't get much out of her because the evenings end in the same way each time. She's scared."

"Scared? Of what?" Richard's eyes grow serious as he listens to me intently.

"I'm not certain yet. I think there's someone who wants to find her. It's a man. She won't tell me his name." Though she alluded to her husband in her dream tonight, I can't be certain now that he is the man she is fearful of.

"What else does she say?"

"She calls out a name. Georgina."

"Georgina? Georgina Bennett is the name of the woman that has been reported missing, and it links with the cloth they found her with. You should file a report, Jane. It could help with this murder case."

"I'll only be damning evidence. Please, don't say anything! I know how it might sound, but I really don't think she killed her?"

"How can you possibly know that?"

"When Georgina appears in her dreams, she's happy – and then she's really frightened of this other man. It's like she wants to protect her, not kill her. I need some more time to find out who this man is that she's so afraid of. But I can't do it if I think the police will come and take her away."

He sighs loudly and moments pass before he says anything. "I don't think that dreams and sleep talking will hold up to much in the court of law. I won't say anything for the moment."

"Thank you." He turns to me with an anxious smile. "How often do you do these evenings? I'll come and pick you up. It's not safe for a woman to be on their own this late at night. And the buses are never reliable."

"Oh no, I don't want to be troublesome. I'll be alright, thank you."

"Come on Jane, it's just a lift."

He throws a glance towards me.

"It's not that," I say.

"Then what is it?"

I struggle to find an answer and we exist in silence until we reach my home. The lounge window light shines through the drapes. He turns the engine off and he lowers his gaze to the bottom of the steering wheel.

"Would you like to come in?" I ask him.

"Another time, you seem tired. I have an early shift tomorrow." His gaze settles gently on me. "I wish you would let me help you. I don't like the thought of you taking the tram home this late at night and I might not know it if you miss it again."

I don't want to tell him that I'm too afraid to let myself depend on him. I don't want to be dependent on any man. I can't afford to let him into my life too much. I have Jasper to worry about too. He needs me to remain stable and secure. We are only inches apart yet the distance between us seems like a mile compared to what we were last night.

"Thank you for the lift home." I manage a smile and climb out the car. "I'll be in touch." He tips the outer rim of his hat down like a salute and smiles back at me.

As I walk up the stairs to my home, I'm suddenly aware that something was awry tonight and not in keeping with the usual nightly routine in the hospital. I wrack my brain around in concentration.

"Cleo," I say out loud to myself in the middle of the stairwell. Cleo wasn't in her cell.

CHAPTER
TWENTY-TWO

1952
Georgina

Charles had come back but we spoke no more of the Beaumont and why he left. We had learnt to be civil with each other for the short amount of time he was back as only a week later, he told me that he was spending yet another two or three days on business.

Lillian came in, calling my name around the house.

"Hello? Georgina! Are you in? I've made an apple sponge cake for you! Georgina?" She found me, curled up on an armchair in the sitting room, staring out the window. "Georgina, are you feeling off?"

"Charles is in Luxemburg again. I don't know when he'll be back."

"Oh. Well, how about you and I do something together?"

"No, I don't think I feel up to it."

"I heard Whitley Hall's just opened to the public again. I've always wanted to go for afternoon tea there. Come on, let's go.

Take your sad, old mother-in-law out, what do you say?" she says with a hopeful smile.

"Girls' day out?" I say, feigning an interest.

"Girls' day out!" she exclaims. "Let me nip back and change. These old clothes won't do!"

Whitley Hall was near to an hour's bus ride away, then we had to walk from the bus stop for about fifteen minutes before we got to the entrance of the Hall. The place looked more like a grand hotel than a stately home, its lobby was exuberantly decorated with Italian marble floors and gilded archways with life sized portraits of the earl and duchess who lived there in the 1800s. The restaurant waiters and waitresses were all dressed in black and white Edwardian uniform, greeting us as though we were royalty and leading us to a table by a large window with a spectacular view of the gardens. We ordered an afternoon tea to share although I was rather overwhelmed by the size of it when it arrived in a beautiful tier of three silver plates.

"Please tell me that you feel more settled now, Georgina?" Lillian asked. "Do I see you also making a friend? Who is she?"

"I'm feeling much happier, thank you, yes. My friend's called Alma. She's very kind to me."

"I'm glad to hear it. It can be a lonely place if you have no one to talk to." I watch her pinching a small cucumber sandwich between her finger and thumb and eating half of it.

"What about you? Do you feel lonely?"

"Me? Not too much. I like to keep myself busy." When Lillian wasn't around at ours, there was always something to do or someone to help whether it was the church, the Crowbeck dance every month, the summer fayre for which she wanted my help at the tombola stand, I felt as though she was always occupying herself to avoid something else. Her own thoughts perhaps. With all the hours I had spent with her since we'd moved, I just wished that she would be a bit more still.

"But what about real friends? Or, maybe, a man? I'm sure Charles wouldn't mind."

"Oh! No, I don't think so. I'm passed all that now! Quite happy to die alone and join his father then!" said Lillian.

I smile and twizzle my cup of tea around in its saucer. "Was he around much when Charles was growing up?"

"Edward? No more or less than normal I suppose. He owned a bakery on the corner of our street before he got very ill, and then he lived his remaining days in hospital. Charles was young and only remembers his dad as the baker."

"What happened to him?"

"To put it bluntly, he went mad. Insanity is the most dreadful disease. Destroys everything around you."

"I'm so sorry, Lillian."

"It's all in the past now. Let us enjoy the days we have left."

I looked out the window again and watched the people stroll amongst the floral borders under the afternoon sun, when I thought I saw Charles walking amongst the trees. I had to do a double take as I thought that I was going crazy myself. He told me he was in Luxemburg. What was he doing there? He was walking alongside another woman whose face I could not quite see at first because of her wide brimmed hat. But the moment she turned to face him and planted a kiss on his cheek, I was sure it was Cassandra, his co-worker I met at the Leeds cigar shop opening. I stared and stared at them through the glass, hoping it

185

was just my imagination, but I spotted Charles's very distinctive limp, and I would have bet everything I had on the fact that it was him.

"Are you alright, Georgina?" Lillian asked. "You've gone a little pale. Did you hear what I said about the summer fayre?" Her voice brought me back to the table where the delicate pastries and tarts were still abundant on the stand.

"Sorry Lillian, I thought I saw…" I looked over to the spot where I thought I had seen Charles and the woman that had accompanied him but they had somehow vanished and all I could see were other people strolling in the grounds. "Never mind, I must have dreamt it." She looked at me quite puzzled, but it didn't seem worth mentioning anymore. "I'm sorry Lillian, suddenly I don't feel that hungry, I actually feel a little nauseous. Do you mind if we go soon?" I feigned a smile. On our way home, Lillian chatted away but my thoughts kept drifting back to Charles and Cassandra in the gardens and the more I held that image in my mind, the more unreal it seemed. Is this what going mad feels like?

As soon as the bus was back in Crowbeck, I told Lillian that I just wanted to pop in to see Alma and asked if she'd be alright walking back to her cottage on her own. She seemed to look rather disgruntled, but we parted ways, and I headed straight for Alma's. Her house was empty when I arrived, I didn't know what to do. I rested on the step of her porch, the confusion and loneliness crept its way in until tears uncontrollably streamed down my face, and I sobbed into my knees. What seemed like hours later, she appeared.

"Georgina? Goodness, what's happened? Are you alright?" she asked. I must have looked like an awful state.

"It's Charles. I saw him with another woman."

"Oh Georgina, I'm so sorry. Come in, come in! You must be in dire need of a drink!"

She poured us a couple of glasses of rum. I took a sip, and she studied me with worry. Bit by bit, I told her my story. I told her about all the trouble Charles and I had trying to conceive and how desperately lonely I had been feeling, even before we moved up here and she listened with quiet patience until there was nothing left to say.

"Do you think that's why he's cheating on me?" I asked her. "Because I can't give him a child of his own?"

"No, of course not my dear girl! Whatever the reason is – if he is doing it – then it can only be because he's a fool!"

I took a large sip of the strong mixture which was doing well to numb the pain and collapsed against the back of her couch.

"Are you hungry?" she asked.

"No, thank you. I'm never really hungry."

"Yes, I've kind of noticed that about you."

She lit a cigarette and clutched it between her fingers. I soaked in the view of her sitting room, all the stylish trinkets and ornate sculptures and artwork she collected. On the mantlepiece was a photo of her wedding day. She looked happy and carefree, wearing a simple lace gown, her arm linked with Howard's. A few quiet seconds passed between us.

"Do you ever feel like you've lost control of absolutely everything in your life?" I said. "I feel like the only thing I can control is how much food I choose to pass through my lips. I think I deliberately starve myself, to feel a sense of power, and to punish myself somehow. Not so much that I'd drop down, dead. But just enough to have that constant feeling of hunger ticking along. I've done it for so long now, that I don't even feel like I need to eat anymore."

"Oh, Georgie, don't do that to yourself. Food is one of the only pleasures in life, even with the rationing – especially with the rationing. Don't deny yourself any good things. You deserve love, not punishment." She placed a hand over mine. I smiled wryly, knowing how ridiculous I must have sounded and tried to hold back the tears. "Wouldn't it just be so much easier if we were men! They get to parade around doing whatever they want, answering to no one, taking accountability for nothing."

"Wouldn't it just!"

She bolted up and her eyes gleamed. "Hold that thought!"

"Where are you going?" I called after her as she raced upstairs.

"Just a second! Don't move from your spot!"

Baffled and amused, I did as I was told and sat very quietly until I heard a giggle coming back down the stairs. I waited until she appeared back in the lounge and there she was.

Alma, with her hair scraped back, dressed from head to toe in Howard's pinstriped suit, holding a lit cigar carefully between her fingers.

"Alma!" I cried!

"You're right, Georgina. It really does feel good to be a man!" She gently sucked in the smoke and puffed it out choking. "Jesus! They're a lot stronger than cigarettes!"

We burst into laughter.

"I must say, only you could make a man's suit look incredible! The most distinguished gentlemen I've ever set my eyes on," I said.

"Oh really?" She strode over to me and held out a hand. "Would you care to dance with me, my lady?"

We played a record and did the jive until our legs tired out and we were out of breath. The tune played out and another came on, a slower tempo. She took my hand, pulled me towards her, I laughed as she swayed me side to side, but I soon realised that she was no longer smiling.

Her eyes doleful and her lips parted.

"You are so beautiful," she said quietly. Her hand reached out to feel a lock of my hair between her fingertips.

Very slowly, she leaned in with her delicate, pink lips and placed them ever so lightly onto mine. My skin tingled with her touch. My mouth opened slightly but the rest of me could not move. Paralysed and stunned, my head spinning from an intoxicating concoction of rum, anticipation and fear. Fear of what I was capable of and fear of awakening the desires I had been hiding from everyone, including myself. She lifted her face away and looked at me. Her eyes wide, full of wonder. Her cheeks glowing and blush.

We stood in silence until the record stopped playing, and then it was just me. And her.

And then impulse took over me. I kissed her, deeply, passionately, slipping Howard's jacket off her shoulders. I undid her tie, like I had done countless times before for a man, unbuttoning his shirt to expose her satin bra. She stared at me, her eyes penetrating powerfully into mine. She raised her hands behind her back to unhook her bra and exposed her breasts to me. My heart pounded in my chest and heat surged through my blood. I had no idea that another woman could make me feel this way.

We made love that night. It was the most tender thing I had ever experienced. When we finished, exhausted and lying with our limbs entangled, we continued to caress each other's bare skin. We were quiet for a long time, until she finally raised off the bed and got us both a drink. She lit another cigarette, tapped the ash on to a glass tray beside her and lay back down beside me.

"Three cigarettes," she said, breathing out the smoke.

"I'm sorry?"

"It's how long I spend with Howard when I visit him at the Beaumont." She stared up into the drapes of the ceiling. "Three cigarette's worth of time is as long as I can handle."

I swallowed back my surprise. "I – I didn't know. How?"

"Battle fatigue, the doctor called it. I didn't want to tell you because Howard hated people knowing and I suppose I just wanted to feel like I was the same as any other housewife with a simple life." A tear rolled down her cheek. "After six months in there, he tried to come home, but it didn't go well. He'd be angry over nothing, or he would get so worked up he'd start crying. He never slept, never came to bed with me." She looked me directly in the eyes. "He never ate either. So, he had to go back. It's been about two years now – or more. I don't know if he'll ever return, he's in a bad way. He barely even recognises me."

I propped myself up on my elbow. "I'm so sorry, Alma. You could have told me, I am here for you."

She gave me a helpless smile.

"I love him, he's a great friend. Or was until… But I'm not sure if I ever really was in love with him." The look in her eyes was captivating. "It's not like what you and I have. You make me feel… different." She lifted her face to mine and kissed me, her lips slowly making their way down by body. We explored each other's bodies and talked until the sun peaked over the horizon and tiredness sunk in.

But when the effects of the rum had worn away and I opened my eyes to the dull skies, I saw her sleeping peacefully on the pillow beside me and the conviction of my feelings I felt for her in the night had somehow dissolved into something unpalatable. I quickly dressed, ashamed of everything I did from the moment she let me into the house. Maybe she had just given me the attention I had been craving for so long that I allowed this to happen, but this wasn't what I wanted. Was it?

She stirred when I pulled my final stocking on.

"Where are you going?" she asked, her voice, drowsy and barely awake.

"Home."

I couldn't bring myself to look at her and just let myself out.

CHAPTER

TWENTY-THREE

1953
Jane
Day

*A*s a guard leads me through the secure block, I look into Cleo's cell to check that she's in, but the cell is empty.

"Where is Cleo?" I ask the guard.

"Who's Cleo?" he says.

"The girl in Unit 5."

He shrugs and opens the door to the meeting room for me. I watch him close it behind him and dread fills me. I pace around, planning my next steps. I need to move quicker. I have to get my patient to reveal more. The door opens again a beat later and Mary supports my patient's arm as they walk in. She is about to sit her down on the chair opposite me.

"There's no need," I say, learning that any pleasantries I give her go unappreciated. "Please could you bring in a wheelchair. I'd like to take her out." She retrieves one without saying a word and I can tell that she is unhappy at the thought of me taking my patient outside again. I ignore her sly stares, place a blanket over my patient's knees and wheel her outside, away from Mary's line of sight as quickly as I can.

I wheel her straight to the memorial gardens, but I don't stop there and head to the other side. There are some wooden steps down a steep embankment before the railway line and the white cottage at the top of the hill is present. Dare I take her there? Where they found the body? I falter and look back from where we came. Even if we make it past the steps and over the railway track, the thinning tyres of the wheelchair will not cope with the rugged farm track to the top.

I stoop down to meet my patient's eyes. "Shall we walk?"

Draping her blanket over her shoulders, I gently place my hands under her arms and encourage her to stand, and she follows my direction. I lead her down the steps slowly. The wooden treads are smooth from years of use, and I have to make sure that she plants her feet securely each time so she doesn't slip. We pause at the railway line which cuts through a narrow forest. The wind pushes past branches of trees, making them sway and rustle.

"Let's cross over."

She shuffles along next to me, and we make our way across the woodland and through to the trail at the bottom of the hill. Her steps are slow and steady, and it is not long before the sky becomes thick with threatening clouds and a breeze picks up. I hunch my shoulders around her to protect her as much as I can.

The path weaves its away to-and-fro through barley grass that brushes against our legs. With each step, doubt worms its way in – I'm making a mistake. I'm going too far. We are not even halfway up towards the cottage yet and the sky's growing darker. I know turning back would be the sensible thing to do but her silence pushes me onwards. I do not want to leave with nothing gained. At the bend where barley turns into a wheat field, her footsteps begin to slow even more until not even a nudge or tug from me encourages her to walk any further.

"Are you tired?"

Her eyes stare blankly into the distance where the path lays ahead. I step forwards and pull at her arm again, but I am met with resistance. Her arms do not follow the direction I try to guide them in. Rather, I see her pulling back, unwilling to move any further. I watch her carefully, but her expressions give nothing away.

"What's wrong?" I look around me. "Do you recognise this place?" We must be near where it all happened. I detect a faint change in her face. The colour from it has drained and turns a shade of ghostly white.

"It's alright. I'm right here. You're safe."

Her eyes very slowly turn to stare at mine. I feel my heart stop as she acknowledges me for the first time and we both stand facing each other. Her lower lip drops.

"Do you want to say something?" I ask.

Three. Long. Seconds. Pass.

Her head starts to shake, like a flicker of a burning candle flame.

"It's alright, you can trust me. There's no one here to hurt you now. You're safe," I say again. But the shaking does not stop. It starts to catch through the rest of her body, from her shoulders, arms down to her knees. Her entire body trembles like a frail leaf in the wind. I do not know what to do. We are alone.

I gasp some air and place my hands on her arms firmly, trying to steady her with my touch.

"Please, let me know what's wrong. Is this the place where they found you? Did someone die here? Did… Georgina die here?" At this moment, I feel as crazed as she could be. All my training flies out the window as I desperately throw questions out at her, begging her to react in any way she can.

And she does.

Her eyes are so wide, they are almost perfectly round and bulging out of their sockets. She drops her jaw down, opening her mouth wider than I had ever seen anyone do. And a terrifying scream releases from her lungs. It is ear-splitting and pierces the air between us. I jump back and my hands flit from my ears to my head, grasping at my own hair as I struggle to know what to do. Not even in her nightmares, does she sound so loud. I am left staring at her, allowing her the space to keep screaming although there is no hint that she will stop. I look around us, there is no one else there. What have I done? What have I done?!

I tentatively take her hand and hold it. I cannot tell if it is my hand or hers that quivers.

"Alright, feel my touch." I don't know if she can hear me because the screaming continues. I screw my eyes shut, praying it will end.

Eventually silence breaks. I look up at her. Her eyes are wet, tears cover her cheeks. She stares into the distance, but her gaze is different – not vacant anymore, and full of intent. I follow its direction. The white cottage sits at the top of the hill looking seemingly harmless. I turn back to her, and her eyes are fixed on it with hardly a blink.

"Do you know that cottage? Have you been there before?"

She is still again, and I realise with my grasp of her shaking hand, that it was really my own trembling all along. Without warning, a swathe of rain pours over us, and her hair and blanket are soddening in seconds. Black clouds above us crack and roar, showing us the heaven's anger.

"Let's go."

By the time we reach her wheelchair, we are both soaked through to the skin. Tolsy stands guard at the rear entrance underneath the eaves, just shy of the sheet of rain gushing down from the roof, her feet a shoulder width's apart and her hands on her hips. I quickly tuck my patient inside the threshold of the doors where Mary waits and wheels her away, but Tolsy acts like a wall in my way and I am left, exposed to the rain.

"It seems we have a reoccurring problem with you leading our patients out of the grounds, Mrs Galloway."

Droplets of water run from my hair into my eyes, blurring my vision, making me squint as I look at her. "I'm sorry. I didn't mean for us to get caught in the rain. I had no idea the storm was coming."

"Of course you didn't think. And now thanks to you, the patient has missed her medication."

I sigh.

"Do you think you could let me in, please? I will speak to Dr Blythe now."

"Dr Blythe is not here and not in charge! Sir Feyman is. And Sir Feyman has ordered us not to take the patients out of hospital grounds. I ought to report you to him right now!"

"I am not employed by Feyman, *Minerva*." I glare at her, ready for anything coming.

"You'd better watch yourself, Mrs Galloway. When Dr Blythe leaves, you will have no job or any protection."

Dr Blythe had never once mentioned that he was thinking of leaving. I believe Tolsy says that just to bring a reaction out of me. Sick of standing out in the rain, I push past her.

"Why are you so against my help? Don't you want her to get better?" I spit.

"I've worked here for long enough to know that many of them will never get better. You may want to carry on as you are, but the rest of us have to deal with reality." The attendants around us turn in our direction and I storm past them, their eyes following me as I try and find the lavatory. A cart full of fresh linen and towels is parked outside a ward and I pick one up to dry myself off as much as I can, but the weight of my damp clothes cling on to me. When I open the door, an attendant outside mops away the trail of water I had brought in. There is a bustle of activity leading into the dining room and the large clock on the wall indicates that it's dinner time. The attendant drills out his daily commands. All the patients take seats and I scan the room. Mary and my patient are in the far corner. She's wearing a clean, dry gown, her hair is now neatly scraped back from her face and plated behind her. I'm relieved to see that she's alright and has resumed her normal routine but it's hard to shift the horror of her scream from my mind. It was the first sound she's made in the daylight since I've met her.

Nurse Tolsy wheels her trolley of pills into the room, bringing me back to the present. The last person I want to see is her, but I also have someone else I'm concerned about.

"Where is Cleo?" Tolsy glances at me and continues with her patients as if she did not hear. "Nurse Tolsy, where is Cleo?"

Tolsy eventually connects her eyes with mine.

"The isolation cell," she says.

"What? Why?"

"She tried to attack an attendant. It comes with consequences."

"Can I see her?"

"If you could, Mrs Galloway, then it wouldn't be called 'isolation'. Tolsy pushes the trolley past me and dispenses a cup of pills to another patient. "You should go home and get dry. We wouldn't want you to get sick." Her tone is saturated with sarcasm. I take a final glance over to my patient and make my way to the secure block. A guard stands at the door to the entrance.

"Where is the isolation cell please?" I ask him. He gives me a set of directions and I hurry off down the corridors before I forget them. I funnel pass several secure blocks when finally I get to a wide and empty passage. It's dark and smells of damp and rust. No natural light makes its way through here and although the rhythm of the arched windows continues along the length of tiled walls, the openings are bricked up. A single room is situated at the end, unlike any others I had seen before. As I approach it, hearing only my footsteps, I feel myself getting nervous at what I might see. A circular window at eye level serves as a window into the cell, padded and covered cream leather panels, discoloured from years of use and what I think are human stains.

In the corner is the poor shell of a girl I remember. Cleo. She holds her knees tight up to her chest, her head, bent down low and her dark sullied hair droops over her face. Her head jerks awkwardly from side to side and she mutters:

"Michael, I'm sorry. I'm sorry. Papa, Papa, Papa. Michael, I'm sorry. I'm sorry."

I know the door would be locked but I take my chances and push against it anyway. It rattles and the sound of it makes her jump. She jerks her head and brings her hollow eyes up to meet mine.

"I didn't do it!" she whispers, so quickly, I nearly couldn't catch it. All the spark that existed when we first met, is lost. Even through the thickness of the door, her haunting stare affects me, and I feel the need to step back.

I turn around quickly and collide against another body, gasping with shock.

"What are you doing here Miss?!" I stare into the eyes of a guard. "No one's allowed here apart from authorised personnel!"

"Sorry, I'm sorry! I didn't realise. I just wanted to check on the patient."

His eyes scan over my visitor badge and his expression remains unimpressed.

"Don't do it without going through the proper security protocol next time."

I swiftly make an exit and leave the building by the nearest set of doors into the gardens, welcoming the fresh air and suck in the smell of damp earth. The grounds are quiet whilst everyone is inside eating and I drop my face into the palm of my hands, feeling despair suffocate me. This place is not a place of healing. It never was.

When I pick Jasper up that afternoon, I hold him tighter than normal.

"Argh, Mama! You're squeezing me too hard! Why are you so wet?!" His squeal is of delight rather than worry.

"I'm sorry, Jay. I really missed you today! Did you have a good day?" I say, planting multiple soft kisses on his cheek and he recoils, pushing me away and giggling. The other mothers hurry past me with their children. I ignore their side glances flowing over my frizzy hair and damp dress.

Jasper gives me an enthusiastic minute by minute account of his day. Usually, I don't really listen and am happy to let him chatter on, but I realise after seeing Cleo, how precious every moment of sanity really is. Along our path, we see Richard walking on the opposite end about to cross the road. He's still in uniform and his helmet casts over his eyes but we see a broad smile stretching over his face and he waves over to us. He waits until the traffic passes and crosses over.

"Hello Jane, hello Jasper!" His friendly face makes me smile. "Got caught in the rain?"

Embarrassed at how damp I look, I pat the curls of my hair down and tuck a loose strand behind my ear.

"Are you on a shift?" I ask.

"I've just finished work actually. And I'm famished!"

"We're heading home now. We'd love for you to join us for tea if you like? Nothing fancy though, I'm afraid. Meat and potato pie?"

He follows me upstairs and I pop into the bedroom to brush my hair and change into dry clothes. When I walk out, Richard's casually standing against the kitchen counter, looking pleased. I head towards him and pull the pie I bought at the butchers out of a brown paper bag. My sleeve brushes against his as I place the pie inside the stove.

"How was your day?" he asks.

"I've had better."

"Oh? What happened?"

"It's the hospital. I'm worried about my patient." I look at him carefully. "Promise me you won't tell anyone at work?"

He shifts with a look of concern.

"Well, it depends if its unlawful. Is it? Unlawful?"

I am unable to hold his gaze.

"Jane, if someone's in trouble, you have to let me help. It's the right thing to do. You have to trust me."

"I'm worried that my patient is in danger." I think of Cleo in her dank cell.

"How do you mean?"

"I took her for a walk today, along the track where they found her towards the white cottage at the top of the hill."

He nods his head. "Chalk House. It's where they found the car and the body."

I check that Jasper is still engrossed with his picture book on the floor by the couch. "My patient wouldn't move past the field. She froze, and then she screamed at me – I don't know why. But what I was most afraid of, was that I couldn't do anything to stop her. Every time I think I'm getting somewhere with her, something happens the next morning that seems to pull us back. I don't know if I can help her. I'm scared that they'll operate on her, and it'll all be over."

Richard looks at me steadily.

A thought comes quickly to my mind.

"Her husband, I know she has one."

"Right?"

"She's been saying that he's not with her anymore, that it's a secret… Why? Why would a husband leave unless he was having an affair?"

"Maybe he was."

"Maybe, but there's another reason why family members just disappear and are never talked of again – when they're mentally unwell and end up in hospital. What if he's in the Beaumont?"

He nods. "Can you find out?"

"Possibly."

"But if he is, wouldn't he be seeing your patient most days anyway? Surely, he would have recognised her already, and if he can't, it's not possible that he can be a reliable witness, given that he is being cared for because of his mental disposition."

"I'm not sure. They usually keep men and women separate, apart from occasions like… the Coronation dance. A patient came charging over to Mary that night like he knew her. But now that I'm thinking about it again, maybe he was going for my patient! I'm going to find out about him tonight."

"Can you at least let me pick you up?"

I smile and say, "Yes".

CHAPTER

TWENTY-FOUR

1952
A letter to Alma

10ᵗʰ July 1952

Dear Alma,

I am sorry that I've not been in touch since we last saw each other.

Lillian tells me that you've rang and have tried to visit. The truth is that I couldn't face seeing you again.

I will keep this short. It pains me to give you this news, but I cannot see you anymore.

What we did was wrong. We are both married women and we must remain true to our vows. If Charles ever found out, my dreams of us ever having a happy marriage and family would be ruined. And even if he ever did find it in his heart to forgive me, then I know that God never would.

I love you as a friend, but we can never be anything more. Had I known that this was where it would lead us, I would never have answered the door to you the first day we met because the regret and the shame has been eating away at me ever since that evening.

You are a truly wonderful person and I wish more than anything that we could continue our friendship, but I don't think it would be wise. There were things we said that we can never take back… things that we did, that cannot be undone.

I hope for nothing but happiness for you and your future.

Sincerely,

Georgina.

CHAPTER

TWENTY-FIVE

1953
Jane
Night

"Are you alive? Please wake up!" My patient's calls swell around walls of the cell.

"Tell me what you see."

"It's dark. I can't see much. Georgina, she – she's fallen." She turns to me, her eyes, filled with panic. "You have to help, please!"

"How can I do that?"

"You have to help me wake her, before he gets to us!"

"Who? Who will get to you? Who will get to you?"

"I – I…"

"Is it your husband? Does he want to hurt you?"

She starts to sob, tears roll down her face.

"Let me help you out of this nightmare. It's Jane, your counsellor. Tell me the name of the person who's hurt Georgina."

"It's so dark, I can't see. I'm so scared."

"I know. I promise you; you'll be alright. I'm going to make sure of it."

I wait.

"It's too late. No one can help me." Her voice is slow, drawling. I hang on her every word.

I draw in a deep breath, realising that it's no use trying to get more information out of her about this night whilst she's locked up in her own trauma and fear. She is suspended in this moment in time. But if she can hear me now, if I am able to reach her subconscious mind, I can try and steer it to another time.

"Alright, I'd like you to take three deep breaths. And then I want you to take your mind back to the day before this night. It is daylight."

There is a long pause as she stares right through me. Then she turns her head to face the ceiling and I see her chest rise and fall slowly, three times.

"Can you tell me where you are?"

"At the Beaumont."

I frown, questioning if this could be right. Is she confused?

"The Beaumont?" I repeat. "This is…" I quickly flick through the file of notes under the flashlight and find the date they found her. "This is the morning of the 31st December? 1952?"

She nods her head awkwardly.

"What were you doing at the Beaumont?"

"Visiting Georgina. She is a patient."

This was new information and I check to see that the tape is recording every word. I jot a reminder in my notebook to search for Georgina in the hospital records.

"What is Georgina here for?"

"She's been sent here because Charles and Lillian think she's ill. She hit him during an argument. I've come to see her to help her escape."

I write the names Charles and Lillian down in my notes. I've not heard their names come up before, but I don't ask now – I just want to keep the flow of the conversation going.

"Tell me about those plans."

"I'm going to meet her tomorrow night at my house and then drive us far away from here."

"Who is going to take her to meet you?"

A pause.

"A nurse."

"Do you know her name?"

Another pause.

"Weaver. Nurse Weaver."

My mouth parts in surprise. Nurse Weaver has known about my patient and Georgina all this time? Flashbacks of Serene and her little room flare before me. Her smile, her soft friendly voice. If she knew who my catatonic patient was all along, could I trust her anymore?

I open my notepad up and scrawl down *Serene*, circling her name twice. I pinch the bridge of my nose, trying hard to concentrate and not let the distraction of this betrayal affect me but anger starts to blur my mind. My next questions must be precise to be able to get as much information as possible.

"Why will Nurse Weaver help you?"

"She knows Georgina doesn't belong here. She knows the things that Alexander does."

"Alexander? Alexander Feyman?"

"Yes."

"And after seeing Georgina in the morning, what do you do?"

"I visit my husband."

"Where is he?"

"At the Beaumont."

I shake my head. "Why is your husband at the Beaumont?" I narrow my eyes at her. They were both here at the same time?

"He is ill from the War. He's always been at the Beaumont. Doesn't want me to tell anyone because he's ashamed."

"What do you say to him when you see him?"

"I'm leaving. I've fallen in love with someone else. I'm sorry."

"And how does he respond?"

"He doesn't say anything. He can't. I don't think he recognises me anymore or remembers he was ever married. Too many drugs."

Husband – also a patient, I write, confirming my suspicions.

"So, after you have said goodbye to him, what do you do?"

"I go home. I pack my bag."

"Where's your home?"

"Chalk House."

I scribble the notes down messily as she speaks and then watch her carefully. I've still got her, captured in a hypnotic like state, and I think it could be finally time to ask the question I had been wanting to know all along.

"What is your name?"

There is a pause, it could have been two seconds long or shorter, but it felt like an excruciating wait. In the dark, she opens her lips.

"Al…ma…

…My name is Alma."

My heart skips a beat. And just like that, it all starts to come together. The entangled web of confusion and silence unravels before me. Alma didn't want to go any further up the hill, because that house belongs to her. Richard told me that Chalk House had been abandoned. I am sure now that it is because her husband has been in this hospital all along. That patient that came up to us at the Coronation dance… that must have been him! They took him away as soon as they knew what he was going to do… to see to his wife. Why?

I scrawl down 'ALMA' across the pages of my notebook in large bold capitals and look over to the tape recorder and make sure it's on.

"Thank you, Alma, that was lovely to hear. You're doing really well. What happens next?"

"After I finish packing, I write a letter to my mother. I want her to know that I'm moving and will contact her again once I have settled. I'm heading outside to post it now… wait, someone is at my door."

"I'd like you to answer that door again, Alma, and tell me who it is."

I wait whilst I imagine she's going through these actions in her mind before she sees who it might be.

"Charles."

"Georgina's husband?"

"Yes."

"Can you tell me what Charles is saying?"

But she cannot. Instead, her whole body starts to tremble, from her shoulders right down to her feet where the chains around her ankles clang heavily against the bed. I need to act quickly before she gets too distressed, and I cannot take her away from this moment. He's doing something that's terrifying her. And then I remember that I am in control of the situation.

"Alma? Alma, I'd like you to listen to my voice, and only my voice. Now take a deep breath in and hold it for five seconds. Then, very slowly, breathe out. I'd like you to go back in time, just a minute before you open the door to Charles. When you open the door, I want you to put your fear aside, and remember that you're going to be alright. Whatever happens, I am here for you. I'm going to start counting down now."

I'm not sure if this will work and all I can do is watch her in the darkness of her cell and wait for her shaking body to stop.

"Five. Four. Three. Two. One. Breathe."

The shaking miraculously stops, and Alma rests her body, taking stagnant air deeply into her lungs.

"Good. Now we know Charles is on the other side of the door. Stay calm, remember to breathe. Whatever he says to you, think of my voice protecting you from any harm. Alright, let's open the door."

"It's Charles. He's… looking for Georgina. He's angry. His eyes are red – bloodshot. He's been drinking, I can smell it."

"Hold on to my voice, Alma. You're doing great."

"He thinks she's with me, but she's not. She's still in the hospital. I don't understand how he thinks she's missing already. I'm confused. He's pushing me aside and knocks me over. I'm on the floor but he doesn't care. He just steps over me with his cane nearly hitting me. He's pacing around everywhere in the house, opening all the wardrobe and cupboard doors. He's back downstairs now, in the kitchen, smashing everything he sees like a mad man." Her breathing quickens and her legs start to kick.

"Alma, stay with me. You're in the past – nothing can hurt you now. Breathe. When I see that it's getting too much for you, I'll count down from three and then I want you to–"

"Please Charles, she's not here. I don't know where she is!" She throws her hands up to her throat and coughs and chokes.

"Alma, are you in pain?"

Her breath continues to splutter, and I fear that her grip around her own throat is too tight, her hands, possessed by her own memory.

"Alma! Come back to me in three. Two. One."

Her hands instantly relax down onto her chest and then drop down by her sides. Her breathing, still rapid, just like mine is at this moment.

"It's alright, Alma. I'm still here. You're safe in your bed. You can sleep now."

Charles, searches for Georgina, angry with Alma, I write. I stay with her for at least a quarter of an hour more, wanting to be sure that she's drifted into a restful sleep, listening to her gentle breathing and syncing mine with hers. I look at the list of names I've made: *Serene, Husband, Charles*. All the people who were present on Georgina's last day on Earth. It's too much to take in. The tape recorder next to me clicks. I turn to see that it's run out of tape, indicating that it was time to go home. I remember that there is a home for me to return to. My son. And the promise of Richard, waiting for me outside the doors.

213

When I am ready, I tap on the door. Raymond opens it. I'm glad that is one of the few that I can trust because when I make my way out of the secure block, I turn to face the direction of Serene's room.

"Mrs Galloway?" Raymond says, breaking me from my thoughts, or rather, intensions. "You ready to go?" No, what I want to do is to find Serene now, and ask her why she's been lying to me since we met, withholding the most important slice of information that is crucial to the reason why Alma's here, why she cannot communicate, why Georgina's dead... Why? But I decide within the few seconds Raymond gives me, that it would be wiser to take stock of what Alma's told me tonight first. Tomorrow. I'll speak to Serene, tomorrow.

Outside, Richard's full beams of his car turn on and I see him waving towards me in the front seat. I quicken my steps and hop inside next to him, securing my hand over my hat as I duck my head in.

"Good evening, Jane, how are you?" he says with a warm smile.

"Hello. Tired. You must be too?"

"I'm alright. Let me have the pleasure of escorting you home."

As he steers around the circular driveway, I stare into the windows of the hospital lit dully from the inside, wondering what other secrets it's hiding in there. He pulls up outside Mr Nichol's chemist and we sit in quietness for a few seconds.

"Richard?"

He lowers his hands away from the steering wheel and gives me his full attention.

"Georgina. I think I know who murdered her."

CHAPTER

TWENTY-SIX

1952
Georgina

Charles came back yesterday after another two long weeks away. He came breezing in through the door like he had only left that morning.

"Hello darling, what's for tea?" he asked.

I stood in the doorway of the lounge with my hand on my hip, glaring at him.

"Where've you been?" I felt anger boiling up to my throat.

"Well – work. You know how busy it is."

"Two weeks?! You've been gone for two weeks! And you never thought to tell me how long you would be or when you would return, and you just expect that dinner would be laid out for you nicely on the table?"

"Darling, I'm sorry. Here, how about I make us a drink, and we'll talk."

"You've not answered my question."

"Which question is that?" he asked as he filled the kettle up.

"Where have you been?"

"London, Luxemburg, Belgium. I couldn't tell you really, it's been rather hectic to say the least."

"Whitley Hall too perhaps?"

He stopped in his tracks, his back faced towards me and the kettle half in the air. I hadn't truly believed what I saw, but it only took that split second to validate that my eyes didn't deceive me that day. His head rose slowly, and I could sense his mind working at speed, trying to come up with the right words.

"Why do you ask that darling?"

"Because I saw you, with Cassandra."

He turned around.

"Cassandra? She left work weeks ago my dear, I've not seen her. It must have been somebody else you saw."

"Don't lie to me, Charles. I know what I saw. I can recognise your walk from a mile away."

It seemed that it dawned on him that there was no way out and although I really had hoped he would prove me wrong, his piercing blue eyes showed me all the guilt and betrayal.

I broke down before him.

"How could you?!" I screamed. "I moved here for you! I did all of this, gave you my body, tried so, so many times to have your children and they've all died, I did it all – for you! I thought you loved me!"

He edged his way closer to me.

"Darling, I do love you. Please, please, just take a seat. Don't let yourself get so upset."

He tried to take hold of my arms but as frail as I was, I shook him off like something crazed and trapped. I cried so hard, air could hardly make it into my lungs, and it hurt me to breathe.

"Georgina please! You're losing your mind!"

I saw red at the sound of those words. I grabbed the glass vase of flowers at the centre of the table and smashed it. Glass, water, discarded flower heads scattered in every direction.

"That's enough!" he roared now. "What do you think you're doing? How dare you treat our home like this!" I crumbled to the floor and sobbed into my hands. "Georgina, you have a good life here. I provide all of this for you. I work hard for this! I think you must be acting this way because you're not well in yourself. Perhaps we need to see the doctor."

I could not believe my ears. I screamed at him some more awful things. Told him he was a liar and that I hated it here. That he was the only reason that I wasn't feeling well.

"Honestly, I don't know what's gotten in to you. Is it that Alma?"

"How do you know about Alma?" Did he find out about our night somehow?

"People in Crowbeck talk, Georgina. You seem to be spending a lot of time with her and it's only since then that you've changed so much."

"No, it's not Alma, Charles. It's you! It's you leaving me for days on end on my own in the middle of nowhere with your mother and next to a lunatic asylum!" Instinctively, I grabbed a shard of glass and pointed its sharpest end towards him. "It's you, you've ruined it all!" My hand started to bleed from gripping at the serrated edges of the glass, its pain seared through my skin, but I found its release nourishing.

At that moment, Lillian, walked through the door and screamed. I dropped the glass immediately in shock.

"Georgina, what on Earth are you doing, child?" Of course, his mother would walk in at the right time – when I was at my weakest.

"Come this way, Mother," Charles said calmly.

I watched Lillian slide over to him, skirting around the broken glass and he whispered something in her ear. All the while, her eyes never leaving mine. Although whatever he said was inaudible to me, I knew my life would be ending.

CHAPTER

TWENTY-SEVEN

1953
Jane
Day

ap, tap, knock.

Three more louder knocks.

Still no answer.

My fist rises to the door again and I'm about to rattle another knock when it finally opens.

"Jane?" Serene stands in her room in her bedclothes and dressing gown with her hair tied up tightly in a bun. Her face glows like it has just been washed and I had interrupted her nightly routine. "Come in – something the matter?"

I've hardly slept and my mind is fuelled with jagged, cluttered thoughts. Richard wanted to know all the details, but I struggled to tell him. It was hard enough to formulate everything in my mind in any sense of order. Nothing made sense. I just wanted to be home, see that Jasper's safe, and listen to the tape recording again.

"Would you mind if I listened to it with you?" Richard asked.

I eyed his curiosity with cautiousness.

"I don't think that would be appropriate. I have to place my patient's interests first."

He nodded and insisted on walking me up to my apartment anyway.

"Would you like to come in?" I asked as we stood outside my door. It was more out of curtesy than wanting his company tonight. Thankfully he declined but wanted me to know that I could call him any time I needed anything. I nodded gratefully and he leant his face over to the side of my cheek, brushing his lips softly against my skin and I felt a faint fluttering in my chest, but the pull towards Alma was stronger and I watched him walk down the stairs before I closed the door.

I drearily step into Serene's room. She closes her door firmly shut.

"What can I do for you, Jane?"

I look around the four walls of her cosy room. "I think it's best that we sit down first. I have some questions and I'd like you to answer me as honestly as you can."

Unease spreads across her face.

"Very well." She lowers herself onto the nearest chair.

"This might come as a shock to you, but I've been seeing my patient at night not just to monitor her sleep, but because she sleep-talks."

"Oh?" she says with a genuine look of surprise.

"I'm telling you in confidence. Promise me that this goes no further than this room."

She nods slowly. "What kind of things does she say?"

"She re-lives her last night outside of the Beaumont every night. It's a reoccurring nightmare – or a memory. In fact, I'm pretty certain it is a memory. The reason I'm tell you now is because last night, whilst in her dreams, she managed to relive the day before she ended up here." I become acutely aware of Serene's intense gaze and how quiet she is as she listens.

"She said that before her friend, Georgina was killed, she spent some time in here, at the Beaumont." I pause to gauge a reaction, to see if Serene will knowingly nod to this piece of this information, but her gaze doesn't falter, and she holds for my next words. "She told me that she had planned to help Georgina escape from this place. And that *you* were helping her do it."

For a good long moment, Serene doesn't move or even blink. But then she cannot hold her ignorant guise any longer. She swallows and her expression changes into something pained.

"She also told me her name is Alma," I continue. "But I think that you already know that, don't you? I need you to be truthful, Serene. Not for me, but for Alma." Moments of silence pass before she speaks.

"I tried," she murmured quietly. "I tried to help her. But in the end, I couldn't."

"What happened?"

She sighs heavily and it turns into a nervously sarcastic laugh, and she shakes her head.

"I'm not sure where to start."

"From the beginning?"

Her eyes roll towards a small clock on her desk. Either she is feeling tired after a twelve-hour night shift, or she wants me gone to avoid revealing the truth.

"If I tell you everything, you have to understand that I've not lied to you because I had any ill intent."

I stare at her, wondering what on earth she'll divulge that would make me think of her as bad. She's been the kindest person to me here since I started my job and I like to think of myself as a good judge of character, able to see people for what they truly are. Can I get it that wrong? I give her a slight nod, prompting her to start.

"I'm… not widowed. I've never been married. I lied to you when we first met because I needed a story that was different to my own. The truth is that I grew up here as an orphan. A distant aunt – I don't know – three times removed, led me to this place. She told me that Alexander Feyman would look after me. He wasn't a Sir yet, it was before all the medals he gained from the War."

"Why didn't she send you to a fostering agency?"

"No one would take me. I was… I am still, epileptic. I used to have seizures once or twice a day. They didn't know how to deal with me. Alexander opened his arms to me. I'm a child of the asylum." She smiled whimsically but there was a sadness in her eyes. "I'm thankful for it. My fits didn't lessen until I reached adulthood and by then, I had become too used to living here, scared of what the outside world might do to people like me. Alexander offered me training and a job here instead so I could still be protected. I'm sensitive to the sun's rays. It's why I do the night shifts."

I'm fascinated by Serene and the fact that she's been spending the majority of her years in the confines of this hospital, never seeing any daylight. It is hard to believe but I do not want my pity for her distracting me from the reason I came.

"How did you meet Georgina?"

She raises her eyes to meet mine and shifts awkwardly, as if she knows I sense her need to divert the conversation.

"Alexander brought her in to see me for a physical assessment. I told him that nothing seemed to be wrong apart from some emotional distress, and he took her away. But when I found out she was confined to a cell in the secure block, I questioned him. He told me she had tried to attack her husband. As you know, I do the night runs, but she was never asleep by the time I reached her cell. She'd whisper through the bars, 'Let me go, please! I'm not crazy!'

I felt for her, I really did. I didn't want her to end up like me. To only see life within these walls."

"So, you tried to help her run away?"

She nods. "I found out that her… lover, was going to meet her so I intercepted."

"Her lover? Alma?" I lean back. "I didn't realise. What happened next?"

"It was a secure plan until we got found out."

"Who found out?"

She starts to nervously scratch her neck and avoids meeting me in the eye.

"I can't say. I still work here, and I don't want to lose my only home."

"Alright. Whoever it was, what did they do when they found out?"

"I'm not sure. I had to get back – I couldn't leave the hospital running on its own, it was my shift. I thought she was in safe hands." Her eyes brim with tears and she bends her face into her hands, her shoulders shaking. When she finally lifts her face back up to meet me, her cheeks are red and wet. She looks around her table and grabs a handkerchief. "I was just finishing off my shift that night when the doors burst open with a handful of guards and a half naked woman. But it wasn't Georgina this time, it was Alma. And there was blood all over her, so much blood!

"I rushed over to her immediately and tried to take her away to give her a wash, but Alexander wouldn't let me get involved. They rushed her away, straight into the secure block. I couldn't get a glimpse of her until the night after. I was desperate to find out what happened. What happened to Georgina. But when I finally managed to get to her, she couldn't speak at all. I don't think she even recognised me. She was lost."

"When did you find out what happened to Georgina?"

"On the radio, the same night, just as I was drifting off in bed. It was awful, awful news. I cried myself to sleep that night."

"It wasn't an accident, was it? Charles, Georgina's husband was there. Alma told me. He did it, didn't he? He murdered Georgina!"

"Shhhh!" she hushed me, her voice turned into a harsh whisper. "I don't know, I just don't know. Listen to me, you must be careful. Now, more than ever! If you get caught snooping, you'll get yourself into a whole world of trouble."

"Do you really think I care about that?"

"You care about your son, don't you?"

The mention of Jasper took the air from my lungs.

"What are you saying? That if I help Alma get her voice back, if I help Georgina get justice and find Charles, that my life and my son's life will be at risk?"

Serene's eyes harden and her voice becomes cold, speaking in short, quick sentences. "I don't know who killed Georgina and you have to believe me when I say that. But if anything links you back to this place then it's not going to bode well. Like I say, I'm a child of the asylum, I've seen everything. All the changes throughout the years, and all the things that haven't changed. Alexander has been good to me, he's become the only father I've known, a father of the hospital. But he's ruthless if you do anything to ruin the reputation of the Beaumont."

I stare at her, baffled, unable to judge if she's warning or threatening me. And Jasper, I must protect Jasper and put all the things into place to secure his safety whilst I keep working. I must keep working.

"I'd better go and see Alma." I stand and head to the door, wanting to just leave. Serene's deceit has hurt me. I was completely wrong about her. If she's managed to fool me with a complete fabrication of her life, then how can I be so sure about anything else she tells me now? Did she really try and help Georgina escape? What if she's trying to lead me onto a false trail? I drive myself crazy thinking of all possible avenues my own investigation into Alma's life could lead me to. I rush down the corridors, ignoring all the murmuring ill patients until one attendant turns a corner. He wheels a patient in a chair with a bandage around her head. As they pass, I recognise those deep, black eyes. Cleo! She leans to the side of the wheelchair like a rag doll, her head lolls over one shoulder and she stares down at her legs.

"Cleo! Cleo!" I call. The attendant continues to walk on, but I stop him and place my hands firmly onto the arms of the wheelchair. "Wait!"

"I'm sorry Miss, she's on her way to surgery."

I check over Cleo quickly. "Cleo, can you hear me?" I look straight into her eyes, her pupils seemingly permanently dilated. From drugs? I hold up a finger in her line of sight and run it from one side of her head to another and there's no acknowledgement from her that she can detect anything. There's blood seeping through the bandage at the top of her scalp. Fresh blood.

"Surgery? She looks like she's just been through one. What's happened to her?"

"Lobotomy. The last one didn't go as planned."

"What do you mean?"

"Well, you can see the results here."

"You mean you've completely removed her ability to move, speak or feel anything?"

He pushes Cleo pass me, forcing me to stand and he moves through to the next section of the corridor. "You've mutilated her! Stop! Cleo!" I shout. I rush to try and follow him but he's too quick and locks the gate behind him. I grab the bars of the gate and shake them in frustration. "Cleo!" I shout again. "Cleo!"

I practically run to the meeting room in the secure block and wait for Mary to bring Alma into the meeting room, pacing from one end of the room to the other, back and forth. I need to know that Alma is safe. Safe from the hands of an eager surgeon wanting to slice Alma's brain open. I don't want her to suffer the same fate as Cleo's. I want her to retain her memory, as painful as it is, so that she can get out of here. So that she can get justice. I tremble with worry as I watch the movement of the long hand of the clock turn as I pace. Four minutes late… Ten minutes late… Thirteen… Where could they be?

The door opens and Mary brings Alma in like everything is as normal.

"Why are you late? Was something the matter?" I blurt out.

"Just needed an extra change," Mary says, gently cupping Alma's elbow as she leads her onto a chair. I watch them move in slow motion but feel my patience waning. We can't afford to take all the time in the world now. Mary gently guides Alma onto her seat and turns to leave the room again.

"Before you go Mary–" she turns around. "I have some questions I want to ask you. Do you have the time?"

"What kind of questions?"

"Nothing out of the ordinary. I'm just wanting to fill in some blanks. Please, take a seat."

"I need to make sure that her tea is prepared."

"Tea – surely she's just had dinner? This will only take a minute of your time. Please."

Although clearly reluctant, she does as I ask and waits.

"When did you say you started working here again?"

"Once this patient came into hospital."

"You haven't been here before until then?"

"No."

"What did you do before you came here?"

"I was a carer for an elderly woman in another town, but she died."

"Sorry to hear that." I move on quite quickly. "Which of the nurses do you work with the most here?"

"I – don't really. I don't talk to anyone much, I'm just here for this patient."

"You're never following anyone else's orders? The charge nurses? Nurse Tolsy? Nurse Weaver?"

"No. I'm familiar with the routine. I take the patient for her meals, for toileting and bathing, and I bring her to you." Her voice is quiet, but steady. Her eyes shift to Alma and back towards me.

"Are you aware of what else goes on beyond your times of caring for this patient?" I ask, testing to see if she knows about my night sessions. She shakes her head, she does not, or at least, she's not letting on that she does.

"What about Sir Feyman? Was he the one that recruited you?"

She nods. "I had one interview, he employed me the next day."

"Do you know anything about the patient's history before she arrived?"

She shakes her head. "What's this about? Why are you asking me these questions? I'm just her attendant."

"Just her attendant. *Just* hers. No one else here, as far as I can see, has their own personal attendant." I stare at her, keen to see if there is the slightest change in her expression but blank eyes stare back at me. "Throughout these months – apart from the flicker of her hand to the music at the coronation dance, have you noticed any changes to the patient, no matter how small? Any movements at all?"

"No."

"If you did, would you report it?"

"Of course."

"Who would you report it to?"

"I – I don't know. Nothing's happened yet."

"But you said you saw her move her hand. Did you not feel as though you should have reported that to anyone?"

She sighs quickly. "Well, you were already there. She is your patient."

"So, if you did see anything more, you would report it to me, correct? Because she is *my* patient?"

"Yes," she says.

I take a quiet moment to observe her. Her cheeks have flushed into a deep pink. I know that I've unnerved her and fully suspect that she's hiding something from me. Just like Serene was hiding something from me too. I notice the irony in this, as Mary doesn't know that I already know Alma's name and that she talks to me each night. We all exist here, with secrets to hide. I'll find out what Mary's is sooner or later.

"Thank you, you can go now and come back in an hour."

She gets off her chair and leaves the room to Alma and I. I gaze at Alma for a long moment.

"Alright Alma, let's begin."

CHAPTER

TWENTY-EIGHT

1952
Georgina's Diary Entry

I couldn't help myself. The last few weeks had bought nothing but loneliness. I've been so confused and scared after my outburst against Charles, I didn't know what he was going to do to me – I really thought he was going to send me away that day, but for one reason or another, he decided not to.

Just in case it ever got to that point though, I would be ready. I packed a small suitcase of belongings and hid it at the bottom of my wardrobe. If I ever felt the threat again of being sent away, I would run away.

I thought I had done the right thing by casting Alma away from my life. Out of sight, out of mind. But there's not a second that goes by when I don't think about her. She exists in every waking thought and within my dreams at night. I missed everything about her, her presence, her laughter. She's the only one I could trust. I kept thinking back to the last time I saw Alma and her beautiful soft features, the touch of her skin against mine. I drowned in regret, sorry for quitting our friendship when it was the most honest thing in my life. My only hope now was that she would forgive me.

I had to see her again. It was out of innocence at first. I appeared at her door – thankfully she was in. She stared at me like I was a ghost walking back into her life. She had every reason to be mad at me, but she invited me in. We started talking about nothing in particular, the weather, what we had been occupying ourselves with over the weeks. It was very polite and reserved, like we were just acquaintances. But there was a longing there that I don't think either of us could suppress any longer.

I cried, so much, begging for her forgiveness over and over again. I didn't know what to do. She held me in her arms and whispered reassurances and forgiveness in my ear. Being able to feel the touch of her, the smell of her, was like being a child back in a mother's loving arms, so entirely and unconditionally loved.

We agreed to keep all our meetings a secret. Not that Charles would find out anytime soon. He was never here at home anymore, and when he was, it was very fleeting.

Alma and I met. In the dead of the night the next day. I snuck out after knowing that Lillian was asleep and crept past her cottage. Alma would pick me up at the bottom of the track and we would drive deep into the Dales at a waterfall which we named ours, where we knew no one would follow us to. The water cascaded over the rocks into crystal clear water, and we stripped down to just our undergarments and sank ourselves into the water under the full moon. The shock of the ice-cold water took our breaths away, but once we submerged our bodies into it, I felt invigorated – I felt alive!

"I love you," she whispered to me in the water. I smiled back at her, tentative at baring my feelings so plainly, but she didn't mind

that I wasn't quite ready. She kissed me so softly it felt like the petal of a sweet smelling rose, brushing against my lips.

She dropped me off at the bottom of the track again in the early hours of the morning as we didn't want the car's engine noise to wake Lillian up. We promised we'd see each other again in two days, same time, same place, and kissed each other goodbye. The sun was just peeping up above the fields. I looked into the windows of the cottage and saw that her curtains were still closed and sauntered up dreamily down our driveway, still basking in our last kiss.

I swept aside my damp towel and took out the keys from the small pocket of my bag. I unlocked the door, stepped inside, and gasped. There, standing in the middle of the gloom of the hallway, staring straight at me, was Lillian.

I calmly greeted her, trying to hide my shock, and asked why she was up so early. She told me that she woke up, thinking that she had heard something outside her house and came in to check that I was alright. Only then, did she find out that I wasn't there. She went up to my bedroom and saw a pile of letters on my dressing table, thinking that they could be from Charles and wandered over to have a look – all out of innocence, she said to me, whilst holding the letters that Alma had written to me.

Her face was hard as she demanded to know if I had sneaked out to meet Alma and I couldn't reply. She rushed over to me and shook me by my arms, crunching up the letters in her hands and telling me that I had lost my mind and that I had to stop seeing Alma completely! I cried and told her that I couldn't – I would never let Alma go, that she was the only thing that was keeping me from losing my mind. And then the fury set in. I was already tolerant of her coming and going from my own home as and when she pleased, having most meals with her, letting her control what we ate, going on outings with her to keep her company. I did it because I felt like it was the right thing to do. But for her to go through my personal things, for her to read my letters so she could see every vulnerable part of Alma and I, for her to judge us and berate me for trying to find an ounce of happiness – it stung deeply. I lashed out and told her to leave, to never come inside uninvited again and she threw the letters on the floor and stormed out.

I scooped up the scattered, creased letters from the hallway, bound them with string, and hid them in the suitcase I had pre-packed. If I could have bottled up that feeling of Alma that night, and opened it up whenever I needed to relive it again, I would have. This diary is the only way I can keep those memories alive because I'm not sure how many more of them I can make. Thank God that Lillian never found this!

Next time I see Alma, I'll be taking my suitcase.

CHAPTER

TWENTY-NINE

1953
Jane

I quickly hand in my visitor badge at reception and look at the clock. There was no chance I could make it in time to pick Jasper up from school and the thought of his little face worrying about where I was, panicked me.

"Please could I borrow your telephone? I'm late picking up my son and need to call the school."

The receptionist hands me the receiver and I try calling Kirsty at home.

"Hellooo?"

"Kirsty, hello. I've been held up at the hospital and Jay finishes school soon. I was wondering if you could help out?"

"Now?"

"Yes, but if it's too inconvenient right now, it doesn't matter. I'll give the Head a call."

"No, no. I should be able to pick him up. For three o'clock, right?"

"Please."

"Don't worry. I'll set off now."

"Thank you so much, Kirsty!"

When I return to our block of flats, I give Mr Nichols, the pharmacist, a wave and head up the stairs, feeling the excitement of seeing Jasper again. But then I hear laughter filtering through to the corridor. As I reach the top of the stairs, two distinctly recognisable voices come from the inside of Kirsty's apartment – Kirsty's and Richard's. I knock at her door, and nobody answers. I feel as though my knock is drowned out by their enthusiastic chatter and feel a surge of irritation. How much longer must I have to stand outside on the landing to wait to see my son? And why does Richard seem like he's enjoying Kirsty's company so much? I take in a deep breath and impatiently tap on the door with my knuckles, harder than was probably rational.

The door swings open and Kirsty welcomes me with a wide smile, her hair tousled like she's been playing with it. My eyes pan over behind her. Richard sits on the settee and gives me a smiling nod.

"Jane! Come in!"

"Where is Jay?" I direct the question to Kirsty, but it is Richard who responds.

"Just doing some drawing in the other room." He stands to greet me, but I feel strangely out of place, like I have just interrupted a fun afternoon between friends, or something more. "I came to see you but found Kirsty and Jay walking in instead."

"Would you like a cup of tea, Jane? You look exhausted and somewhat flushed," asks Kirsty.

"No, thank you, I won't." Jay hears my voice and runs over. I bend down to hug him. "Jay! Mama missed you! Ready to go home?" he nods and I tell him to get his things. I turn to Kirsty. "Thank you for picking Jay up for me, that was very kind of you."

"Oh, you know it's never a problem! You have a good evening! Richard, are you staying or are you leaving too?" I didn't wait for an answer and was already across the landing unlocking my own door and heading in.

"Jane?" I turn around to see him in the landing.

"Yes?"

"Is something wrong?"

"No, I just thought you were having a nice time catching up with Kirsty. I didn't want to disturb you."

He smiled a sort of confused smile and walked up to me. "You know I came to see you, didn't you?" He took hold of my hand. "Are you alright?"

"I'm fine. I just need a bit of a rest."

"Do you want me to take Jay out for some tea so you can have a lie down?"

"No, honestly, I'm alright. Why did you come? Was there something you needed to tell me about the case?"

He seemed taken aback by my bluntness. "No, I just wanted to see you. But if you're not feeling right, it's probably best I come another day?"

I instantly feel guilty. I don't know what I'm doing – pushing him away?

"Just let me get Jay ready for bed first. I'll be out in a moment."

I take him into his room and settle him into his bed. I tell him I love him and how much I wish he would stop growing so fast. Of course, I do not wish that of him, but there is this irrational fear that he loves me less with each day that passes. Am I too suffocating and too protective? Or am I being not protective enough by leaving him with my neighbour each evening? And if I am able to do that, why then am I feeling suspicious of everyone including Kirsty who has only helped me countless times? When I leave Jasper's room, Richard is standing in the middle of my sitting area, waiting.

"Would you like a cup of tea or a glass of wine?"

"Wine would nice, thank you." I pour red wine into a couple of glasses, remembering the last time we tried to do this, he had to leave without drinking a drop of it and I wondered how much of it he would manage this time. He slowly walks over to me. I pass him his glass and I sip the cool red liquid down my throat and feel instant relief, but it is made uneasy by Richard's gaze on me.

"Are you alright?" he asks, his voice, soft.

I am still for a moment, and then start to shake my head and bow it into my hands. A surge of emotion rises through me, and I cannot resist the urge to release it and tears pour out.

"Hey, hey," he strokes my back. "Shhh," he whispers and brings my body closer into his chest. I rest my cheek on his shoulders, so close to his face that I can breathe in his cologne and the day's stubble tickles my skin. He lifts his hand up to my chin and strokes it with his thumb. I lean into the warmth of his palm and close my eyes for a long second. "What's wrong?"

"It's all just getting a bit too much with work, and not spending enough time with Jay. I feel like I'm failing at everything. I'm sorry."

"You must know that that's not true. I look at how dedicated you are to your work and how much you've already helped your patient, I can't see any other counsellor who would work day and night to help anyone. And I see how Jay absolutely adores you and you adore him." I shake my head and smile weakly. "And then there's also the fact that I, also adore you…"

I dare not look up because I'm frightened at what might happen next. I had taken years to build walls around me, and this man might be the one to break them. I'm scared that they'll come crumbling down with nothing left to protect me and everything that I've kept buried will come bubbling to the surface.

Hesitantly, I raise my eyes to meet his.

His gaze is longing, pained, but undemanding. It pulls me towards him, and without a thought, my lips rest on his. At first our kiss is gentle, so soft, it is hardly there, like the brush of the finest feather. But urgency consumes me, and I press so hard against him, our glasses of wine are knocked over. Red liquid floods the table and onto the floor but neither of us take notice, neither of us care. He kisses me, invades me with his tongue. I push my hips against his groin and moan against his lips, biting them. He withdraws with a sharpness and blood starts to seep out from his bottom lip. A look of shock flits through his expression. But as instincts take over, I know how to look at him, to give him the lust in my eyes that are meant only for him, just as he knows how and where to touch me.

I lead him into my bedroom, and I let him take my clothes off. I let him soak every inch of me in with his eyes and his kisses, take all my worries away. I did not know how much I had missed this feeling.

* * *

I lie in the bed on my own. The toilet flushes and Richard returns to his side of the bed, still naked. We smile at each other, and I rest my cheek on his chest.

"You know you could have anyone." I say, it's more of statement than a question.

He laughs. "I'm not entirely sure what you mean by that."

"Of course, you do. You must know how handsome you are and how you make all the girls giggle and swoon just by walking past them on the street!"

"Well, first of all – they definitely do not do that or there'd be a significant rise in hospital admittances. And secondly, I don't want just anyone." He turns to face me.

"A married woman with a child? You'd choose scandal over innocence and decency?"

He wraps his arm around my back and strokes my shoulder.

"I know what you've been through, none of it is your fault. And I like you. Really like you. You are no plain Jane." He kisses me on the forehead when there's a knock on the door.

I grab my dressing gown, thread my arms through its sleeves and tie the belt around my waist as I make my way to the front door. I check through the spy hole first before opening it. Oh dear – it's Kirsty.

"Hi Kirsty." I only open the door slightly, so she doesn't see the extent of how undressed I am.

"Oh sorry, Jane. I didn't want to disturb you. It's just that, well, I'd normally be over at yours by now, babysitting Jasper? I didn't think you needed me tonight with Richard... anyway, I just wanted to make sure!" Her eyes dart through the gap behind me. I look back and it's Richard in just his trousers, getting a glass of water with a smirk on his face. I turn back around to see Kirsty switch into a shade of crimson. "Oh, I'm so sorry, I should have just rung you on the phone!"

"No, no, it's alright, Kirsty really. I appreciate that you've come round to check. I think I need a night off. You should have one too."

Kirsty smiles awkwardly, and makes a half turn back towards her own apartment.

"Kirsty, wait. I'm sorry if I was rude before. I'm just very tired. I'm always, always grateful for you."

Her smile warms up fully. "Goodnight, Jane. See you tomorrow."

I walk back into the bedroom where Richard lies and raise an eyebrow.

"I suppose you thought that was amusing?"

"Yes, it was quite!" he says with an infectious grin.

"Poor Kirsty! She'll be too afraid to come round anymore!"

"I'm sure she's seen it all before! So then. What happens now? Now that you've had your wicked way with me? Should I head home before the sun rises and everyone in the block sees me?"

I laugh. "Probably yes, you should! Especially before Jasper wakes up!"

His face falls serious. "You should know that you do mean a lot to me."

I should know by now, not to trust so easily but hope is an odd thing. It can make one believe that the impossible is attainable. Hope entangled with love is worse because the power of belief can make one dangerously reckless.

CHAPTER

THIRTY

1952
Georgina

I rang Alma at her home that evening several times, but she wasn't in, or she didn't pick up. I was wrought with worry and paranoia and could not get to sleep until very late. In the morning, the sound of someone in the kitchen roused me. Already I felt my temper rise, knowing that it would be Lillian completely disregarding what I had said and letting herself in again.

I threw on my dressing gown and stormed downstairs only to be stunned by the person standing before me.

"Charles! You're back!"

"Morning, Georgie." As I stood in the hallway, he was standing by the breakfast table with a cup of coffee in his hand. His voice was low and solemn.

"Is something the matter?" I start walking into the kitchen and notice Lillian sitting to the side by the window with a cold glare and I take in a deep breath.

"Mother's told me everything."

"Everything?"

"About your affair with Alma." I swallowed hard, frozen in the same spot. "I'm not mad at you Georgie."

"You're not?"

He shook his head.

"Charles – I'm sorry. I really am. I didn't mean for this to happen. I just got so lonely and Alma, she was there for me and–"

"I know. I know what a hard time you've been having here, and I know I've not been here for you, but I'm here for you now." My eyes flicked over to Lillian whose gaze was now fixed on the view of the driveway outside the window. Charles walked up to me and took hold of my hands. I wanted to wrap my arms around him and feel his reassurance through an embrace, but I held back, knowing that I didn't want to be here anymore, that my heart had changed and Alma's face came into my mind's eye.

"Darling," he continued. "I should have done this sooner, but I thought you'd get better. You need help."

"What do you mean?" He looked at me with an apprehension that I had never seen in him before, and then it dawned on me what he meant.

"I've spoken to Alexander again. He really is very kind and said he'd give you a private room in the Beaumont." Instantly, I pulled my hands away from his and noticed in the corner of my eye, Lillian turning to watch.

"No! No! You can't do this!"

"Georgie, listen. You have to trust me. They've got the top doctors of Yorkshire there, you'll be really well looked after, much better than Mother and I can do for you at home."

"I don't need looking after! I was just – just –"

"Sad, lonely and miserable! I know! And now, I come back home to hear that you're also engaging in, in … I can't even speak of it, it's deranged and – and shameful!"

"Shameful?"

"Yes! An affair! With a woman! I mean – you can't tell me that you're proud of it. Don't *you* want to change? Be better again?"

"Please don't send me away." My voice turned into a mere whisper, but he continued.

"How is that going to make me look in public? An affair is bad enough to utterly ruin my reputation! But it's not even with a man! It's completely emasculating!"

And then I felt the heat rise in my chest. "You think that this would have even happened if you didn't go and have one yourself? An affair?"

His eyes grew dark. "Don't you go twisting this back onto me! This isn't about me!"

"No, no you're right. It's not just about you, it's about us – and how unhappy we make each other. I wish I had woken up to this realisation earlier, but I haven't been happy in a long time because of us, and I tried, so hard."

We stood in the middle of the kitchen in silence for a long moment before the quiet was interjected by Lillian's voice.

"They've arrived," she said.

Through the window, I saw a white Wolseley reach the top of the drive and I turned to look at Charles and Lillian who stood guard in my kitchen, watching me tentatively, like I could try and make a run for it at any moment.

"So, that's it? I'm to leave now? Don't all the years we've been together mean anything to you, Charles? All the love we've ever felt for each other. All the babies I've carried and lost? Our babies. Now you don't feel anything for me at all?" The back of my eyes burned with the prickling of my tears.

"Of course they mean something, Georgie, they mean everything. That's why we're getting you the best help there is."

"The Beaumont isn't help, it's a prison!"

"Do you think we're absolutely stupid?!" Lillian threw at me. "Don't you think I see everything you do? You and that Alma, messing about like adolescents as if what you do has no consequences?!"

"It's no worse than what your son has done to me," I said quietly. Two men in long, dark, double breasted coats and matching caps climbed out of the car. They reminded me of the pictures I'd seen of Nazis in the papers and not that long ago, their faces, just as frightfully stern, devoid of any human emotion. Their eyes panned over the front of the house, and they made their way towards the door. I stared at Charles who refused to return my gaze, I wished I could have willed him to look at me. The Charles I fell for so long ago was in there somewhere, surely. If he'd only raise his face a little and allow me to see the betrayal in his eyes.

"What's he done to you? What has *my* son done – to *you*? You selfish, pathetic, ignorant child! All he's done, all we've both done, is try and make you happy here, pandering to your every whim! You have the best man, the best house, the best dress, the best food! – not that you bother to eat any of it! I know myself that I did everything I could to help you settle in! But you had to go running off with that girl instead!" Lillian spits.

"Are you somehow thinking that because I happen to love a woman, that it's worse than if I ever went off with another man? I'll tell you this now, Lillian. I don't love Alma because she's a woman, I love her because of her heart. She's shown me more generosity and kindness than I've ever had from anyone. I once thought Charles loved me that much. At least another woman wouldn't expect me to have children."

"Enough! The both of you!" Charles turned around, his face hot and red. He straightened his shirt and lowered his voice. "What's done, is done. There's no use dragging it all up and picking it apart. That'll help no one." There was a loud onerous knock on the door, and he briskly walked straight past me. I tried to grab hold of his hand as a last, desperate plea to stay but he shook it away.

It was the signal for the end, the last chapter. The fire in my gut, suddenly stamped out as Charles greeted the guards at the door. Their footsteps made their way down the hallway. The Beaumont Nazis, were here now, coming to collect me. I was as good as dead. Their ungodly presence filled the kitchen.

"What's the matter with her?" one guard asked as if I wasn't there, although he looked right at me.

Before Charles could say anything, Lillian intercepted.

"My daughter in law's suffering from deep depression. She won't eat and goes through some upsetting outbursts. The other day, she smashed a vase and threatened my son with broken glass. Thank the Lord I came in just in time! Sir Feyman knows the rest."

"What's her name?"

"Georgina Bennett," I say defiantly. "And I am perfectly well. I do not need to be taken away."

Everyone in the room acted as though I had not spoken.

"We know Sir Feyman personally, he's a dear family friend and has offered her a private room for a good cost. Please could you ensure that that's put in place for her?"

"Certainly sir."

"No, please Charles, you can't do this to me! I'm your wife!"

The guards dragged and pulled me out the door. I begged and pleaded until my heart burned and I was too exhausted to struggle against it. He pushed my head into the car and drove to the Beaumont. At the hospital, they ripped my clothes off me and slung an oversized gown over my head. An attendant in a white jacket took over and led me to a cell.

"Where are you taking me?!" I demanded. "You're locking me away in confinement? I was told I would get a proper room! Answer me!"

He threw me in so that I stumbled over my feet into the middle of the room. By the time I was able to turn back around, he slammed the cell door shut, making me jump at its loud clank.

"You can stay here until the doctor comes!" he said through the window.

I collapsed onto the bed and wept into my hands.

"It's not that bad here lady, you'll get used to it," said a voice coming from another cell. I decided to ignore it, but she kept talking, although it didn't sound like it was at me.

"One day we'll be out of here, won't we Michael? He'll soon see that we don't belong. Even if he doesn't love us, he doesn't need to keep us here."

The door to our block opens.

"Pa?" the woman calls out. "Pa! Let us out! Let us out!"

The footsteps tap along the corridor until they reached the door to my cell. The lock turned and the door opened.

A tall, suited man with a well-groomed moustache, stooped under the door frame to walk in. I recognised him immediately as Alexander. His eyes, stern and cold, observed me and I felt as though I was completely naked under his scrutiny.

"Good afternoon, Georgina," he said. "Welcome to the Beaumont! I'm sorry about the cell. It seems that my colleagues didn't get my message. I'll have you transferred to a much nicer room this afternoon. How are you feeling?" He sat next to me on the hard bed. I stared out to the small slit of light near the ceiling where my freedom lay. "I'll need you to speak if you'd like me to help you."

"Why do people keep saying that's what you do here – help?" I asked.

He laughed as though I had just told a small joke. "Well, we have the means to help you here, yes. Like we discussed at our first meeting, if you're feeling sad, low, confused, angry, frustrated, any of those things, we can help with that through medication or other more, advanced methods – some very new techniques that not all hospitals are able to house but we're lucky enough to have the space, equipment and knowledge. All the treatment and procedures we have performed here have had immensely positive results, our patients come out with much clearer, happier minds. It's all about good communication, diagnosis and the monitoring of treatment. I like to think that we pride ourselves here on establishing a good relationship with our patients for the best outcome possible. We want you all to feel better in yourselves."

His voice had a resonance and hypnotic quality to its tone, that I was almost touched by their persuasion. Perhaps he was right, perhaps I needed some help. I hadn't felt happy for a long time, even before I moved up here. It wasn't just due to loneliness and the feeling like I've failed in everything God had made me for, I had sunken into darkness for so long, I lost myself to it. Alma saved me, and I found joy when I was with her, but that carefree girl from London might never return. I looked around me at the yellowing, stained walls that appeared like someone actively urinated against them.

He looked through his clipboard of notes. "It says here that you have been engaging in relations with another woman, would that be correct?"

I did not say or do anything to respond.

"Right then, I'm going to prescribe you a couple of pills first. You're in luck actually – these are completely new to the hospital, and you may find that your symptoms ease much quicker once taking them. The nurse will be doing the medicine rounds soon. Then we'll get you moved to somewhere much more comfortable!"

He scribbled something in his notes, looked at me and smiled. Afterwards, he left the cell, locking the door behind him but he didn't leave the block immediately and I heard him whispering to someone.

"Charlotte," he said.

"Pa, don't leave me again please! Let us go with you, we won't be any trouble I promise!"

"You know I would if I could."

"We won't be any trouble, we won't!"

"I'm sorry, Charlotte."

I heard some shuffling before she screamed, "Don't leave Pa! Papa!" and the door to the corridor slammed shut before she wailed. Her voice made my blood run cold.

"Michael. Papa. Michael," she continued until her screams died down into a murmur late into the night and weeded its way into my dreams.

CHAPTER
THIRTY-ONE

1953
Jane
Day

There will not be many more times I will be able to sit here and wait to see Alma's docile face. Dr Blythe will leave soon, leaving without a trace of his work here. And where does that leave me? The girl I have come to know seems to be part of the reason why I exist, and without that, I am unwanted and redundant.

I flick through Alma's file when Mary enters the room with her.

"Hello, Mary. Please could you do me a big favour and get me a cup of tea? It's been a busy morning and I forgot to get myself a drink."

Mary very subtly narrows her eyes at me which I try and ignore but without saying a word, she leaves the room and I watch Alma very carefully.

I bring the phonograph in again today with a new song.

"Thank you so much Mary, could you come and pop it down on the table please."

She hesitates and then steps in. The attendant closes the door, and she makes her way over, placing the tray next to the phonograph. She lifts the teapot up and starts to pour tea into the cup.

"Oh, don't worry, I'll take it from here, thank you," I say, when her hand slips. She drops the pot, tea floods the table and spills over the vinyl and her own hand. She yelps and in one reflexive motion, jerks her hand sideways, knocking the needle out off the record. Steam rises from the puddles of hot liquid and Mary's hand is red and scorched. I jump away from the splash but see that Mary, with her good hand, moves Alma out of the way just time before she also gets burned.

Silence fills the room until a sound, so quiet it is almost inaudible, emerges. At first, it's hard to place where it comes from. But I stare at Mary and am sure that it's not from her. Mary in turn, gazes at Alma, her eyes, wide and startled.

"Ma." It's clear this time and I see Alma's lips parted to form the word.

Mary and I are both so still, we hardly breathe.

I watch on as Alma's head turns to Mary's stunned face.

I wait for either one of them to say something, anything.

"Ma," Alma says again for the third time, her voice, croaky and dry. Her eyes draw down towards Mary's burnt hand and her fingers stretch out away from her body, as if reaching out for Mary.

I see Mary's Adam's apple move stiffly up and down her throat like she's swallowing something hard and resistant, and I look at her scorched hand that's slowly blistering up. Could it be? Alma's personal attendant all along was really her mother? What would possess her to hide that from us and above all, from Alma?

Mary places her other hand over it and sees the incredulous look I give her. Without saying a word, she runs out the door, leaving Alma and I alone together in the cold room. Alma's eyes, still glazed and grey, but now welling with tears.

"Alma?" I say.

An attendant blunders in with a mop, interrupting us.

"Where did Mary go?" I ask him.

"Gone to get some cold water on that hand of hers I think," he mumbles.

I wait for him to finish cleaning up to leave us alone again, he lets the door slam shut and Alma jumps at the sound. She's reacting to everything around her. I want so desperately to hold on to this, but I know how fragile the moment is, like cupping an empty eggshell in the palm of my hands. I bring my chair close to hers.

"Alma, did you just call Mary, your Ma? Is Mary your mother?" The clouds part from Alma's eyes and she raises to meet mine. For the first time, I see someone who is finally aware of me.

"I'm going to get you a wheelchair, let's go for a little walk around the grounds."

We leave through the back entrance and walk down the path through to the garden of the dead and unnamed and I position myself on a bench next to her overlooking their graves. We sit in silence for a long time as the sky alters from grey to blue and a moment of sun exposes itself.

"Is Mary your mother Alma?" I ask her again.

Her face expresses nothing.

"Would you let me in, Alma? Would you trust me like you do in your dreams?" I turn back to the field of grass, my words catching in my throat. "It's Jane. I am the same person and I know it must be hard for you to trust anyone. But believe me when I say that I don't want you to be another patient that's buried underneath this ground."

"G…"

I turn to her quickly. She stares towards the graves.

"Yes?" I say.

"G… Ge…"

"Georgina?" I say. "Alma, is it Georgina? What do you want to tell me about her?"

More tears form in Alma's eyes. Slowly, she nods her head and closes her eyes.

"Georgie…" she says. Her face changes, and moves, showing me the anguish she's shown me a thousand times before during the night. I try and console her by placing my hand over hers, but at my touch, she forces her eyes on me and clutches my hand, wrapping her skeletal fingers around mine, gripping them until they hurt.

"Alma!"

She bares her teeth at me and grunts, "Georgie!" She uses both of her hands to pull my arm, dragging me towards her. "Georgie!" she cries.

I am shocked by her strength. "Alma, what do you want? Tell me!"

"Where? Where!"

"Where is Georgina?"

"Where!"

Her breath becomes rapid. I try and push her hands back down and remain balanced, so I don't fall over her.

"Alma, please let go! I need you to listen. Take a deep breath, and a long breath out."

I wait until she's able to calm her breathing. Her grasp loosens but her hands tremble as I place them back down onto her lap.

"Not long after the hospital found you, the police found Georgina. I'm afraid she died in an awful car accident." I didn't want to tell Alma that they found Georgina in Alma's car and that they had set it alight. I look into Alma's eyes with the deepest sorrow. "I'm really sorry Alma, but Georgina has passed away."

I know she hears me as her pupils react to my words, so I keep speaking.

"You know who I am, don't you? My name is Jane Galloway and I've been coming to visit you, day and night. Today is the first time you've talked since I started working with you, but at night, you speak to me through your dreams. You speak very clearly. I know that you loved Georgina deeply and that losing her has sent you into such shock. You relive your last moments with her in your dreams too. You are troubled by them. I think that you must feel some sort of guilt. That perhaps you feel as though it might be your fault that Georgina died.

"I'm here to tell you, Alma, that it's alright. There's no need to bear this burden. It wasn't your fault. I know you only tried to help Georgina escape from this place. That's all you tried to do."

I wait a while, but she does not say anything further. Her face is drained from colour, like the shade of the clouds drifting over us, and it stalls me from asking her more questions about Mary. I don't want to overload her when we've come so far already.

"You must be tired. It's alright if you don't want to speak anymore today. I'll take you back to hospital now and I'll come again to visit you tonight." I hold onto her hand. "I want to free you from your pain."

I wheel her back to the hospital, through the corridors, and as I pass the dining room, Nurse Tolsy almost corners us.

"Ah, there you are!" Tolsy says. She is in the middle of distributing pills to the patients and begins to crush a couple of tablets onto a spoon ready to feed Alma with. All seems like normal around the hospital, but it feels strange to not have Mary hovering over us. Why did she run off like that? What is she hiding?

"Where is Mary?" I ask Tolsy.

"She seems to have disappeared. I can't find her anywhere! If you see her, tell her to come and find me immediately."

She places the spoon into Alma's mouth who seems, for the first time, to resist against it. Tolsy reacts to this despondently, not noticing that my patient has started to show reactions, and pushes the spoon against her lips with more force until Alma has to open them. I frown as I watch her tip the powder onto her tongue and clamp her mouth shut with her hand.

"I trust your appointment has ended now?" Tolsy directs at me. I nod and notice Alma's deep gaze into my eyes and think she's trying to communicate with me using a look alone. I gently smile at her, hoping that she's remembered that I will be with her tonight as Tolsy wheels her back to her cell.

I draw in a deep breath and head to Dr Blythe's office.

Before he can even address me, I blurt out:

"Mary is Alma's mother."

"What?" he says, gesturing me to sit down.

"Alma spoke. Just now and not asleep. Mary was there. She called her 'Ma'. We both heard it."

"Ma? Mary? Alma's mother?" Dr Blythe repeats in dismay. "How can that be?"

"I don't know but it's clear that Mary's been trying to hide it all along because she ran! That explains now why Mary has been the only person to care for Alma. And now Alma's finally saying something, she's gone. Something is really wrong, Doctor."

He nods. "Did Alma say or do anything else?"

"I took her to the memorial garden, and she really reacted. She got hold of me and asked me where Georgina was. Not in so many words. She found it difficult to form any full sentences, but I got the gist of what she wanted to say."

"So, what did you do?"

"I explained to her that Georgina had died not long after they found her. She started to cry, but didn't say anything else after that." I sighed. "It was like it was all she needed to know."

"Gracious. Mary. Her mother! Could it really be? I would never have guessed it. It makes me wonder if Alexander Feyman knew."

He scratches at his balding head.

"So, what do you intend to do now, Jane? Are you back tonight?"

"Yes."

"I want to free her from this burden. I'm not sure how I'll do it yet, but I want to take control of her vision of that particular night and talk her through her steps. Show her somehow that she did all she could to save Georgina. It wasn't her fault."

"And you're so sure about that yourself?"

"No… and yes. It doesn't matter what I believe. I need her to believe it so she can lift the guilt away. And if she can do that, then maybe she'll be able to speak freely."

He nods at me through narrowed eyes.

"Good, carry on doing what you are doing. We are so very nearly there."

Night

"Georgie, I'm sorry, I'm so sorry…" Alma murmurs.

"Alma, it's Jane. Your counsellor. Hold on to my voice. You're in a dream state and you are able to speak freely. You are safe and I am here to protect you."

There is a pause, long enough for me to question whether this different path I take tonight will backfire.

"Jane?" she breathes. "Jane."

"Yes. Where are you? What do you see?"

"Georgina. I see her. She's running towards me. She's so happy to see me. But I'm scared. I cannot save her now." She throws her hands to her face and starts to weep.

"Talk me through it slowly. I'm right here."

"Georgina is meant to meet me here, at my house and then I am going to drive us away. We are starting a life together. But…"

she swallows and shakes her head. "Charles appeared at my door. He's found me at home, and he's been waiting here. He knows Georgina is coming. He is going to take her back to hospital."

"What happens next?"

"I'm afraid. Charles won't leave. He's waiting for her. I can see a figure coming up the hill… It's her! I run towards her and hold her tight.

"Georgina, you have to leave! She doesn't understand. I'm trying to warn her about Charles but can't get the words out in time. He's coming. He's coming up behind her from my house. I turn Georgina around to face him and she screams at him."

"What does she say?"

"She tells him to leave us. That there's no future for them anymore. He doesn't care. He just wants to take her back. He's grabbing hold of her arm and pulling at it. His other hand is holding his cane, he's not very steady. She keeps shouting at him, telling him to let her go! I'm trying to hold her back but even with just one hand, he's overpowering us."

Alma suddenly gasps.

"What is it?" I prompt.

"Georgina's kicked his cane away. He's fallen. She's holding my hand and we're running to my car. NO! Georgina!"

I curl my hands into fists, feeling the same tension she feels.

"Oh no, no, no!"

"Alma, it's alright. Remember that I'm here and that you're only reliving a memory. Hold on to my voice. You have complete control."

"I can't! I can't! Help me! Please! Georgina, she's hurt! Oh my God… Is she still breathing?" She releases a deafening wail into the cell and throws her hands to her face.

"Alma, I'd like you to take three deep breaths and move forward from this point. On your last exhale, you're no longer there at your home with Georgina and Charles. But you are going forwards in time, and you're at the Beaumont."

Her panicked breathing at once calms and I count her breathing.

"Alma, you're at the Beaumont now. Is Mary with you?"

A pause and then a reply. "Yes," she says, her tone, calm and quiet.

"What's Mary doing?"

"She's feeding me. I'm not eating much."

"You cannot speak, can you?"

"No."

"But your thoughts are clear?"

"For now."

"How do you know Mary?"

"She's my mother. I think she's my mother. Sometimes I don't remember. I – I'm confused."

"Do you know why you're here?"

"No," her voice drifts off.

"Do you remember Georgina?"

"Geor… Georgina…"

I realise at this point that by bringing her into the days after that fateful night, she enters a trance like state, she is catatonic not only physically, but her mind will slowly become placid too.

Probably it is to protect herself from her suffering, sheathing her from the reality of Georgina's violent end.

"Alright Alma. It's time for you to rest now. On a count of three, I'd like you to go back to a deep sleep until the morning. One. Two. Three." I wait until her breathing steadies into long, deep breaths. "Good night, Alma. See you tomorrow."

CHAPTER
THIRTY-TWO

31ˢᵗ December 1952
Georgina

I had been in my cell for what seems like days or weeks. Alexander never moved me to a private room like he said he would. In fact, I never saw him again. The nurses gave me medication just before every mealtime and watched me swallow them down. They didn't tell me what the pills were or what they did but I knew that a short while after taking them, my senses would numb, my movements would be slow and my memory of anything would be vague.

I heard a shout through the corridor.

"Units one to five! Bath!"

The door to my cell opened and a guard stepped in.

"Come with me, lady. Time for your bath." They always called me 'lady'. The odd, friendly one would call me 'love'. I wondered if they even knew my name. I thought that if I stayed here long enough, I would forget that I ever had one. Every activity throughout the day was structured to a strict routine like a prison. We all wore the same gowns despite some of them complaining that they had bought their own clothes to change into. They stripped us entirely of our identity and when the five of us patients lined up outside the baths, they stripped us of our clothes too. The patient in Unit 5, the cell next to me was more resistant than the others, they dragged her naked body towards the furthest bath, showing us what would happen if we didn't comply, throwing her in and pushing her under the water as she choked and cried. It took two women to hold her down as she slipped around the tub and flayed her limbs with water splashing and slopping onto the tiled floor.

A female attendant tugged my gown down past my shoulders so hard that the fabric burned my skin.

"In you go!" she said, giving me a shove. I was faced with a large bath filled with grimy water. I watched as the others climbed into their own baths and gasped as they sank into it, filling me with more apprehension. "Go on, this is the only wash you'll get for two days so you'd better make it good." I would have rather stayed dirty, but I lowered my feet into the water, it was ice cold and I held my breath as I sat in it. The attendant came over with a cloth and started scouring me with hard, vigorous strokes as if she was scrubbing clothing against a washboard. Then she took out a brush and started tugging the knots out of my damp hair. I winced with each tug, feeling strands of hair being pulled out with each stroke.

"Get up!" she ordered and rubbed me down with a stiff towel. She threw a clean gown over my head whilst I was still damp and the water from my hair dripped down onto it.

At mealtimes, I would be led into the big hall, and they would sit me at a table with the other celled patients, away from the 'safe' ones. It was always the time when I would feel like myself the most, when the morning's drugs were starting to wear off and my senses would come back to me before the next dose after dinner. This was when I was able to take a good look at the woman in Unit 5. She always talked to someone called Michael who existed only in her mind. I would spend my hours just listening to her conversations with him. I found them strangely interesting even though it was all nonsense, especially in my drugged, dazed state.

She came and sat opposite me this dinner time and I watched her sweep her wild, dark hair aside only for it to fall over her face again. If you were to picture a person who was locked away in a lunatic asylum, she would be it. A slop of dinner caught in strands of her hair as she placed a spoonful of gruel into her mouth. I played around with my own gruel with my spoon, glad that I was used to not eating much.

"Bleurgh. Always so disgusting," she moaned whilst another woman next to me shovelled it down her throat eagerly.

"It's not that bad. Beats starvin'!"

"I'd rather starve! Lucky Michael doesn't have to eat anything." She caught me staring at her and I shifted my eyes awkwardly back to my bowl, immediately feeling my cheeks burn. "Who are you?" she asked, fixing her dark eyes on me, contorting her strange face into a frightening smirk. I swallowed.

"Georgina," I replied, managing a weak smile. "And you're Charlotte?" I remember hearing Alexander addressing her in her cell.

She suddenly moved her face over the table so that it was only inches away from mine and I recoiled.

"Charlotte's dead," she whispered harshly, and I caught a faint whiff of her breath. "It's Cleo, now." She threw her arms in the air. "Resurrected!" she shouted, so loud that everyone in the room turns to her. Her grin fades quickly as she slumped her shoulders back down and lowered her face, whispering again.

"Psst," sounded the patient next to me who had wiped her bowl clean, but seemed less crazy. "They're the same person, Charlotte and Cleo, in case you hadn't figured that out already." I nodded, grateful for the clarification.

"Do you know who Michael is?" I asked her.

"Her brother. She killed him. Didn't you, Cleo?" she started to chuckle.

Cleo gave me an unnerving cold glare, smacked her hand against her tray so food splattered around her bowl. She turned to her side, tilted her head as though she was listening to something, or someone, and shook her head.

I furrowed my eyebrows, unaware of how appalled I looked, and Cleo glared at me.

"What you lookin' at!? I didn't do it! I don't think I did it! Did I? I didn't do it." Her muttering continued and I kept my eyes down on my tray, breathing in slowly so no one could detect any movement from me.

"Cleo! Pipe down!" shouted an order from the nearest attendant.

"You havin' that?" said the patient next to me, still hungry. I shook my head, and she took the bowl off my tray and started spooning its contents into her mouth too. From the corner of my eye, I saw a white coat approach me and I was sure I was in trouble.

"Come on lady, you have a visitor." I looked up at his stern expression.

"Me?" I asked.

"Yes, you. Come on, up you get."

I got off my chair and all eyes were on me as I followed the guard out of the room, down the corridor and into another. He opened a door for me and seated at a table in the centre of that room was the face I never thought I'd set my eyes on again. Sitting up straight, in a blue skirt and matching buttoned jacket, her hair tied neatly in a bun and a hat with a bowknot veil perched perfectly on the side of her head, was Alma. She looked as beautiful as the first day we met, but also different. Neater, and her carefree energy I fell in love with seemed to have been stripped away and I hardly recognised her. I wanted to run to Alma but remembered which side of the cell I belonged in. I was no one, dressed in no one's clothes with no one's name. I started to panic, spun around and tried to leave but the guard was blocking the doorway.

"I can't be here." I whispered to him.

"Georgina, wait. It's alright, please," I heard Alma's voice call, and I sank, turning around to show her my hollow face. She held out her hand towards me, her eyes brimming with tears. I shuffled back to the table and sat down opposite her.

"What happened to you my dear Georgina? What have they done to you?"

"Charles… he sent me here. We had an argument. He thought that I wanted to hurt him and then he found out about us." I couldn't meet her in the eye.

"Oh Georgie." She clasped my hand, and I pulled it away from her, glancing back at the guard to check if he was watching.

"What are you doing here?" I asked.

"I wanted to see you! I've missed you so much. Don't you want to see me?"

"I can't. Not anymore. They're trying to change me. Cure me of… it's too dangerous."

She swallows. "Georgie, listen to me. I'm leaving Howard." She eyed the guard at the door and lowered her voice. "I'm going to get you out of here, you hear me?" I shook my head, not knowing how that would be possible. "I know the charge nurse in the evenings. She can help us. You and I, we're going to leave this place together."

My eyes raised up to hers, not knowing if I had the courage to hope again.

"When?"

"Tomorrow."

CHAPTER

THIRTY-THREE

1953
Jane
Day

"Mrs Galloway, good morning," the receptionist says.

"Morning, Patient A please."

She flips through the diary. "I'm afraid she's not available right now."

"Not available? She's a patient. Where is she if she's not available?"

"I'm very sorry but I'm not able to dispense the information. Would you like to speak to the charge nurse?"

"Please."

She picks up the phone.

"Mrs Galloway wishes to speak to you." She puts the receiver down. "The nurse will be with you in a moment."

I wait for at least ten minutes and I'm about to pester the receptionist again when I hear the familiar chink of keys to someone's steps along the corridor. Of course, it would be the usual not so friendly Tolsy that I see.

"Mrs Galloway. How can I help?"

"You surely already know why I'd be here. Why am I being prevented from seeing my patient?"

"She's sleeping right now."

"Well then, I'll wait."

She stares at me for a long moment and huffs.

"Go through to the meeting room. I'll bring her in."

I glance at the receptionist who looks awkwardly back at me, and I follow Tolsy down the corridors to the meeting room and wait in my chair.

Nearly an hour had passed by when the door opens and an attendant I do not recognise brings Alma in. She is profusely shaking. Her hair is not braided as usual and hangs messily around her face which is pale, wet from sweat.

I turn to the attendant.

"Where's Mary?"

"Not in today." He doesn't wait for a response from me and shuts the door.

"Alma, where's your mother?"

I guide her to her seat. Her hands are trembling and I take hold of one, feeling its iciness, I try to cup it in my hand and steady it. I move her sleeve up to feel her pulse. It is faint and slow, and a discolouration of her skin on her wrist catches my eye. It is mottled by hard bruising in the shade of blues, purples and greens. I slide her sleeve further up her arm and in the crease of her elbow, several pinpricks expose that she has been given medication of some sort intravenously.

I flick through her file which mentions nothing that I've not entered myself.

"Alma, who's been doing this to you?"

She doesn't say a thing but continues to shake. I place a gentle hand on her shoulder and use the other to feel her forehead. Her skin is damp and cold.

"Alma. It's Jane. Remember me from your dreams? Tell me what happened to you?"

Her trembling suddenly ceases. Her sallow face starts to recede further into a shade of green and her eyes peel open so wide that they bulge out of their sockets. Her chest starts to heave, she opens her mouth as if she is about to speak. Then vomit spews out of it, over the table. Splatters of undigested gruel bounce off it's hard surface and splash onto my dress.

"Attendant!" I call out, jumping back.

The attendant swings the door open and heaves a large sigh.

"Clive! Need a mop! Now!"

"What's happened to her?" I ask him.

The guard, Clive, opens the door and Tolsy follows in closely after him. Alma continues to retch although nothing more can come out. Tolsy immediately digs a hankie out of her pocket and wipes Alma's soiled face and strands of hair.

"Nurse Tolsy, her left arm is bruised and full of injection points. What has she been given?" She fails to meet me in the eye and frustration in my stomach rises into heightened vexation. "Nurse Tolsy, I have the right to know what my patient has been administered! If you don't tell me now, then–"

"It's anaesthesia."

"Anaesthesia? For what?"

"Electroshock therapy."

"What? Since when? Who has permitted this?"

She throws her hankie in the bucket and sighs at me. "Sir Feyman."

"He's not meant to interfere with medical prescriptions or treatment. Who's administering the injections? It looks like an amateur."

"I did. Mrs Galloway." I'm astounded but I see that her glare softens and she turns to Alma with a subtle shake of her head. "Poor soul," she says quietly. I finally see that she didn't agree with the procedure either. The attendants shuffle the tin bucket around as they mop up the sick whilst Alma stays seated on her chair. They leave the room but the smell of half-digested warm gruel and bile still lingers around us. I wait until the door is securely closed.

"Why did Sir Feyman do it? She's catatonic. She doesn't require ECT."

"It doesn't take long to realise that Sir Feyman operates on his own agenda. There's no reason for many things he does. The longer the patients are here with no family visiting, the more likely he'll take matters in his own hands. He answers to nobody."

"So, you just let this happen under your watch? These experiments he undertakes on innocent, helpless people? You'll just sweep it all under the rug?"

"Sir Feyman is a powerful, manipulative man. He knows people in high places. If anyone of us said a single word against him, we'd be out, not just out of the Beaumont, he'd make sure that we'd have no future. We do what we need to survive and if we have to sacrifice the people who have no hope of any future anyway, then so be it, there is no choice, do you understand me?!"

I can hardly believe my eyes or ears. How can she just accept the monstrous actions of the superintendent as routine? She directs the next sentence to me like a warning. "I'd get out of here as soon as you can if I were you. You're not suited to this place." She straightens herself up and hardens her expression again. The small glimpse of the nurse she might have been will not be seen again by me. "This girl needs cleaning up. I'm sure you wouldn't mind your session interrupted just for today." It reminds me that Alma usually has Mary to look after her needs.

"Where's Mary?" I ask Tolsy.

"No idea, hasn't been in since yesterday."

I storm straight towards Dr Blythe's office, ready to knock his door down, suspecting that he must have known about all of this, but I'm only halfway down the corridor when I notice that his door is partly open. He stands at the side of his desk, filling up a cardboard box and spots me in the doorway.

"Hello – come in, Jane, how are you?"

"Dr Blythe?" I ask.

He sighs. "I'm leaving, Jane. Feyman's kicking me out."

"What? Right now?! He can't do this!"

"I wish that was so, Jane."

"But – where will you go?"

"I'm being transferred full time to Wakefield."

"Dr Blythe, won't you just stay and see this case through? We are so close. Alma has come so far. If we don't continue, she may regress back to be being catatonic. They've been taking her in for ECT treatment – did you know that?" He glances at me and shakes his head. "She's suffering from side effects. If they keep doing it, it could have severe impact on her memory. I'm afraid for her future, she doesn't belong here."

"Yes, yes, I know! Jane, listen. At the rate these institutions are carrying on, no one will be here soon so I wouldn't spend too much time worrying about her rotting away in a cell for the rest of her life. She will be forced out into the community one day."

"And who will care for her then?"

"Society. Or she has a mother now apparently who has been caring for her all along – maybe she will learn to come back and do it properly."

"But Dr–"

"Jane, I admire your passion, I really do. But it's pointless. There's nothing I can do to help this woman further. You've been here for months now, and she can say... Ma? One word. She's not the only case who suffers like this. There are hundreds. We've tried our best." He continues with packing his boxes.

"We have to look at the positives. I couldn't work in this environment for much longer anyway, Jane. The care here is diabolical. Feyman doesn't care, at best he is controlling and insistent on continued Neanderthal practices. For Christ's sake, he still believes in phrenology! Imagine if we all walked around assessing patients just by looking at the shape of their skull! It's a good job the place is shutting down."

At last, he stills for moment and looks up at me. "I've really enjoyed working with you, Jane, and I'm sorry that I dragged you into this mess. I was like you – wanting to help her. Hopefully our paths will cross again. It just wasn't meant to be this time."

"I don't understand. What does this mean for me – am I still employed here?" I ask.

"I'd say that until they take that visitor badge off you which could be at any moment, then yes. If you want to continue helping Alma, make the most of it. Which reminds me, you haven't come across the collection of tapes have you?"

"Tapes?"

"The recordings of your night sessions?"

"No, I gave them all to you."

"Yes, hmm. I can't seem to find them anywhere. I was meant to hand them back over to you. Nevermind, they can't have gone far. I'm sure they'll turn up once I've packed everything away."

He's rummaging through the stacks of paper, files and books on his desk, and I realise how much he's aged over the past few months. I feel lost, like a member of my family is leaving at the point I need them the most.

"Do you need any help?" I ask.

He raises an eyebrow and smiles.

"I'll be fine, thank you Jane. You look after yourself and I'll see you at the next hospital."

I have a strong urge to throw my arms around him and hug him tight. He's been my rock and my sounding board in this hospital, and I fear that without him, I'll struggle to hold my head up high against the likes of Sir Feyman and Nurse Tolsy, especially now that I know Serene hasn't been truthful. I leave his office for the last time, walk down the corridor to a junction and wonder which way to turn. Back towards Alma's cell, or to the exit of the hospital. Or do I walk to the other wing where Sir Feyman might be? Do I find him and have a conversation about his intensions, confess to what I've been doing with the patient ever since I met her, use that information to guide him, change the direction of her fate? My heart starts to race, knowing that it might cost me my job, but it looks like it may be ending anyway. I make my way to his office.

I pass the endless rows of doors again and the dining hall where attendants and patients start to congregate for their next meal. An attendant pushes a patient in a wheelchair past me and gives me a nod. I return the nod, somehow feeling guilty or self-conscious like I was entering a place I shouldn't be.

Eventually, I reach the door with Sir Alexander Feyman's name on the plaque. With everything that's happened so far this morning, I feel shaken and uneasy. I knock tentatively but instead of having to wait for an answer, the door becomes ajar. I call out his name and still, there is no answer, so I push the door open slightly more, and I realise that there's no one in his room.

I glance over his office and see several glass jars with liquid and something organic soaked in them, lined up on rows of shelving. What were they? Organs of some sort? The rest of his room is ornately decorated with a grand ebony desk and his array of medals on the walls. On his table, a lone file sits. I poke my head back outside into the corridor to check no one's approaching. Carefully, I step inside the room and close the door behind me. My heart is pounding, knowing that I was in prohibited territory and ignoring the fact that he could come back at any moment. It will only take a second.

I flick through the file discarded on his desk. Patient A, Alma's records up to date. They appear to be the very same that

I review every day. Except that they're in a red folder stamped with "undisclosed" on the front.

I open it to the first page, and it does not take me a second to see a list of medication given to Alma on a daily basis in the morning, drugs that were not shown in the record that is handed to myself daily. Sedatives that are to be kept hidden from my knowledge and ones that would easily cause limited movement and speech. My heart thuds against my chest as I take this in with only one suspicion on my mind. Has Sir Feyman been preventing Alma from speaking all along?

I skip to the next page where scheduled appointments and treatments are listed.

Lobotomy. Tomorrow morning at 8am.

Voices and footsteps echo closer towards the room from outside. I panic and place the file back on the desk, not knowing where to hide. I try the sash window and to my relief, it slides open. I climb out the window, a small jump to the soft ground. I hear a key enter the lock and it begins to turn and I quickly slide the window shut.

I feel blood boiling to the surface, raising fury and fear with it. I crouch down, trying to keep my escape discrete. In the distance, I see someone standing upright and staring at me. Mary? Has she returned? I keep my pace up, skirting the outside of the hospital, hoping she won't say anything to anyone.

CHAPTER
THIRTY-FOUR

1952
Georgina

That night I tried to recycle Alma's visit over and over in my mind, not wanting to ever forget it in case it was the last time I ever saw her, but it was difficult to keep hold of that thought when my brain felt like it had turned to slush after another dose of pills made their way into my nervous system. I needed to find a way out of having to take them so my mind could stay clear. Every so often, under the dim, orange light, Cleo's whispering would drift in and out of my dreams.

"Don't worry, Michael. Pa will come soon. I know he will."

When I was more awake, I knocked on our wall. Her muttering ceased and she knocked back the same number of times, in the same rhythm as if she was ready to play a game.

"Who's that?" she whispered.

"Georgina."

"Georgina," she echoed. "Who was that you went off to see earlier?"

"Oh, a friend."

"Must be nice to have those."

"Do you not have any?"

"Ha! Just Michael."

"Can I ask you a question, Cleo?" She went quiet and then I heard a tapping against the wall again. Three taps in a row in quick succession. I assumed that meant yes.

"Do you know Alexander Feyman?" She answered with another three taps.

"Do you call him, Papa?"

Tap. Tap. Tap.

"Is he your father?" There was a very long pause this time and I thought she would never answer. But then three taps sounded by my ear.

"Why has he put you in here?"

She started murmuring something I couldn't understand, which morphed into a low, miserable cry. "Because I killed his Michael! But don't you see! He's not dead! He's right here!"

I woke up that day and followed the routine as normal, waiting to be collected, or some sort of a sign that it was time for me to escape. I wasn't sure what I was looking for but I knew I had to stay alert so I hid the tablets they gave me under my tongue and prayed that they would forget to ask me to lift it. They didn't forget and forced me to swallow them down, so I drifted back into my fog, tired and numb. The memory of waiting for anything or anyone was slowly slipping away. The sun skulked behind the horizon and the evening charge nurse with mousey blonde hair came by with the medication.

"Two pills, pop them in quickly," she said softly, but when she handed me the paper cup, it was empty. She passed me a cup of water when I handed the cup back to her, she gave me a subtle nod and visited the next cell. The hours passed but still nothing happened. Perhaps Alma didn't want to go through with it after all. It would have been too risky, and who could blame her.

The lights went out, plummeting me into darkness. All was quiet apart from the low hum of snores from the other cells and the odd outburst of Cleo's demonic wailing. Then a click in the distance. My eyes widened, searching through the black. The lock to my cell turned and the door slowly swings open. A figure stood in the doorway, and I thought I had met my doom.

"Come," the figure whispered. The charge nurse came back but wore no uniform, just normal clothing and a big shawl wrapped around her shoulders. It was hard to really see her features because of the poor lighting but I didn't recognise her.

I rose from the bed. Whether she was leading me to freedom or to my death was still unknown. I followed her out. She shut the door gently and we trod quietly down numerous corridors, weaving left and right until we reached a small, wooden door at the end.

"Head straight over the graveyard, down to the railway track, cross it and straight up the hill to the white cottage at the top. Alma will meet you there. This is where I leave you. Take care of yourself." It was only then, that I could hear her Irish accent. I hung on her every word. My life depended on it, I was sure it did. I could tell she was risking her job by doing this for me too. I wanted to reach out and hug her but not here, not now. Perhaps another time when we were just normal, free people meeting under better circumstances, but really I knew that I was never going to see her again.

She opened the door, unveiling the outside world that I hadn't seen in days. I stepped out tentatively onto it, my feet, bare and frozen, feeling every roughness of the earth under the soles of my feet. There was a wintery breeze in the air and I tremble. I turned back to her, and her eyes showed me fear and sympathy.

"Hold on," she said, and slipped off her mules, passing them over to me. I took them gratefully and tucked my feet into each one. She then took her shawl off and passed that to me too. "Be careful. Good luck. Remember, straight over the graveyard to the railway track and up the hill."

"Wait – what graveyard?"

"It's a wide stretch of grass. There aren't any headstones on it. Our patients are buried there."

She closed the door on me leaving me in the night on my own. My body shook uncontrollably as I made my way out of the grounds from cold and fear. I looked all around me, checking no one saw but once I reached the graveyard, I felt terribly exposed. I stood with my back against a hedge for a moment of protection as I stared across the lawn. The wind howled through the emptiness, and I took a deep breath, willing my legs to move. Somehow the confines of the hospital now felt safer than it was being out here.

As I made my way across the grass, I was treading on countless graves of the patients that never made it out of the Beaumont, I had awful visions of my steps disturbing them from their rest. One by one, they rose from their sleep, their skeletal hands reaching up through the earth, penetrating through and grabbing at my ankles, their groaning half-dead voices begging me to save them – or join them. A feeble scream escaped from my lips and my steps picked up in pace until I was sprinting towards the woodland. The mules the woman had given me were loose and I had kicked them off during my run, but I didn't care anymore, I wasn't about to run back to retrieve them. I just needed to make it through.

I finally found the railway track and looked up at the white cottage, standing like a lighthouse, a beacon of hope, Alma's house. I scrambled up the track towards it, cutting my feet against the stones along the path and as I reached the top, through the darkness, came a voice.

"Georgina."

I turned to it and her warm arms embraced me. I held on to her and cried with relief.

"Sweet Georgina," she said as she planted kisses over my face, over and over again. "I'm sorry, I'm sorry, I'm so sorry."

"It's alright. I'm safe now," I said, feeling deep relief.

"No, you're not safe. I'm so sorry Georgie." I pulled away from her, confused. I realised in that moment, it was terror filling her eyes, and she shook her head. "He's here!"

"What?"

Her eyes pan over to my left and behind me. She dragged me backwards and turned me around.

"You can't hurt us!" she shouts into the night. I narrow my eyes, but I cannot see what she sees.

From the thick of the gloom, a foreboding shadow emerged with a gait, so distinct, I would always recognise to whom it belonged.

"Charles?" I breathed.

"You couldn't have just stayed at home and been a good housewife, could you?" he replied, his face coming into view, angry and sinister. "We would have been so happy just doing what we were doing."

"We were never that happy Charles. If anything, we got too good at lying to ourselves."

"And each other," he finished, looking over at Alma.

"I didn't mean for things to happen with Alma. I was lonely. She's just a friend."

"Do you know what would happen to my reputation if word got out about what you're doing? As if it wasn't bad enough that I had to send you away to the Beaumont!"

"I've not done anything that's any worse compared to what you've done to me!"

"See this is what I hate about you! Why do you always have to argue back! I just wanted you to be quiet, and good!" Charles spoke with gritted teeth, his hand gripping onto his cane, so hard his knuckles bared white. He lunged for my neck and gripped on to it tight.

"No! Charles!" Alma shouted.

My hands fumbled around his wrist, trying as hard as I could to release his grip, but it was no use. I could feel the blood drain away from my head as the world started to fade when I hear a thud and his hands let go. He was on the ground. There, standing over him, was Alma holding a rock in both her hands. He wasn't moving. The ground beneath him gradually dampened with his own blood.

"We have to go," she says to me quietly.

Just as Alma pulls me up, I screamed and my knees slammed against the ground. Charles had pulled me down by my ankle. I curled my fingertips into the soil as he dragged me backwards on my stomach.

"Georgina!" I heard Alma screech. And everything went black.

CHAPTER

THIRTY-FIVE

1953
Jane

I duck my head low below the windowsill and cling against the wall so that Sir Feyman can't see me as he walks into the room. I check to see where Mary's standing, she's gone, disappearing like an apparition.

There is a shadow gliding along the perimeter of the grounds. I run towards it, knowing that it must be Mary and I follow her into Crowbeck. As she weaves in and out of people, she disappears again, and I only just manage to catch a glimpse of her heading towards the end of a side street. She turns around. I tuck myself into the threshold of the nearest house. My heart stops sure that she has spotted me, but she crosses the road and I wait, following her with my eyes to see which direction she takes next. She slips down a narrow street to the right; Hudson Mews, a row of tightly knitted terraced housing.

My pace quickens before I lose her completely and catch her standing at the door of number fourteen. I carefully position myself in a ginnel and watch her dig for her keys. She opens the door and steps inside. I cross over and stand outside the same door she walks through. And I knock. A few seconds later, she opens the door. Her sleepy eyes widen clearly in recognition of me and she tries to swing the door shut but I hold up my hand and push against it. I am stronger than her and it stays ajar.

"What do you want?" she hisses.

"Mary, I know that was you. You saw me climb out of Sir Feyman's office window, didn't you?"

"So, what if I did?"

"What were you doing there? Why haven't you come back to look after Alma?"

Her weight against the door relaxed and she stares at me.

"How do you know her name is Alma?"

"She told me. Mary, please. I just want to talk. I'm here only out of kindness."

"Kindness? Kindness means nothing. Kindness given me nothing but this miserable life. Go!" She tries to slam the door, but once again my hand stops it.

"Mary, I know you care for her. Your daughter – Alma. Let me help."

"Are you deaf? Go! Leave me in peace!"

"Peace will never come if you abandon her now," I say.

"No one asked you to come! Everything was fine until you turned up. She was content with exactly where she was."

"Content?!"

"She was safe! You have no idea what you have done!"

My hand must have relaxed as she manages to fully shut the door in my face, and I hear the lock turn. I knock at the door loudly, shouting over and over, "Mary, please! I just want to talk!" but she doesn't come back, and I feel helpless, not knowing what to do next. The only thing I can do now, is to wait until night when I'm back in that cell with Alma.

I head back to the high street of Crowbeck and board the next tram back to Bramley. It won't be long before I have to pick Jasper up from school. When I get off the tram again, there are two policemen walking in my direction and I realise one of them is Richard and in dawns on me that I could ask him for help. He spots me straight away.

"Jane? Are you alright? You look a bit shaken up?"

"Could I have a word with you? In private?" I glance at the other policeman who seems to catch on quickly.

"I'll walk on up ahead," he says to Richard. Richard extends out a hand to hold mine.

"What's wrong?" he says, and I shake my head. "Is it Jasper?"

"No, it's my patient. I think she's in danger."

"How do you mean?"

"The superintendent's been hiding information about her from me. I found out that he's been injecting her with drugs. I think he's purposefully trying to stop her from talking."

"Why would he do that?"

"Evidence? I don't know. She's been telling me some things about the night that her friend, Georgina, died. I think he's found out somehow about my night visits and now he wants to give her a lobotomy which means taking out some of her brain... She might not even remember who she is afterwards." The words tumble out of me, I'm rushing them in case I run out of time.

"I'm sorry, I shouldn't be telling you any of this, but I don't know what to do. My supervisor who knows everything has been sacked."

"Do you have any evidence of this?"

"Feyman had a separate medical file for Alma – one that I've never seen before. I found it on his desk when he wasn't around and nearly got caught looking at it." Richard looks down the street, seemingly to check for people who might hear us, and gently pulls me to the side.

"Jane, do you know how important Sir Feyman is? Our chief inspector is a good friend of his. I don't think it's wise to snoop around in his things. You just said you nearly got caught."

"I know but I can't just stand by and see innocent people get hurt. Surely you can understand that?"

He observes me with worry until he eventually nods.

"I'll try and get hold of the sergeant in charge of Bramley and see if he'll send anyone down to have a look, but promise me that you'll stay out of this from now on?"

"Yes, yes, I will."

"Leave it with me. It might have to be tomorrow though. Will you still be assessing your patient tonight?"

"Yes. I have to pick Jasper up first."

"Alright, I'll pick you up again?"

"Thank you, I really appreciate it."

"It's under my job description to help," he smiles gently. "Make sure you get some rest before you head out again, you look worn out." He dips his head to brush his lips against my cheek. "It's going to be fine," he says softly.

Everything is dark in the space I'm in, but there are still images I see that are fractured and make no sense. I'm disorientated and cannot seem to control where I'm heading to, when the sound of tapping drifts into my thoughts. I look around me and cannot see where it could be coming from. The tapping is incessant and only gets louder.

"Mama, there's someone at the door!" Jasper's voice comes across as muffled and I try to answer him, but he can't hear me. "Mama! Wake up!" I feel my shoulder shake and I jump, forcing my eyes open to see that I'm back in my living room with Jasper's face right in front of me.

"Sorry, I didn't know I'd fallen asleep." The knocking continues. I look at the time, it's got to be Kirsty coming to look after Jasper. My body feels heavy as I rise off the couch and try and calm my dishevelled hair as I approach the door. Upon opening it, a woman, not Kirsty, turns around.

"Mary!"

"Can we talk? Please?" She wears an anxious look, and glances towards the stairs. "Could I come in?" I nod and open the door wider for her. She stands in the kitchen fiddling with her gloves.

"Would you like a cup of tea?"

"Just water, please." I get her a glass of water and ask her to take a seat at the dining table. "I've come to give you these." She gives me a stack of letters tied together with cotton string. They are all open and addressed to Alma. "They are all from Georgina."

"Thank you. Why the change of heart?"

"I see what's happening in that hospital. I think you should know why."

I feel the paper of the worn envelopes with Georgina's writing in my hands, as precious as rare artifacts. I take a moment to think.

"A while ago," I say, "I received a phone call from a woman. She told me that I must be careful and then put the phone down on me before I could find out who it was."

Mary nods her head. "It was me. I wanted to warn you because you had no idea what you were getting yourself into. And I was scared. I didn't want to truth to be revealed – I was worried for Alma's safety.

"Alma and Georgina were… seeing each other outside their marriages. They were more than just friends. They tried to keep it a secret, but I know my daughter. She only needs to give me a look and I know what she's thinking. When Howard left home and she started spending more and more time with this new friend of hers, I knew at the back of my mind that it was something more than that. There was a change in her. I turned a blind eye, but I was always aware and afraid of what people might do if they found out."

She took a sip of water and carried on.

"And then Georgina's husband – Charles – did something awful. He had her sent to the Beaumont. Alma was distraught." Her hands started to shake. "Do you know what they do to people like them? What Sir Feyman does? Not just chemical castration and lobotomies, but other experimental medication with unimaginable side effects. He sterilises women… its beyond anything a doctor is allowed to do. I wanted so much to help her but had no idea how. Then she came up with a plan to escape with her. I warned her not to, it was too dangerous, but she wouldn't listen. When Alma and a body were found on the same morning, I knew what Charles had done. But I was too afraid to go to the police."

"Why were you afraid?"

"Do you know that Alexander Feyman is Charles' Uncle? He has a law of his own. You accuse his nephew of murder and he'll find a reason to incarcerate you too. It was almost lucky that Alma had lost her voice – he wouldn't have the need to hurt her if she couldn't say anything or give any evidence. When you came onboard, Feyman started giving her drugs, new ones that he'd never tried on other patients before, in the hopes of keeping her quiet. But she never stayed quiet in the night, and you discovered that."

"Did you know that she sleep-talked as well?"

Mary falls silent and shakes her head.

"How did you know that I found out?"

"Nurse Serene told me. She's known us for a while because we used to go and visit Howard a lot. She always wanted to help. She told me that she never gave Alma her evening medication because she knew that it was doing her more harm than good, but when you told her about the sleep talking, she thought that the lack of drugs might be helping – she was able to be free enough to talk through her dreams.

"I should be grateful that you've taught my daughter to talk again. But because you have, he's going to destroy her. She knows too many things about that night and about him." Mary's eyes start to well up, soon tears cascade freely down her cheeks and she lifts a hankie out of her bag to dab them away. "I need your help, Mrs Galloway. I don't know what to do anymore. How do

I save my daughter?" I get up immediately and walk towards the telephone.

"No, we mustn't do anything or say anything to anyone!"

"What? Mary, we must!"

"If you ring the police, at best he will deem you as crazy as the patients he owns. At worse, he will kill her!"

"We have to do something," I say, worried that I had already jeopardised her safety by talking to Richard and asking for his help. What if I've also sent him to get hurt too? "There must be something we can do."

"There is nothing. They are all under his control. Do you remember Cleo?" I nod. "Cleo isn't just a schizophrenic girl taken off the street with an invisible friend called Michael. Cleo is Charlotte Feyman." A wave of realisation hits me.

"Alexander's daughter?"

Mary nods. "If he can imprison his own daughter, he'll do it to anyone."

I sit back and think hard. There must be a way to get Alexander Feyman seen under the eyes of justice. I think back to the secret file of Alma's, and of the mounting list of family members that Feyman has incarcerated. Alma, Charlotte... And a thought comes to me like a bolt of lightning.

"We have to go, now." I grab my coat. "Jasper, time to go to Kirsty's."

"Where?" says Mary.

"The hospital."

"They won't let me back in."

"Not through the front. I know a way. Come on, we have to be quick." I was aware that Alma's lobotomy would be tomorrow and we had to act fast, and I would think of a plan on the way there.

CHAPTER

THIRTY-SIX

1952
Charles

"What have you done?!" Alma's voice came out, half a whisper, half a scream with despair in her eyes.

I hardly knew. Georgina, my wife, lay on the ground lifeless before me with blood pouring out from her temple. I didn't do that, surely? That's not the man I was, not the man I was raised to be. I was no killer. My own vision was blurred, my head, throbbing with pain from being hit, but I could see Alma running into the house.

"Wait, what are you doing?" I shouted after her.

"What do you think I'm doing? Calling for help!"

"No, you can't."

"Are you out of your mind?!" she screamed back at me.

"No! This – this, isn't my fault!" I gestured towards Georgina.

"Charles. You have to let me call for an ambulance, please. She could still be alive, we could save her and you wouldn't be in trouble!"

"I can't." The ache from my crooked leg spread up to my hip but if Alma was going to turn me in, I would do anything I could to stop her. I grabbed her hand.

"Let go of me!"

"You call for help and I'll turn you in! I'll make it look like it was you that hurt her!" I said through gritted teeth and dragged her over to my car.

"Let me go! Why do you have to do this?" she cried. "All of this time, you made us feel like we were the mad ones, when it's been you all along!"

"Don't you dare call me mad! I'm not like you at all! I'm not like anyone who belongs in that God-awful asylum!" I opened the boot of my car. At the front of the boot was a large can of petrol. I unscrewed its cap and lifted it out.

"What are you doing?!" She tugged and scratched at my arms so hard, her nails drew blood from my skin. I flayed my arm, trying to shake her off and threw the petrol over Alma, soaking her dress in toxic fluid. It made her scream like a trapped witch, and she immediately let go of me.

The pain still seared through my head and blood from my scalp dripped into my eyes. I limped over to her car and started lugging pools of petrol all over it.

"I won't let you escape!" I pulled out a lighter from my pocket. "No one knows that I'm here. But everyone will see your letters and know that she escaped to meet you. Your sad affair left you crazed, so you lured her up here in the night to end her life."

I flicked down the striker and a flame came to life at its tip. It was only the size of the nail of my little finger, but its heat was enough to burn the skin of my thumb. I threw it at the windscreen of the car, it slid down towards the bonnet. Nothing happened at first but then a miraculous explosion burst the windows out into the night. I shielded my face with my arm and shards of glass sliced through my shirt. Alma's car was in flames, and I stood there, mesmerised by the inferno. Suddenly I was aware that I was no longer gripping on to Alma and she was no longer tugging and scratching at me. I looked around the grounds of her house, she was nowhere to be seen.

"Alma! Alma!" I yelled. A shadow flitted past the flames towards the house.

I limped over to her house in so much panic, I was almost galloping with my bad leg trailing behind. The door was wide open but there were no lights on. I stepped inside.

"Alma?" I called out. "Alma, I know you're in here!" I looked around her living room and the kitchen. "Alma!?" The telephone receiver was hanging off the wall. I walk over to it and hold it to my ear. The line was dead. I looked around me again, worried that she had called the police and I rang the only person that could help me now. Alexander picked up almost immediately like he had been sitting in front of his telephone waiting.

"Yes?"

"Alexander. It's Charles."

There was a pause. "What is it?" he said with a hint of agitation.

"Georgina. She escaped from hospital. I found her at Alma's house, we had an argument and… and she fell. She's lying in the middle of Alma's front lawn. I'm not sure if she's still alive. I think – I think she is, but Alma's threatened to call the police and I can't find her."

I heard him sigh.

"Is there something you're omitting from your story, Charles, or am I supposed to believe it word for word?"

"What? No, we just had a disagreement. It all happened very quickly, I got upset – very upset. But it wasn't my fault! Please Uncle, you have to help me! If anyone found out that I hurt Georgie, or – or…"

"Killed her?"

"I'll lose everything. Everything I've worked hard for."

"Fine," he said.

"Fine, what does that mean?"

"It means that I will clear up this mess."

"Wait – Uncle?" He waited as I tried to clear the lump in my throat. "If Georgina is alive. I want her to be taken to the hospital, but please – don't hurt her, don't do what you do. She's still my wife."

"Do you honestly think you're in a position of bargaining, Charles?"

"No. But I'm begging you as your nephew… and as Michael's cousin. You remember what you did to Michael, don't you? And Cleo? What you made me keep quiet about?"

There was a long, excruciating pause and I worried that he had put the phone down on me, that my threat didn't work, and I would be left alone to face the consequences.

"Find Alma and bring her to me when you do."

"What if I can't?"

"Then make yourself disappear, once and for all!"

He hung up on me. I searched Alma's house, high and low, but she had disappeared. I rushed outside as fast as I could, but my leg was now in excruciating pain, and I had no idea where my cane was. I searched for anything I could find as a substitute – there was an umbrella stand by the door and I grabbed the largest one there which had a hook for a handle and I used that to steady myself.

Alma's car was engulfed with flames, illuminating everywhere in sight, including Georgina's body on the ground. I walked up to her slowly. Her head was almost fully facing down and tilted at an awkward angle, and her arms were bent and crooked, one by her side and one stretched out in front above her head. I had seen countless dead bodies in the war, many that I had killed myself, but this was my wife. I felt a wave of nausea ripple through my stomach and make its way up to my throat and I vomited right next to her body.

I was wiping my mouth with the end of my sleeve, my eyes stinging with tears, when I noticed a slight bit of movement in her hand. Her fingers extended and flexed. I blinked the tears away and looked more carefully. Her back rose and fell softly. She was breathing. I gasped. At that moment, white beams of light shone from the bottom of the driveway and a white Wolseley approached the house. I quickly retreated to the side wall, where no one could see me and prayed that it wasn't the police.

Two men driving the car got out the front seats. I knew at once that they weren't the police as soon as they opened the rear door of their car and hauled something long and seemingly heavy out of it. I was watching from a distance, but it looked like something similar in size and shape to themselves. One of them unzipped the bag. The other approached Alma's burning car with a crowbar and forced open the driver's seat. He then proceeded to join his partner, and lift out the contents of the bag. A body of a woman, with long untied hair. Her arms, dragging along the grass as the men carried her by her ankles and armpits towards the car. They flung her body into the seat and slammed the door shut.

One of the men's arms caught on fire and they speedily dampened it down. He turned his head in my direction. I felt my heart thump double time as they stalked towards me. This was it, I thought. I knew I shouldn't have trusted Alexander. Deep inside, I knew I was a dead man too. But instead of closing in on me, they stopped at Georgina's body, lifted her up and placed her in the back of their car. They drove off, like phantoms in the night, not leaving a single trace that they were ever here.

I staggered up to the burning car, holding my arm to my face as the stench of burning flesh began to fill the air. Why did they put another woman's body in the car? Who was it?

I dove into my car and rushed back home. Dawn had arrived and I had to get away before any news got out about the finding of a body. As quick as I could, I dragged my suitcase from the top of the wardrobe, threw it on the bed and chucked the most essential belongings I had inside. I opened my briefcase and made sure my passport and money were safe.

"Charles? Are you in?" said my mother shouting from the hallway.

"Up here!"

I heard her footsteps slowly make their way up.

"Off again?"

"Yes... Business trip," I replied absentmindedly. "What are you doing up so early?"

"Alexander called me."

I saw her face turn pale and I turned to stone.

"What did he say?"

"It's Georgina, Charles." She walked slowly towards me. I dared not say anything until she had finished. "She managed to leave the hospital and they found her shortly afterwards at Alma's cottage. Charles, I'm so sorry – she's, she's dead."

I could hardly breathe, let alone talk. I walked around the bed and placed my hands over her shoulders. I wanted to make sure that my next words were going to be adhered to.

"Mother, you have to listen carefully. If anyone asks you anything about last night, anything about me, you have to tell him that you've not seen me in days. Tell them that I've been in Luxemburg since the beginning of last week. Do you understand me?"

"What? What are you doing Charles?" Her face was full of worry, her eyes searching mine for more answers – answers that I couldn't give her.

"You have to trust me."

"But why do I have to lie?"

"To protect me. You want to protect your son, don't you, Mother?"

"Charles. What have you done? Please just tell me. Tell me and yes, I'll do whatever I can to help you." I went to the bathroom, collecting my toothbrush and toothpaste from the cabinet, ignoring her request. "Charles?!"

I sighed heavily.

"Alright look. Georgina's body… it's not what you think. I haven't done anything wrong, do you hear me? That's all you need to know. I'll explain this another time, when things settle. Just remember what I've told you to say. You've not seen me. I've been in Luxemburg."

"Well, where are you going now?"

"Getting the next flight over there."

CHAPTER

THIRTY-SEVEN

1953
Jane

Mary and I don't get off the tram at the stop for the Beaumont. Instead, we stay on for one more stop.

"Where are we going?" Mary asks me when we don't get off.

"We're getting on a train." She looks at me questioningly and I realise I'm being overly cryptic. "The stop after this one is Guiston Station. A supply train from there still runs to the back of the Beaumont. If we can get on that, we can get in from the back."

"How do you expect to just get on a supply train?"

"We'll tell them we work at the hospital and are there to run an inventory of the supplies."

"Do you think that'll work? How can you be sure there'll be a train?"

"There's a train every afternoon at around this time. I know it's a long shot but it's worth a try." I'm hardly convinced myself, but I need Mary with me. It would be impossible to retrieve the files *and* help Alma escape on my own, but I know from my tightened chest that I'm nervous, that I need Mary there for moral support as much as physical. I may not like her or know her well, and I know her even less than I thought I did after her revelation, but at least I can be sure that we now have one common goal, and that is that we want to get Alma out of there.

We arrive into Guiston Station and ask a kind conductor if the train to the Beaumont had already left this afternoon.

"You mean the supply train?" he says. "Who's asking?"

I show him the badge that I never handed from my visit today because I had run off after Mary instead.

"I'm a counsellor at the hospital and I'm with one of the attendants. The superintendent asks us to do an inventory of everything coming off the train as soon as it arrives. Usually, we're already at the hospital to do the checklist, but we've had to pop into Guiston today to assess a potential patient – the plan was to get the same train back. I hope we're not too late?" The words instinctively reel off my tongue and even I'm impressed with how persuasively I can improvise.

"You're in luck actually! There's been a fault on the line that has taken most of the day to fix which has delayed the train from setting off. It's docked at platform three." He points over across to the track on the other side of a footbridge. "Should be leaving before the hour."

"Thank you so much!"

We hurry to find the right platform where the train to the Beaumont is already waiting. To my relief, we manage to board it without anyone questioning us at all. This is too easy, I think to myself, but I don't say a word to Mary. I want her to feel safe and confident that our plan will work.

We arrived at the back of the hospital and open the door from our carriage as soon as the train grinds to a halt. A man who I assume was on the train catches sight of us and shouts something inaudible, but we are already halfway into the woodland, on the way up to the memorial garden. We cut straight across it to save time and see one large mound of freshly dug up soil next to a rectangular pit, just large enough for a coffin. I immediately assume that it is not just for another patient of the Beaumont with no family members to collect them, but it is one of Feyman's victims. I just hope that I'm not too late and that it's not Alma.

"Quickly," I say to Mary as we pass it. Once we reach the grounds of the hospital, we crouch down a little as we walk, making ourselves look small as much as we can although I have never felt as exposed as I do now. We pass the White Block and I peer in through its windows. The rooms are dark and deathly quiet, but I know that will be where Alma will be in for her brain surgery in a matter of hours. Finally, we get to the back door, and I try to open it but it's locked.

"What do we do now?" Mary asks.

"Come with me."

We work our way around the stone walls of the hospital and find the exact window that I'm looking for. The familiar patterning of Serene's drawn curtains against the glass, seen clearly from the outside. When we get there, I tap against the window, my knuckles repeatedly sound against one small pane in quick successions and I'm praying that she'll be in and awake enough to hear me.

A few seconds pass and there is a twitch in the fabric from being pulled at one end. And then I see her sleepy face appear in the light. It takes her a moment to realise that it's me knocking. Her eyes turn to Mary and back towards me.

"What are you doing here?" she calls from inside.

"Shhh." I hold a finger up to my lips and gesture for her to slide open the sash. She rolls her eyes but does it and then stares at me, waiting for an answer. "We need your help." Serene immediately starts shaking her head. "Just, a minute of your time. I know you can offer me that because we're friends, aren't we? Not every moment we had was false, I'm sure of it. And I know despite everything that's happening, you want to help Alma."

"What are you going to do? Help her escape? I've tried that one before and it didn't end well, did it?"

"It's going to be different this time. You have me." I glance over to Mary. "And you have Alma's Mother." Serene's eyes widen at Mary and Mary nods.

"Well do you have a plan? How are you going to get past the guards and attendants?"

"I can't – but you can."

"That'll cost me my job. And my home! You know this is where I live!"

"I think there's a way we can do this without Feyman finding out. But we can't talk here."

"Then where?"

"The church next to the memorial gardens. Meet you there in ten minutes."

We find ourselves a pew in the middle of the small, stone building with a simple cross at the altar.

"I've got to be quick. I don't want anyone knowing that I've gone out. It'll raise questions."

"It's going to be very quick, Serene. Don't worry."

"So, you want to steal Alma away from her cell?"

"Yes, but not until tonight. I need you to do one thing for me this afternoon please. Can you access Feyman's office?"

"I – I don't know. He keeps his own set of keys. Why do you need to be there?"

"There's a file for Alma – Patient A – that's disclosed. It's not the same as the one that's being passed to me during the day. It shows a record of the medication she's been receiving, including a lobotomy that's scheduled for tomorrow. I saw it accidentally once. I'm sure there's more than one of those. Not just for her. But for other patients too."

A look of realisation creeps over Serene's face.

"What? What is it?" I ask.

She shakes her head. "I – I've heard him speak about some files like that before, it was a long time ago now and I didn't think anything of it. He called them the grey files."

"Grey files? No – the one I found for Alma was red, it wasn't grey. We specifically need those ones. If we can get a hold of them, then we can send Feyman down."

"Send him down?! Are you mad?"

"I might be, but I will not just stand by and watch these poor helpless people being as good as tortured! Will you?!"

"No, of course I don't want to. But how are we supposed to do this?"

"I can only think of one way. We need you to get into his office. He could be there, say you need to talk to him about a patient that's been worrying you. You'll already have let both Mary and I in before then. Once you're in Feyman's office, Mary's going to create a distraction that'll lead Feyman out of the building."

"What kind of a distraction?"

"She's going to set the fire alarm off. Everyone will need to evacuate. Everyone will be trying to get out, including you and Feyman. But I need you to make sure that he doesn't lock his door so when you both leave the room, I can get in and access his files."

"How on God's Earth am I supposed to do that?"

"I don't know, knock the keys from his hands by accident or something?"

"That's a terrible plan."

Then I remember that I had managed to escape from his room once before, through the window.

"Say you're suddenly feeling faint and need some air. Get to the window and open it. Make sure it doesn't get locked. I'll access it from the outside when you both leave the room."

"Gosh, Jane, I don't know. This all sounds very risky and highly likely to fail."

"I just need a few files. He won't look at them until the morning and by that time, we'll have left with Alma and informed the police with the evidence."

"And how do you plan on taking Alma?"

"That should be the easy part. I'll come for the evening session as normal. Raymond will be there to open the door for me, I know he'll help because he's Dr Blythe's friend. Please Serene. This is Alma's life we're talking about."

"And what will you do with her once you have her?"

"I'm taking her to another hospital. Back under Dr Blythe's care."

Serene thinks long and hard. Mary has stayed so quiet throughout the entire conversation that I nearly forget that she's there, but I know that she's listening acutely. She wants to save her daughter as much as I do.

"Alright," Serene finally says. "Just give me an hour to take care of some things. I'll meet you at the back door."

I nod. "One hour."

Mary and I wait by the back door and an hour and ten minutes have passed since we spoke to Serene. Our eyes continuously search the site around us, scouting for anyone that might spot us and see that we look out of place. Out of the sunlight, the cool temperature of the alcove of the door makes me quiver.

"She's not coming, is she?" Mary asks. "She's telling someone we're here, I can feel it."

"Shh. You don't know that yet, Mary. Could just be something silly holding her up. Another patient or something."

Just then I hear the sound of metal against wood. It's the bolt of the door sliding on the other side. The handle turns and the door opens. My heart pounds and images of Feyman's face greeting us frightens me, but it is Serene that appears and I'm relieved to know that phase one of our plan is about to begin.

"Took longer than I thought," Serene says, stepping aside to let us in. "Minerva was on duty and asked what I was doing up so I had to come up with some excuses and then I had to wait for her to leave."

"Thank you."

"Right. I'll go to Alexander's office now. Mary, you know where to sound the alarm. Give me about twenty minutes to get settled in his office first. Jane–"

"I'll be waiting outside his window."

Serene nods. "Let's go then."

I turn to Mary and place a hand on her arm. "You alright?"

"Yes."

I practically crawl my way around to the next block where Sir Feyman's office is and hide behind a hedge facing it. I watch through the gaps of the bushy foliage and wait for the signal. Just like clockwork, I hear the sound of his sash window slide open and a glimpse of Serene's head pop out a little. Her voice, sound frail as she pretends to feel unwell. She tucks her head back in and slides the window shut, and I pray that he doesn't go to lock it. Only a second later, the fire alarm sounds.

I count to five, giving them enough time to leave the room and run towards the windows before swathes of patients and attendants start to flood the grounds. I tuck my fingers under ledge of the wooden sash and push it upwards. It slides up, for an inch and then it jams. No! I try pushing it and pushing it, feeling sweat form all over my skin. No! Not now! Come on! I thread my hands under the narrow opening and curl my hands around the windowpanes, pulling it up with all my strength. The jam relents and the sash slides up with a jolt. I heave a huge sigh of relief and climb through.

I open every filing cabinet there is and find nothing. They must be here somewhere! I think, searching every corner and crevice of the room. Where would I hide them if it was me? I scan the displays of medals he's won on the walls, the jars which I now see labelled as preserved brain tissue and have an impulsive need to pick each one up and smash them against the floor. The corridor outside the office begins to fill with the sound of attendants shouting out orders to the patients and there is a shuffling of hundreds of feet passing by the door. I see the shadows of them across the floor in the slit just below the door. Hurry. I need to hurry.

I turn a full circle around the room and spot his drinks cabinet exhibiting an array of spirits and tins of exotic teas. It looks extravagantly large and much deeper than anyone would need, especially within an office of a hospital. Something within in me wills me to walk over to it.

I run my hands around its varnished top and down the sides of the doors. I pull the delicate handles of it out and see more bottles of spirits. My heart sinks and I feel dejected, wishing so much that I had got it right, that everything I was looking for was hidden in here. I start putting the doors closed again when I see a glimpse of something, dull red in colour, behind a bottle of unopened whisky. I lift the bottle out and can now see more clearly, a stack of red folders, tucked in right at the back of the cabinet. As stealthily as I can, I take the rest of the bottles out as well as the files and I also see the tapes of my nightly recordings. I shuffle through the files, acknowledging each 'undisclosed' label on every front cover. Sure enough, every patient I listed that were here. All their names, amongst others, over a dozen of them, maybe even two dozen in total, have been changed to the name Grey.

Patient: Howard Grey, real name: Mr Howard Ingham
Patient: Alma Grey, real name: Mrs Alma Ingham
Patient: Charlotte Grey, real name: Miss Charlotte Feyman
Patient: Georgina Grey, real name: Mrs Georgina Bennett
Patient: Michael Grey, real name: Mr Michael Feyman

My heart races as I flick through their most personal history.

Charlotte, Alexander Feyman's daughter, admitted in 1933 at the age of eleven.

Diagnosis: Schizophrenia. Symptoms: Sees visions. Hears sounds and voices, mainly that of Michael Feyman. Calls herself Cleopatra. Lobotomies undertaken: Two. The last page, showing her death certificate and the date of it being last Tuesday, wrenches my heart out of my chest. *Cause of death: Post lobotomy complications.* No!

Michael Feyman, Alexander's son, admitted in 1930 at the age of sixteen.

Diagnosis: Sexual deviation. Treatment: Chemical castration and aversion therapy.

And then, another death certificate dated in the year 1932. Cause of death: *Post lobotomy complications.*

The papers start to tremble in my hands as the truth sinks in. Feyman has not only been incarcerating members of his family, he's been using them for heinous experiments in the most grotesque form, inflicting his obsession to cure homosexuality on his own son. And in his last sickening move, killed him. Michael was not just a figment of Cleo's imagination – he was real and her brother. Feyman used her illness against her to make her believe that she murdered him!

I force myself to move on, knowing the clock ticks. Any second now without warning, Feyman would start unlocking that door. I look at the next file. It's Alma's. I've seen it before and know the damning evidence that exists inside of it, but I quickly flick through to make sure that the contents are still there. They are, and I look at the next.

Howard Ingham, admitted in 1950 for battle fatigue. Treatment includes ECT and a long list of trial medication. Location: Male Block, Blue Ward.

Georgina Bennett, Alexander Feyman's niece-in-law, admitted in 1952. Diagnosed with a manic-depressive insanity. Escaped two months later after admission, re-admitted again on the same night post escape and relocated to Secure Block B. Treatment also includes ECT and trial medication.

"Re-admitted?" I say softly to myself. She's still here? She's alive?!

I suddenly notice that the corridor outside has gone deathly quiet. Everyone must be outside, including Feyman himself. Soon he will realise that it has all been a false alarm and he will be making his way back here. My hands shake as I try quickly to hold all the files in my arms and then realise that I can't hold all of them. What if he decides to look at them this afternoon? If I just take a couple, then he's less likely to notice. My fingers feel clumsy as I place the tapes and files back, save Alma's, Georgina's and Cleo's. I try and remember where the bottles of spirits were placed before I took them out and close the cabinet doors.

I grip onto the files hard, like my life depends on it and escape back outside, making sure that the window is firmly shut behind me, and I run. Mary is already back at the church waiting for me. Our plan seems to have worked so far. I just need to get these to Richard now before I come back tonight to get Alma.

"Do you think that's enough?" Mary asks. "Alexander's a very powerful man, he knows people in high places. We could all get into serious trouble for this."

"I know. I'm not sure if this will get him. But we have to try."

CHAPTER

THIRTY-EIGHT

1952
Alma

Charles wore a crazed look on his face when he sent my car bursting into flames. I saw him standing, his feet grounded in one spot, watching the fire roar with the blaze reflecting in his wild eyes. It looked like he had frozen in place. I took that as a chance.

I ran indoors towards the telephone mounted against the wall by the kitchen, picked up the receiver and dialled 999. My fingers were cumbersome and too impatient to wait for the dial to spin back around before turning it again. Two seconds passed as I clung on. Pick up! Pick up! I recited in my head, but it felt like one long minute as I kept my eyes on Charles' dark figure still outside. Finally, a man's voice answered.

"Good evening, Crowbeck Police Station?"

I hardly had time to say my name or what was wrong before I saw Charles turn around. He saw me, our eyes connected through the door, he caught the fear in me, and he came for me.

"Help! Chalk house!" I screamed through the receiver and immediately placed it back on the hook but I didn't manage to do it properly and the receiver dropped. Not knowing if my cry would have any effect on the person at the police station, I ran to the side door. Thank God the key was still in the lock. I rotated it and swung the door outwards. Once I was back in the open and felt able to turn my head around to check where Charles was, I saw through the kitchen window that he had lifted the telephone receiver up and placed it against his ear. Was he speaking? Who to? Was he telling the police that I had rung that it was all a mistake? I was back on the front lawn and Georgina was lying lifelessly on the grass. I lunged towards her.

"Georgina!" I whispered. "Georgina! Are you still alive? Please! Please! Get up! We have to go!" Her eyes were shut tightly, like she was in a deep but painful sleep. I tried to turn her body around, to move her in any way that I could, but it was no use. I held her bloodied head against my legs, stroked her face and cried and cried, rocking back and forth as I did so. "Please!" I begged her through my sobs. "Please!"

I glanced back towards the house and saw Charles hobbling up the stairs. What was he doing? Did he think I was hiding up there?

"I'm so sorry Georgina, I have to run. I'm going to get you help. Stay alive for me Gina, stay alive. I'm coming back!" An explosion came from the car, sending a cloud of ash into the air and the span of the flames higher and wider. I shielded her body from the bang, feeling its heat on my back, still sodden with gas. Blinded by tears, my heart heavy with pain, I tore myself away from her and ran. I ran as fast as my feet could carry me through the rough, pitted lane, down towards the railway track, until there was a rumbling in the distance. It was the sound of a car hurtling down towards me from the house, travelling much quicker than I could run.

Was it Charles searching for me? I dared not wait to find out. I clambered over the hawthorn hedge lining a wheat field, lacerating my body against its sharp thorns as if they were barbed wire and sank myself into the field, letting the planting shield me from view as he sped passed me.

I lay there until I was sure he wasn't going to return and rose back up. I didn't want to climb over the hedge again so stumbled along the side of it through the tall blades of foliage until I reached a wooden gate. The petrol in my saturated dress seeped into my cuts. It stung and burned so much that I started to scream. A scream that I released, not only from the pain, but as a deliverance of anguish and self-loathing. I had tried to save Georgina, but from the first moment she escaped that asylum, all I did was sentence her to death.

As I tore the dress from my body, desperate to get it off, my cries filled the night, I didn't care who heard me anymore. My love, Georgina. My poor Gina! If she wasn't dead when I left her, I was sure that she would be dead by now.

* * *

1st January 1953

There was no knowing how much time had passed but eventually, the black sky lightened into a murky indigo, and when the sun started to inch its way up above the horizon, the indigo dissolved into a dazzling sapphire blue, shimmering with golden iridescent clouds. A new day but without a glimmer of hope. Instead, it meant the end. It was Georgina's soul ascending up into the heavens, sending me her final message of beauty and love.

My head and skin throbbed with pain and my throat felt dry and coarse, all I could taste was the foul mix of gas, iron and fertilised earth in my mouth. I longed for water but at least there was light. I took a piece of my dress and pressed my bleeding finger against it. Crudely, I inscribed 'Gina' across it and clutched it tightly in my fist. If anyone found me and I had fallen unconscious, at least they would have this.

Amongst the sweet singing of the morning birds, I heard another engine make its way up the track. Had help finally come? The car pulled up alongside me. Two men dressed in a familiar black uniform stepped out the car. By this time, I was too numb to move.

"Mam! Are you alright?" one of them said.

"Good God, get her covered up!" said the other.

The first one draped his thick woollen coat around me and stared into my eyes.

"What's your name?... Mam? Can you hear me?"

Yes, I could hear him. Alma! My name is Alma! a voice inside my head shouted, but I was unable to respond as I stared right back at him.

They tucked me into their car and drove me to a grand old building that I thought I could recognise. I was sure I had been here before, but I couldn't remember why. Was I here to visit someone? Did I know someone who lived here? Someone I loved?

A man in a long white jacket came up to the car with an empty wheelchair and they sat me on it to wheel me inside. A lady looking like a nurse walked up to me. She was slight but had a stern face.

"Who do we have here?" she asked the man in the white jacket, her voice lacking in any warmth. She spoke as though I was there to answer myself. But then, I did not even remember who I was.

"Don't know. She won't speak."

"Right well come along, let's get you cleaned up!"

She ran a bath for me and helped me in. My mind and my body seemed detached from one another. My movements were slow and stiff, but I was able to shift my legs and arms with her guiding them. I felt so confused, not knowing what had happened or how long I had been like this.

Her hands were rough as she dipped a sponge into the tepid water and wiped it across me. The water turned muddy and red with each squeeze of the soiled sponge. She pulled me up and dried me briskly, the stiff towel, feeling like a scour against my cuts and burns. If I could have flinched, I would have but I was beginning to lose all sensation. Then she pulled a large gown over my head.

"There, good as new!" she said, seemingly proud of her work, and wheeled me down several corridors until we reached one particular door that looked much like the rest.

She knocked loudly and announced herself before walking in.

"Minerva here! There's a new patient!"

A tall man, smartly dressed with a well sculpted moustache peered at me from behind his desk.

"Who is she?"

"No one knows, Sir Feyman, she's not speaking to anyone. We think she may be mute. They found her with this." She passed the handwritten rag over to him. He shook the cloth open to uncover the name and I saw the end of his eyebrow raise with the slightest hitch.

"I see…" he said and folded the cloth back up, tucking it by the spine of a book on his desk. He set his eyes onto me. They were cold and unnerving. "Thank you, Minerva. Please place the patient in one of the spare cells in the secure block for now. I'll give her a thorough examination in the afternoon."

"Yes, sir," the nurse said. She spun me around and headed for the door.

She led me back through the corridors although I could not tell if they were the same ones as before. At first the areas were busy with activity, full of other patients roaming around freely and aimlessly. The further we got into the building, the quieter it got until there was hardly anyone left in sight, but she kept pushing me in the chair until she reached towards the end of a long hallway and there was a man standing outside a large metal door, dressed in the same uniform as the ones who collected me from the track.

"Is there a cell free?"

"Certainly is, nurse."

"Good. She's all yours. She can walk from here, but you'll have to guide her."

He took out a large set of keys and unlocked the door. Was I in prison? But what crime had I committed? The man tucked his hand under my armpit, hoisted me up onto my feet and took me down to the cell at the end. He sat me on the bed with a thin mattress and slammed the door closed. The lock turned and that was the last time I saw anyone until it grew dark.

CHAPTER

THIRTY-NINE

1953
Jane
Night

I knock at the front entrance of the hospital tonight, something feels different in the air. There is a fog hanging low around the building and I am yet to find out whether it will help or hinder my secret. It takes longer than usual for the door to be opened, and when it does, it's not Raymond's familiar face I see. It's someone else, another attendant that I've never met before.

"Jane Galloway?"

"Yes."

"Come in."

I step into the foyer. "Where's Raymond?"

"Called in sick. Here to visit the patient in Unit 1? Follow me."

He leads me through to the secure block towards Alma's cell. He fumbles through his set of keys as though he's not familiar with them and smiles at me when he thinks he's found the right one. He unlocks Alma's door, the door creaks open and I see her lying on her bed with her back facing towards me.

"Thank you, you'll open the door again once I tap on it?"

He nods and closes it shut without the stealth of Raymond. It slams and I jump, turning around, ready to throw an angry glare at him, but he's gone already.

I set up my tape recorder and flashlight as normal and wait for Alma to stir. She's strangely still tonight as I watch her through the gloomy light. I realise too that the curvature of her body doesn't seem like hers. I've become accustomed to the way her shoulder line, side and hip frame the line of her blanket in the evening, it's like a delicate silhouette of a hill sloping down to a valley and up again through to the smoothness of her thighs. Tonight, it is as if someone else's body has replaced her. The thought of it being someone else in her bed makes me turn cold.

"Alma?" I whisper through the dark. "Is that you?"

No answer comes from her bed and dread fills my mind. I rise slowly from the floor and force myself to take a closer look. The body on the bed appears so still, I'm afraid it is a dead one that's lying there.

"Alma?"

Dark strands of hair cover her face. The top of her blanket is up to her cheeks. I gently touch the top of it, holding just the slightest bit of the blanket's edge in between my thumb and index finger. Slowly, I peel the cloth away from her body, revealing a shoulder. Her gown shifts, moving along with the blanket and yet, her body still does not move.

By now, I'm sure it's not Alma. This person is heavier set with thicker hair. I reach out towards her shoulder and feel it cold to the touch. It must be a body and I stifle a scream with my other hand covering my mouth. With slightly more force, I pull her shoulder back and her entire body rolls backwards. I jump back and scream. I leap at the door, hitting it.

"Let me out!" I cry. "Let me out!"

I pick up my flashlight and try and shine it into the corridor through the bars of the door. My heart is beating hard. I turn back to the body. The body's glassy eyes glare straight at me, her lips gaping wide, and her arms and hands are set at strange, peculiar angles. I try and steady my breath as I approach her slowly and light up her body with my shaking hand. Then it dawns on me – she's not real. The body is in fact a mannequin.

"What is this?!" I scream through the bars. No one is there to answer my calls apart from the yells from other patients.

"Shut it!"

"Oi! I'm tryin' ta sleep 'ere!"

"Let me out!" I cry again. "Where's Alma! What have you done with her?!"

I hear a clank of the door at the end of the secure block. Someone's coming. Their steps are slow. One by one, the sound of them nears. A man's face appears in the window of the door. His eyes are stern and full of warning. I recognise him as Sir Feyman.

"Let me out."

"I'm afraid I can't do that, Mrs Galloway. Some members of staff have reported to me that you've been acting rather unstably over the past couple of days. I recommend that you get some rest

here tonight, ready for your full examination in the morning."
He starts to walk back down the corridor.

"So you're going to hold me captive like everyone else you should have loved and cared for? Where's Alma!?"

He turns back around.

"Patient A is no longer your concern," he says and starts walking again.

"My friend is in the police – he comes to pick me up every night. He'll know I'm not there – he'll be waiting for me! Let me out or he'll be asking questions. I know everything you're trying to hide! Who's the woman you burned to death? Where is Georgina?!"

"I wouldn't try and threaten me, Mrs Galloway. It'll only be you who'll end up suffering. You, and… your son."

"You stay away from Jasper! Alexander! You stay away from him!"

I grip on to the bars and pull them with every ounce of strength I have but it's not use. The door doesn't budge, and I press my face hard against its iron poles, with tears running down my cheeks.

"Let me go! Let me go!" I scream, over and over again.

It feels like hours when the door opens once more, and I try and see who it could be. The attendant that opened the door to me comes to the window.

"Please, let me out of here. I've done nothing wrong. I'm not crazy. I have a son, a little boy waiting for me at home. He needs me. You have to believe me."

"Alright miss, calm down now. It'll be alright. Now I'll let you out, but you have to promise me that you'll be quiet. No sharp movements or we'll have to restrain you."

I nod, obediently, willing to do whatever it takes to get home safely. I back away from the door to allow him to open it a touch, only just wide enough to let me squeeze through. As I pass the frame of the door, he suddenly uses all of his weight to pin me to it, winding the air from my lungs. I struggle to regain my breath. A sharp pain pierces through my neck. I try and scream, but no sound comes out. The dim orange lights of the corridor begin to double and cross over. A lead like heaviness seeps its way into my mind, the room becomes clouded over and my legs give way. I know I'm falling but can no longer feel anything.

CHAPTER

FORTY

1952
Alma

I sat in the corner of my cell. My ankles were chained to the end of the bed. I could sense that the sun was on its way down when the door opened again.

The same man I saw in his office visited with a woman in a plain dress. Her dark hair was tied up into a bun and her eyes matched in colour, but there was a warmth there that I hadn't seen in anyone else so far.

She turned to look at the man who nodded at her and she walked towards me with hesitating steps. She knelt beside me and placed a hand over mine.

"Alma, its Ma," she said.

Ma? Who is Ma? I thought. I could shift my eyes a little to focus on her. There was a familiarity about her, but I couldn't place where from. I wanted to speak but seemed to have no control over anything anymore, like my lips were glued shut and

I was wading through thick cloying tar. Only one word could come to me. It rang like a gong inside my head.

Georgina! Georgina! Georgina! I stared at the woman.

"What is it, Alma? What are you trying to say?" Her eyes moved to my lips – were they moving? I couldn't feel them.

Then, a small sound. I think it came from me?

"What was that?" the woman said.

"Geor…" A sound came out, barely as a whisper. The suited man by the door strode towards me. "Geor…" I breathed again.

"She remembers," the man said. His tone was hard and wary. The woman twisted her head towards him and then quickly back to look at me. There was a panic in her eyes.

"Darling, Georgina doesn't exist. She never did." I stared at her, her words confusing me, swirling around and mixing with the sludge in my brain.

Georgina! No, no! She was real! She IS real! Who was this woman? Why was she saying this?! I howled and shrieked but neither the man, nor the woman said anything back. My own voice drummed loudly, my legs kicked and my arms flailed, but all of it was only in my thoughts. Everyone on the outside saw nothing.

"You won't hurt her, will you?" the woman asks him.

"Hurt her? Of course not, my dear! We only strive to mend people's minds at the Beaumont! The way I see it is – and you are free to disagree – there are only two directions you can take. One is to do nothing, and she will continue through life, suffering and mute. Or two, she can be under my care, and I will monitor her daily, assessing her needs and treating them accordingly with medical expertise. Like I said, the choice is yours."

The woman frowned with seriousness. "Can I visit her regularly?"

"Yes, my dear. Visiting hours are between one and two o'clock. Between those hours, they are being cared for by our trusted attendants and nurses. But I would advise that you don't visit for two months that she can get settled with our routine."

There was a pause whilst the woman appeared to consider my fate as if she had any part to play in it.

"Is there a position for attendant work? I'd like to help and care for her myself." I started to notice how my name was being omitted from the conversation now and merely replaced by 'her' and 'she'.

"Well…" the man began. "If you were to take on that role, to care for just her, then you would have to understand it would be purely voluntary and that you are contracted to keep all of the patient's medical information confidential?"

"Yes, I can do that, as long as I can be by her side the whole time. Please, just let me help her?"

He bent his head close to mine and waved his hand across my eyes. He took out a pocket flashlight and peeled my eyelids wide open, one after the other, shining the flashlight into my eyes and then placed it back into his pocket. He straightened his back and addressed only the woman.

"You are to wear an attendant's uniform and act like one of them at all times. You are to clock in at seven o'clock in the morning and leave at six o'clock in the evening. No earlier and no later. You are responsible for her hygiene and her meals, no one else's. We will dispense her medication and ensure that she takes it."

The woman nods profusely. He finally looks at me again.

"My name is Sir Alexander Feyman. You are at the Beaumont Hospital. Because you are incapable of speaking, we are unable to ascertain your name properly. From now on, you will be known as Patient A." He turns to the woman. "As you know she is linked to the most tragic accident up in Chalk House. No one knows what exactly happened, but the police will come round for statements during the next few days. You are to say nothing, and you are not to address this patient as your own child or display any type of affection that would lead one to assume that you have any form of relationship with her." The woman nods submissively and turns to me with tears falling down her cheeks. "Good. Let's get you a uniform."

No! No! I screamed in my mind. Don't leave me here! Help me find Georgina! She needs my help! Still, no words came out of my mouth. Not even tears could form from my eyes.

"I'll be with you for your next meal," she says and the door slammed shut again.

The screams inside my head fell silent and I heard another woman calling in the distance.

"Pa!" she shouted "Pa!" Who was she calling? It sounded like she was locked in another cell, but unlike me, she was loud and frantic. The night had fully taken over now and an amber glow filtered in through the bars of my door. I finally felt one tear roll down my cheek. Too late for that, I thought. No one will ever see you cry anymore.

CHAPTER

FORTY-ONE

1953
Jane

Muffled sounds of doors clanking wakes me from a deep sleep. Consciousness reaches me before I can open my eyes. I feel the cold base of the mattress beneath my back. Male voices throw harsh instructions in the distance and there is a sound of trolleys being wheeled nearby. My eyes seem to be clamped shut but there is a haze of light beyond the sheath of my eyelids. I want to put my hands up to rub them, but they feel restrained. Something fixes them to my side. I try moving my legs. They too, are tied. Panic rises within me and I force my eyes open to see that I'm alone in a cell. Harsh florescent lighting from the tube fixed to the ceiling blinds me until my eyes adjust to my surroundings. I see that they are leather belts tying all my limbs to the bars of the bed.

"Help! Help me!" My cries come out dry and choked. "Let me out of here! Feyman, you bastard! Let me out!" No one responds and I'm shouting and screaming until my voice becomes sore, until my throat relents and I'm feeling a deep, hard thirst for water. No one comes, not even passes by the small, barred window in the door. I start to wonder how long I've been trapped here. Jasper. My poor boy. I hope he's safe. I hope Kirsty or Richard is there for him. I hope he's not dying of worry for me like I am for him.

All of a sudden, the light above me and outside the cell goes dead and I'm plunged into nothing but darkness and the faint orange glow that I'm now all too familiar with. Except this time, I'm the patient, chained to the bed. Tears run from my eyes again, I feel their wet tracks trickle into my ears and dampening the hair around my temples.

Which cell and in which block have I been put in? Alma. What have they done with her? Have they cut her head open, sliced a part of her brain off, changed her memories, changed the way she feels, thinks, loves? Is she still alive? Is she buried with the other nameless bodies in the earth with no headstone to mark her existence on this Earth? My throat still feels raw from screaming but I try to speak, projecting my voice out through the little window as much as I can.

"Who else is here with me? What are your names?" My voice comes out weak and croaky. "Alma? Are you there? It's Jane. Alma, tell me you can hear me."

Just then, through the darkness, cutting through the silence, a voice. A woman's voice.

"Alma? You know Alma?"

My eyes widen and my heart picks up pace.

"Yes! Yes! I know Alma. Who are you?"

She waits a moment before she responds.

"Georgina."

Her voice carries gently through the wall next to my bed and I let out a slow exhale.

"You really are alive," I say.

"Yes. And Alma is too?"

"I – I don't know. I'm worried about her. I don't know how long I've been out. Where are we, Georgina, which block are we in?"

"Does it matter? They'll never let me go. I doubt they'll let you go either."

"They have to. I have people out there waiting for me. A son."

"I thought I had people too. They all lie in the end."

"Georgina, listen to me. We have to get out of here. We have to find Alma and save her and leave this place. Can you walk?" I'm met with silence. "Georgina? Can you hear me?"

Soft laughter comes from her cell.

"How are we going to do that?"

"Surely a guard or attendant must come during the day or night at some point? They must have come to feed you? To help you with your toileting?"

"Can you not smell the stench of your own bowels?"

I look down to my waist and for the first time, I see the stains pooled around my backside.

"Can you walk or are you chained to your bed too?"

"I can shuffle. My ankles and wrists are chained together. You see that slot at the bottom of the door? Like a post box? That's where they deliver food."

What good is that if I'm not allowed to get out of bed or even sit up? I think to myself.

"What have they been doing to you all of this time?"

"Nothing at first. They just left me. If I wasn't crazy to begin with, I'm crazy now. It's what they wanted, I suppose, so they can justify locking me in here. Have you met Alexander yet? He likes his experiments. Wonder what pills they're giving me in the morning. Sometimes they're quite good actually, takes the pain away… Takes everything away."

"Georgina, I'm going to get us out of here."

She begins to laugh again. A sort of deranged and unhinged kind of laughter.

"Tell me more about Alma."

"She's been in this hospital, in a secure block like this one. I've been treating her day and night for months. She was catatonic when she arrived. Yesterday – was it yesterday? When I last saw her, she began to speak again. Her mother's name. And yours. She had nightmares every night, reliving the last night she was with you. She talks in her dreams, not like during the day."

"Did she say things about me? About us?"

"Yes. She still cares for you very much." Georgina doesn't say anything back, but I sense that the validation has affected her somehow. "I was going to see her for one more night but I was too late... Alexander doesn't want her to speak, does he? Surely it can't be just because of your affair that this has happened?"

"Alexander is nothing but an evil conman. He tricks people into thinking the Beaumont is a sanctuary for unhealthy minds and tells them he can heal them. My mother-in-law seemed to idolise him and told me he could help the way I was. The lucky ones just get sedated and are allowed to be with other patients –

the ones that probably do need help. And then there are people like me – I loved someone I wasn't supposed to love."

"Everyone thought you were dead. They saw your burnt body in the wreckage of Alma's car! They must have used someone else, put another person in there! What if they do the same to me? What if everyone just thinks I'm dead!?"

Her voice goes quiet. "I'm sorry, Jane. There's no way out."

"No. No, I won't accept that. I have to get back to my son. My son!! My son!! God, please no!!"

"You're better off getting some sleep and hope that they'll give you a shot in the morning," she says and goes quiet after that.

I try to wrench my hands free from the bounds of the leather belts, but they are wound around my wrists too tightly. I bend my fingers around them as far as I can to try and unbuckle them, over and over again until my hand tires and then I try and do it with the other hand. The straps chafe against my skin until it bleeds and burns but I do not stop until at some point, the lights flicker back on, and I have to clamp my eyes shut because they're too bright.

"Help! Help!" My voice rings out clearly this time. "Guards! Attendants! Nurses! Is there anyone there?! I need your help! It's Jane Galloway! I'm a counsellor here! Dr Blythe called me to work here! You have to let me free!"

The door into our block finally opens and I see somebody walk past my cell.

"Please, talk to me! Who are you?"

The person doubles back and looks through the bars into my cell. It's another attendant I do not know.

"I'll get someone to clean you up," he says and leaves again.

Someone to clean me up. Good. Someone's coming. I'll get them to untie me. Take me to the lavatory. I'll wait for the right moment. And then I'll make an escape.

Time passes and no one comes. I feel as though I've soiled myself again, but it comes with excruciating pain. I long to just relieve myself from the same position on the bed.

"Georgina?... Georgina?" I say louder. She doesn't respond. I wonder if she's fallen asleep or if the last attendant gave her the pills she was waiting for.

The door to the block opens again and I force my eyes open to watch for anyone who passes by. A head appears through the bars of the door. I can tell from the hat that it's a nurse. Her keys clang against each other as she pokes one through the keyhole of my door, opens it and walks in. She glances at me, her eyebrows furrow and she ties a hanky around her face, brings it up so that it closes around her nose.

"What's your name?" I ask her. She doesn't reply but brings in a trolley with a syringe and a vial next to it. "What are you going to inject me with? Is it a sedative? Tell me, I have the right to know." She continues to ignore me and starts filling up the syringe with the clear liquid from the vial after giving it a shake.

"No, wait! Please! At least tell me if my child is safe! I have a son! He's waiting for me outside. Please! There must be good in you, you can't possibly want to do this to another human! I'm just a woman, like you! I've done nothing to deserve this. I'm not crazy!"

She places the empty vial back on the trolley and walks towards me. I start to panic and writhe on the bed, unable to break free from the distance closing in between us. Her needle, long and sharp is upright. She places her cold hand over my forehead, forcing it still. The pressure of her palm, burning into my skull.

"Where's Alexander Feyman? Tell him to see me now!" The point of the needle pierces through my neck. I twitch from the sharp pain and she presses her hand harder to still me. She places the syringe onto the trolley and pushes it out the door. "Wait!" I cry. Oh, Jasper. I'm so sorry. I should have known. I should have stayed out of this mess. I tried to protect my patient, but I should have been protecting you. Jay… My thoughts become muddied, the drugs work quickly and it feels like I'm screaming through sludge before I fall into a deep, troubled sleep.

I wake again. Not knowing how long I've been out for. From the darkness of the room and the dull orange glow, I know it's night again. I rattle my hands and feet which are still tied to the bed, but my hospital gown is no longer damp. They must have changed me whilst I was out.

I try and fumble away at the leather straps around my wrists. I feel dextrously around them, stretching my fingers as far as they will go. And gradually, so gradually, I manage to thread the end of the strap out through the loop. I take a deep breath in and out and hook my little finger under the strap, attempting to lift it away from its metal hook. I fail the first time. And the second. But on the third go… my hand is free! I move quickly to untie the buckle on my other hand. And then sit up, to untie my feet.

I circle my hands and feet and give them a shake to loosen their joints, and I feebly sit up, rise from the bed, and walk softly to the door. It's locked, of course. I try and feel the edges of the door jamb, running along its length with my fingertips to see if there are any weaknesses in the opening. I try and stick my bony arm out through the window bars, but they are too narrow. There is a sound – someone's walking into the corridor. I grab a leather strap from the bed and hide at the side of the door. When someone comes, looks through the window to see I'm not on the bed, they'll come in and I'll pull the strap around their neck, only just tight enough for them to worry about their own life, and to let me go.

The door opens. But instead of me following through with the strap in my hands, I feel my shoulders shake. It's not me who is shaking them. I'm no longer in control of my body anymore and I feel the bonds around my wrists, still tying me to the bed. I'm still lying down on it. I was never free.

"Jane! Jane!" calls a whisper in my ear. "Jane, wake up!"

I prise open my eyes, their lids, heavy from sedation.

"Jane!" the voice says again. I turn my head towards it. I peel my eyes open. Her silhouette starts to form definition and I recognise her face.

A nurse. Serene? Was she here to finish me off? I would tremor and thrash around to break free if I could, but my entire body feels like a lead weight.

"We're leaving," she says. "I'm going to untie you and help you up. You need all the strength you have left – I can't carry you." She quickly loosens the belts around my wrists and ankles and pushes my back up. "Here." She wraps my arm around the back of her neck and lifts me onto my feet. I crumble under my own weight and my ankles give in. "Come on, you can do this. We must be quick."

CHAPTER
FORTY-TWO

1953
Alma

Nurse Tolsy medicated me at the same time every day; at half past seven in the morning and at half past one in the afternoon. Nurse Serene would dispense the last medication at night. It was only at night that things came alive. In my dreams, I felt my mind begin to grind and whir, like the cogs of an old, un-oiled machine. The night would bring me back to life, only it wasn't the life I wanted to be in. It would be the reminder of the last time I ever saw Georgina and the picture of her lying on the ground with hair matted to her face from her own blood.

In the middle of these nightmares, the memory of her and I would float in. Happy memories. I missed her deeply and cherished the vision of her which became richer and more vivid with each night that passed. In my dreams, she too was still alive but by the morning, it all vanished and I could remember nothing.

Then a new doctor became in charge after Sir Feyman left for days on end. Someone needing help from a lady who introduced herself to me as Jane Galloway. From the moment I met her, I felt a change in myself. She bought something different to my life in this prison I've been caged in, a feeling of safety and reassurance. But it had been too long since I had spoken, a cage had built itself around my mind too, I did not know how to begin.

Jane always spoke to me kindly. Most of the time I would not be able to fully understand what she was saying but I knew that she was treating me like I was no different to her. Even though I could not respond and my mind was thick with fog, with each accumulative hour she spent with me, the rock that had been lying heavily on my lungs started to loosen. And with every day I spent with her, small parts of that heaviness would chip away. And then when I dreamed of Georgina at night, it was her voice that I remembered. So clear and powerful, telling me that I was going to be alright.

The day Jane took me to a garden where there was nothing but grass and a mound of soil in the distance. It was the garden of the dead. She grabbed my hands, and her lips mouthed her words so wide I was sure she must have been shouting. At that point, something happened to me. She carried on and the words she spoke suddenly rang out of her and sound came gushing back into my ears. She was pleading with me to talk. Her hands and her face were shaking. Light, colour and clarity burst into my eyes. For the first time I could see. It was an awakening.

I couldn't remember anything about myself, but I knew I did not want to become one of the bodies lying in the ground and I didn't know how I was going to get out. I was trapped, a prisoner inside my own body, isolating my mind from others. That night, when Jane came to visit, because I knew she would, I felt her there. I could speak to her. I needed her to understand what happened to me. I wanted her to see what I was seeing. But in the morning when the lights came on, Nurse Tolsy came with her trolley of pills, those feelings and memories would dissolve into a cloud of confusion again.

The woman I came to know as Mary tried to feed me breakfast one morning. Like most days, I couldn't swallow much. Jane had asked Mary to bring her some tea. She came back with a tray holding a teapot, milk and a cup and placed it on the table in front of me. In the corner of my eye, I saw her pouring the tea into the cup when somehow, her hand slipped, and hot tea poured all over it.

The sight of Mary flinching, pulling her reddened hand back in shock jolted a memory. Fire flashed before me. The sensation of heat spread through me, crawling over my skin from my fingertips to every part of my body. I felt an instant need to itch and scratch it, to scrape my skin off so that it didn't belong on me anymore. Mary's hand was beginning to blister, and I felt the same pain she felt. I wanted to save her. Like a bolt of lightning, jolting me, I noticed the colour of her eyes, her hair, her skin. The fine lines around her eyes and the shade of blueish grey around them. I knew her.

"Ma," I said. I recognised my own lips moving this time when they hadn't moved in months when I had tried to speak before.

My voice sounded strange, but it could definitely be heard. "Ma," I said again.

She stepped back, looking at me with those old, wide eyes like she had just seen me for the first time. My Ma, my dear Ma, who has been looking after me all this time, feeding me, changing my soiled clothing, bathing me… hiding me.

I thought me finally calling her would fill her with joy. I thought she would hold me like any loving mother would if their child recognised them. But she didn't do or say anything except stare at me. A long, silent moment passed, and without a word, I saw her walk out the door. She left. Should I have stayed quiet? Was this not what she wanted?

The next day, Nurse Tolsy and other attendants took over my Ma's chores. Their actions were rough and uncaring. And instead of pills, Nurse Tolsy starting to use needles. It stung as the liquid surged through my veins but I had no way of resisting and the medicine trickled into my bloodstream.

They wheeled me outside and into the white block. Inside was full of attendants and two tables. One was empty, and the other one had a patient lying on top of it, alone, unconscious and convulsing. Despite whatever I had been injected with, I could still see and feel with no one else noticing. Like cold sweat was dripping on the inside of my skin and although I appeared as still as stone, I was trembling from fear. They laid me onto the empty table and strapped me down, forcing something hard into my mouth. I kept my eyes open all the while and saw attendants come and go whilst I could do nothing but wait. Then a tall male figure in dark clothing drifted in and his face came into view. Sir Feyman. Tears rolled out of my eyes. Several more attendants came over to me and pressed their arms along my chest and legs. A hard and violent shock surged through my brain. My body jumped in hard, violent jerks against the pressure of the attendants holding me down. It leaps for one final time, and I hear a snap like a bone in my rib cage had just cracked in half.

CHAPTER

FORTY-THREE

1953
Jane

I stumble down the corridors with my arm draped over Serene's shoulders. She checks with every turn that it's not being guarded or watched. Finally, we reach the back exit. She swings it open and a gust of cold night air hits my chest.

"Come on!" Serene says, her voice hushed but urgent. I hobble along the ground with bare feet, still hanging on to Serene.

"Where are we going?"

"To meet Richard."

Relief should be hitting me but instead I pull Serene back.

"Wait! Georgina! What about Georgina?"

She stares at me. "She'll have to wait. I can only free one person at a time."

"She won't be there once they find out that I've gone."

"I'll take my chances," she says, trying to continue.

"No, you have to go back! I'll be fine. I can walk now. Just tell me where to go and I'll meet you there."

"Alright, fine! But you must keep yourself hidden! Stay along this line of hedges and trees. Keep out of the light of the streetlamps. Once you're at the memorial gardens, you'll be very exposed so cross them as quickly as you can. Make your way to the railway line – you know it?" I nod. "I'll be back as quick as I can."

I follow the lines of hedging for as long as I can before I reach the gardens and swallow, suddenly feeling very aware of my own vulnerability. I have no way of telling the time. A shiver slides down my back, feeling has reached its way back into my body fully, but it is not a pleasant sensation. I crouch down low, trying to conceal myself by a bush. Did Serene tell me to wait at the end of the hedges or to cross the gardens on my own? My mind still feels dizzy from medication. A shuffling noise comes close towards me. It must be Serene, returning with Georgina. I rise a little above the leaves to take a look.

It's not Serene. It's a much taller figure, a man. Richard? Is it Richard? I squint my eyes to focus. Cold wet droplets start to fall over me. Rain. I hardly notice the downpour, soaking my gown in seconds as all my attention is upon this man. I pray that someone I know will come quickly before he sees me.

I duck down below the hedge line and crawl slowly through the thicket, hoping the steps to the tramline will appear at any moment. The wooden treads down to the valley come into view as I reach the end of the hedge line. There's nothing but exposure to the elements now. And exposure to anyone who wants to catch me. Do I lay myself close to the ground or make a run for it. The rain's starting to make the ground beneath me soft and wet and my knees sink into it. I start to cover myself with wet earth, blocking every inch of my fair skin and white gown.

I edge my way down the hill, towards the steps. The rain has made a thin layer of muddy slime over the wooden steps. I slip, letting out a scream.

"Jane?!" A male voice calls out from the bottom. It sounds familiar. I think it's Richard, but I can't trust myself to be sure. Then suddenly a sound of two gun shots release into the night sky. I instinctively cover my head.

"Jane!" he shouts again.

I try and grab onto the rail, but I slide down three more steps, jarring my elbows, smacking the base of my spine on the edge of one of them with a sharp blow. Thorns and nettles tear against my skin as I tumble down towards the train track. A silhouette of a man runs towards me. No! I'm frightened and curl my knees up to my chest.

"Jane!"

"No! Please!"

"Jane?" he repeats, his voice, now, low and soft. "It's alright. It's me, Richard." I feel his hand reach towards me, prising my arm away from my face. I peel my eyes open and see him. He gently pulls me onto my feet. My legs shake involuntarily. "It's okay. I've got you now."

But another shot is fired, forcing me to shut my eyes and duck down again. I dare not open them back up but I hear Richard's cry falling away from me. The shot has taken him out, blowing his shoulder backwards and he falls across the track.

"Richard!"

I crawl towards him. His eyes widen at me, their pupils fully dilated with shock filling them. His shirt's turning a deep shade of red. Blood runs from the top of this chest. No! I push my hand against his wound, trying to stop the bleeding. I tear the sleeve off my gown, scrunch it up and press it down, seeing the blood quickly seeping into it.

Then a scream in the distance. I turn back to see the direction it's coming from. Who screamed? Georgina? I turn back to Richard. He's holding the rag against his wound on his own and his breathing seems stable. I tuck my hands under his armpits and pull with all my strength away from the train track. He eases the burden a little by pushing his heels against the ground and we make it over. I start to cross back over the track.

"I have to go back to Georgina–"

"Wait!" he calls, and holds up his baton. "Take this. It's no gun but if they come near you, knock them out." I run to grab hold of it. "Be careful," he says.

Before I go, I ask him, "Jasper? Where is he?"

"Kirsty," he breathes. "Go!"

I scramble up back up the hill, avoiding the slippery steps this time, back onto the grass of the memorial garden. I'm hunkering down against the grass and see two figures huddled together. I recognise Georgina immediately. She is with Serene! My crawl becomes a scuttle as I get closer and closer towards them.

Suddenly a heavy bolt to my side forces me to the ground, knocking the baton from my hand. My mouth is buried into the grass, my back is pushed against the ground, I feel like my rib cage could break at any moment, and that would be the death of me – fractured bones, puncturing my lungs and drowning me in my own blood. But I'm forced to turn onto my back now and I am faced with the picture of the man attacking me.

Alexander Feyman. His eyes, light and drained of all colour, like the devil's on Earth. He bares his teeth showing me a full face of evil; he grips his large hands around my neck and pushes himself against my throat. I throw my hands around his wrists, trying to prise his grip off me but the pressure is so hard, I can't even choke. I launch a last attempt at stopping him, slapping his face, clawing it, digging my nails into his cheeks and my thumbs into the sockets of his eyes but it only forces him to sink my head deeper into the ground that's turning into wet sludge from rain.

I feel the blood draining from my head and I know that I'm about to black out. My arms collapse down to my side when I hear a loud, ear-piercing screech coming from behind him. I open my eyes and see a flash of an axe blade coming towards me. I try and scream but all I can manage is hopeless, dry, choking coughs.

Suddenly, the grip of Alexander's hands loosen, and instead I'm met with the dead weight of his body. I gasp, desperate to push him off me and get the air back into my lungs. Somebody is there, dragging him off me. I wriggle free and sit up as soon as I can, finding his lifeless body with a fire axe buried into his back. I look up to see who saved me.

She stares at me with her familiar dark eyes, her chest heaving large breaths. Mary! She holds out her hand and pulls me up to my feet. We both run over to Georgina and Serene. Georgina lies lifeless in Serene's arms. Her abdomen is bleeding.

"She's been shot. Call an ambulance, quickly."

Mary runs back towards the hospital when a row of cars with flashing police lights bolt up the road and sharply halt at the gate of the garden. I see her stop at the car and point in our direction.

CHAPTER

FORTY-FOUR

1954. Six months later.
Georgina

Georgie…. Georgina!… We're not safe here… No!! No!!"

In the dark, Alma twists and turns her head against her pillow. Beads of cold sweat trickle down her forehead. I place my hand on her trembling shoulder. Six months on since leaving the Beaumont and she's still suffering from nightmares although the good nights are starting to become more frequent.

"Alma. Alma, darling. Wake up," I say softly, wiping her brow. "It's Georgina. I'm here."

Her heavy breathing gradually steadies but she doesn't open her eyes and instead, floats back into a calm sleep. I take a deep intake of breath and lie back down against her, watching her, waiting until her nightmare begins again. My poor Alma.

When the sun rises, my eyes grow heavy and I feel as though I can drift back off to sleep, but another murmur comes from Alma's lips and I open my eyes to see her smiling back at me.

"Tell me where we are again?" she says.

"Somewhere far, far away from where we used to be."

"How did we get here?"

"We boarded the train."

She closed her eyes again and the sweetest smile spread across her face. I let out a giggle and with my finger, I brush a loose curl away from her cheek. Every day since we arrived, we start the mornings off with the same conversation, like we can hardly believe we're out, alive, intact, and completely free.

I will always remember us standing at the platform of Crowbeck station for the last time. Steam billowing out of the train's chimney. Two small fabric suitcases by our feet – we didn't need much and had already lost everything of any value that we possessed anyway. Mary was holding Alma tightly, not wanting to let her go. Jane was with us too, smiling softly by her side. This was just over four months since we escaped the Beaumont and her speech is still a little broken, although much improved with Jane's frequent home visits. We knew that Alexander's medication had prevented her from functioning, but it was the long-lasting scars of the horror she experienced which took time to heal.

Alma went back to stay with Mary whilst I was transferred to another hospital to recover. I was malnourished and needed some help to come off the drugs Alexander had prescribed me day in and day out. I never realised that I had grown a dependency on the medication, or that that sort of thing was even possible. And it was only the evening after we had escaped, did I start to feel a change in myself. I wasn't drowsy or numb anymore. I was suddenly scared of everything, even Alma. I was unable to control my tongue, or whichever way my eyes looked. It was disorientating and frightening. I had been imprisoned with empty thoughts for so long, that I had lost sight of who I was and was afraid of what I had become. Live your life with the insane and those who control you and your prophecy will be fulfilled. I wasn't safe to be around. Men with long white coats came to get me again, and I thought that I would lose Alma for good.

The new hospital, however, was very different to the Beaumont. It was modern and sterile. The nurses and attendants weren't that much different and I wouldn't trust any of the doctors there either. It was only Jane who could reassure me. Even when I was located over an hour away, she made the effort to come and see me and on several occasions, she would bring Alma too.

Her husband, Howard, never quite recovered from battle fatigue and had to stay on at the Beaumont although it was out of his own choice. I suppose he had become, what people say is, *institutionalised*.

I shake the memory of those days out and bring myself back to the station.

"Are you sure you don't want to come with us, Ma?"

Mary shakes her head and cups Alma's hands in her own. "Start a life of your own with Georgina. You don't need your mother there getting in the way. I'll come and visit once you've settled in."

"You wouldn't be in the way, come anytime you want." The train conductor blows his whistle to call the last passengers on.

"I've… got to go. I'll… call you and write to you as soon as I get there. I love you!" Alma says, kissing Mary on her cheek. Mary dabs her eyes with her hankie. Alma looks at Jane, her eyes are also brimming with tears. She's speechless, not from fear, but from gratitude. Jane reaches out, placing her hand on Alma's arm.

"Take good care of each other. Stay in touch."

I nod at her and smile at Alma. She acknowledges that we have to step onto the train, and we lift our suitcases up, stretching our feet over the gap and finally getting on board. We get inside the carriage, slide the window down with a hard push and wave at them. The train hasn't moved yet and already I see Mary hardly able to compose herself. Jane wraps her arm tightly around her, she starts to shout something at us, but the train pulls away, its loud chugging engine drowning out her words. We keep waving until they become dots in the distance, and the Beaumont only exists like a scar in our memory.

Once we sit upon the velvet lined bench in our carriage, I take a deep breath and let it out slowly, and heavily. There is a faraway forlorn look in Alma's eyes.

"Are you alright?" I ask. "You don't regret doing this?" I always knew that it would be hard for her to leave her mother and Howard, but I couldn't stay here reliving memories, knowing that Charles was imprisoned nearby. Mary's strike with the fire axe didn't quite kill Alexander either so he too, joined Charles in prison. Part of me wanted to relish the irony of Alexander being the one in a cell but mostly, I only wanted him extinguished from my thoughts.

Charles was taken into questioning as soon as he returned from Luxemburg and charged with assault and attempted murder. I still remember the look on his face, refusing to look me in the eye as I stood in court and described what happened that night, knowing that he thought he had left me for dead. But it didn't stop me from visiting him in prison for the first and final time. We were sitting at a table across from one another. He was dressed in his brown uniform in a cold room that reminded me too much of the Beaumont.

"Why did you do it?" I asked him. "You could have just let me free, and none of this would have happened."

He shook his head. "You and Alma is something that I'll never be able to accept. I wanted my uncle to help you, I never meant to hurt you, not like that. Never like that."

"You didn't know? About all the terrible things he had done?"

His eyes reddened. A single tear started to trickle down his cheek and I saw a glimpse of a man I used to love.

"I knew he tried to change Michael when he caught him with another young man. He tried all sorts of things, but nothing worked. When Michael didn't survive his lobotomy, Alexander really changed. He told Mother and I that Charlotte had killed him – that she attacked him in the hospital with a knife and Charlotte was too sick to know anything different. But deep down I knew. I suppose he was always dangerous… but he became erratic too. I think the loss of Michael twisted him even more, but that was a long time ago. Maybe I knew about his past and of his reputation, but he was well respected everywhere, no one dared to touch him. Not even his family."

I told him to take care of himself and that he'll never see me again. After the court trials, I never saw Lillian again either. Once I felt well enough, I went back to Crowbeck House to pack a few things. After months of no one living there, it was starting to look bleak and my secret rose garden had overgrown into a small patch of wilderness. I found all the letters that Alma wrote to me and my diary, and I burned them in the fire, one by one after reading them and I left there, only taking with me a few of my dresses.

Alma gently holds her handkerchief against her eyes, then places her hand over mine.

"Oh no, this will be the one thing in life that I'll never regret. I just feel sorry for Ma. Who will she have now?" she asks, gazing out the window seeing the Dales rush past us like a silent movie. We're heading east towards the coast to begin a new life together where no one will know us or what we have endured.

"She can visit us whenever she likes." Alma smiles at me and nods. In my heart, I know that she won't be coming. Not because she feels as though she'll be in the way, but because I don't think that she'll ever really accept what we truly are – in love.

Alma rises from the bed and draws the curtains of our little bedroom wide open, letting the bright rays of sunshine burst its way in.

"Gosh, what a beautiful day! Come on! Let's not waste it in bed!"

We get dressed and head straight to the shoreline, just a few minutes' walk down a cobbled hill, away from the terraced house we rent – its walls are painted in turquoise, the same colour as the ocean, the sunlight glittering across the water's surface. As soon as we reach the sand, we slip off our sandals. I grab hold of her hand and charge towards the water, the first wave we meet laps over our feet, crashes above our knees, wetting the rim of our dresses and we squeal with delight at the icy coldness of the water and the feel of the silk like sand beneath our feet.

Alma drops her arm around me and plants a delicate kiss on my cheek, her soft light waves perfectly framing her face. I reach out to run my fingers through it. Her eyes rest on mine and I see my own reflection in them. Beyond that newfound contentment, there is pain lingering underneath that I cannot reach. I know it all too well because I know what it is to hide it myself. The Beaumont scar might never truly fade.

She lights a cigarette and sucks it, blowing smoke out delicately to the side.

"Ice cream for breakfast?" she asks with mischief in her eyes. I throw my head back in laughter. An elderly lady walks past us and her dog gallops ahead, its ears flapping with every bounce against the glistening beach. She lifts a hand up as a gesture to say hello and smiles and we smile back. To her, we are anonymous – just two girls having fun by the sea. To us, we are two souls finding their own private slice of peace.

CHAPTER
FORTY-FIVE

1955
Jane

I'm standing at the gates of Jasper's school. Rich, golden leaves hug the foot of a low, brick wall lining the pavement and a breeze brushes through its top layer, bringing them up to dance around the spears of the iron bars. There has been a change in the air, with the temperature falling over night, defining the end of autumn and the start of winter. Not a day has passed since leaving the Beaumont that I have not been grateful for my life.

Soon after the ordeal, Sir Alexander Feyman was arrested, officials investigated the medical practice of the Beaumont and found at least eighteen examples of mistreatment and unfounded reasoning for lobotomy surgery along with other monstrous experiments on patients' brains and other body parts, alive and dead, in the premises.

The body he ordered to be thrown into the wreckage of Alma's burning car was simply one of the patients that had lain dead on the autopsy table inside the mortuary of the hospital, due to be buried in the garden of the unnamed. To him, it was another anonymous nobody to be tested on and mutilated, but that woman would have had a name and a past, and someone she cared for. When I asked Richard why Feyman wanted the body to be recognised as Georgina, he suspected that he wanted Alma framed for the murder as a way of punishing her further for loving another woman. And to an extent, it was nearly believable. It was her car, and they were alone together at her house – something going wrong in their love affair was a strong enough motive.

Feyman was removed from the hospital with immediate effect and another superintendent replaced him. They had asked Dr Blythe if he would take on the post, but he respectably declined, saying that the hospital's state of disrepute is irreparable. I did visit the hospital one last time. I wanted to see Serene, to thank her for saving our lives. On the way to her room, I saw Tolsy walking out one of the wards. The way she dominantly strode around the place hadn't changed, but her observation of me did. It was less of a glare, and more of a steady gaze.

"I'm sorry for what happened to you, Mrs Galloway," she said, her tone was still stern but I guessed from years of being such, it would be hard for her to be any other way. I simply nodded and smiled back at her.

"Take care, Nurse Tolsy."

I knocked on Serene's door, and like nothing had happened before, she opened it with a warm smile, dressed in the comfort of her own clothes before her night shift and welcoming me with her soft, tuneful voice. We had tea and I mentioned that I might visit again soon, but I haven't seen her since.

There is something unusual about the work one does in the night. The air carries a different quality to that during the day, the sound of the night is different, its silence holds more clarity, and one senses things that are out of the ordinary – it is almost mystical. And with that subtle in between where the day filters into the night sky, under the moonlight we are more inclined to reveal truths that otherwise would be hidden. In some strange way, I find myself missing Alma at times because of this bond we shared, especially when the stars are out.

As for Dr Blythe, he offered me a place at Wakefield hospital where he was working. I also respectfully declined and instead went back to study psychology and maintained my contact with Alma to make sure she received the care she needed in order for her to speak and move fully again.

Another mother of a student from the school walks up to the gate and stands next to me. She wears a green beret, and her curly locks loosely fall below it. She smiles and I smile back, although in my heart, the gesture feels alien. Parents know who I am but don't normally want to acknowledge me – I am that boy Jasper's single mother after all.

"Hello," she says. "I'm Dawn, Noah's mother."

"Hello," I say back to her. I pause and then realise that I'm supposed to introduce myself as well. "I'm – Jane. Jasper's mother."

"I know, it's lovely to finally meet you. Noah's been coming home every day talking about Jasper, he's really taken by him! If Jasper would like to come and play after school one day, we would love that."

"That would be really nice, thank you."

We hear the school bells ring and the doors open with a flurry of children running out, eager to find their parents.

"Just wait a minute children! Stand in line until we see that your parents have arrived!" calls the teacher.

Jasper spots me immediately and sprints into my arms. It looks as though he's grown five inches over the last few months, but I've only just noticed. I bury my face into his neck and kiss him on his cheek. I feel my eyes brim with tears, overwhelmed by my sudden desperation to hold on to his childhood.

"Did you have a good day, Jay?"

"Yes Mama!" he looks up at Dawn next to me who's smiling down at him. "She's Noah's Mama!"

"Yes, she is," I say quietly.

"Hello!" he shouts at her like she wouldn't be able to hear otherwise.

"Hello, Jasper! How are you today?"

"Good, thank you. It's my Mama's birthday today!"

"Oh, is it!" Dawn's eyes widen at me. "I didn't know. Happy Birthday, Jane!"

"Thank you." I feel the heat rise in my cheeks from the attention Jasper had thrown upon me. Dawn's eyes shift to the playground and catches her son's attention with a wave. Noah runs over to Dawn and wraps his arms around her waist. It is a welcome distraction. She quickly turns back to me.

"Are you doing anything nice to celebrate?" she asks us.

"Just going out for some tea at the local coffee shop."

"How lovely, I hope you have a wonderful evening. Let's try and arrange something this week. Talk tomorrow?" she says.

"That'll be great, thank you."

I take Jasper's hand in mine.

"Are you leaving for work tonight?" he asks as we walk down the path, and he takes pleasure in kicking the fallen leaves around us.

"No, I won't be doing that anymore, Jasper. I never want to leave you at night for work again."

"Yay!" he says, jumping up. "Which coffee shop are we going to?"

"It's called The Vista! Only opened yesterday. I thought it would be nice to try it out?"

"The Vista!? Sounds very posh!"

I laugh. "I think it is! And guess who's joining us?"

"Kirsty?"

"Yes, and guess who else?"

"Oh, please say Richard!"

"Yes! And look! There he is!"

At the bottom of the lane, holding a bunch of flowers tied up with ribbon is Richard. He casually leans against a wall with a wide grin. Jasper speeds up to him and bowls him backwards, nearly winding him and sending dahlia petals flying into the air.

"I'm sure you've grown another inch since I last saw you!" Richard laughs and I marvel at how it had only been a minute ago that this similar thought came to me as well. Richard winks and holds the bouquet towards me. "Happy Birthday, Jane." He smiles, his eyes bright, full of promise and I thread my arm into his as we walk towards The Vista.

THE END

AUTHOR'S NOTE

Whilst research has been taken on the profession of psychology, counselling, the running of mental hospitals during this era, and conversations have been had with various therapists and many who have experienced sleep talking and have had conversations with others whilst lucid dreaming, I must emphasise that this is a work of fiction and parts of this story that are inspired by real places and people, have been dramatically exaggerated or imagined to tell a story of fear, passion and suppression. For anyone who is or has been suffering from mental health and those who have been abused under similar circumstances, I hope that I have been as sensitive as I could be.

ACKNOWLEDGEMENTS

Thank you to Taryn and Chronos Publishing for believing in this story, and to Lydia Jenkins for her editing. To all my beta readers, Chlothilde Farthing, Emma Phipps, Deborah Oxley and Lily Clark, I am in awe of your ability to absorb novels – your eyes are keen, precise and experienced, and I am so grateful for your feedback on my initial draft. Thank you to Emma Cunliffe, Suzanne Yarnold and Judy Smith for your breadth of medical knowledge and precious time – you have given me such invaluable insight into your worlds that have helped to shape this novel with as much tangible realism as possible, and all the while respecting where I chose the path that may alleviate fact from fiction. As ever, thank you to my family for their support as I navigate my way through this life of creativity – I am infinitely lucky! I love you forever, forever and forever!